A Killing of Angels

Also by Kate Rhodes

Crossbones Yard

KATE RHODES

A Killing of Angels

Minotaur Books
New York

A KILLING OF ANGELS. Copyright © 2013 by Kate Rhodes. All rights reserved. Printed in the United States of America. For information, address St. Martin's Press, 175 Fifth Avenue, New York, N.Y. 10010.

www.minotaurbooks.com

Library of Congress Cataloging-in-Publication Data

Rhodes, Kate.
     A killing of angels : a novel / Kate Rhodes.—1st U.S. ed.
        p. cm.—(Alice Quentin series ; 2)
     ISBN 978-1-250-01431-3 (hardcover)
     ISBN 978-1-250-01430-6 (e-book)
1. Serial murderers—Fiction. 2. Visiting cards—Angels—Fiction. 3. Women psychologists—Fiction. I. Title.
     PR6118.H48K55 2014
     823'.92—dc23

                                                                              2013038929

Minotaur books may be purchased for educational, business,
or promotional use. For information on bulk purchases, please contact
Macmillan Corporate and Premium Sales Department at 1-800-221-7945,
extension 5442, or write specialmarkets@macmillan.com.

First published in Great Britain by Mulholland Books,
an imprint of Hodder & Stoughton, an Hachette UK company

First U.S. Edition: February 2014

10   9   8   7   6   5   4   3   2   1

For Jack, Matt and Frank

'If a man is not rising upwards to be an angel,
depend upon it, he is sinking downwards to be a devil.'

Samuel Taylor Coleridge

PROLOGUE

It's early, but already the heat of the Tube station is more than you can bear. Your shirt clings, and the starched linen of your suit is beginning to wilt. The platform heaves with tourists and commuters, jockeying for position, elbowing you out of the way. You don't stand a chance. Years ago you could have barged through them, and made sure you were right at the front of the queue. But fighting doesn't interest you now. Not even the cut and thrust of work — watching the markets crest and fall, grabbing the best deals. It's hard to believe that you're standing here, shoulder to shoulder with the great unwashed. But your driver called in sick again, which means that you'll have to let him go, even though he's been with you twenty years. You dab the sweat from your forehead with a silk handkerchief. A young woman is jabbering to her friend, her mouth an ugly blur of crimson lipstick. She's not worth a second look, but her voice grates in your ears like nails on a blackboard. Bodies press against you so tightly that you can hardly breathe. Then there's an unexpected reprieve. The crowd shifts like a lung expanding, and you're carried forwards to the ideal spot, at the edge of the platform. For the first time today, your

I

body relaxes. Soon you'll be strolling through the finance district, watching the pinstripes race to their desks.

The train's approaching at last. You sense rather than hear it, the air circulating more quickly, a faint ringing sound rising from the tracks. And that's when you feel it. Someone's touching you, tugging at your briefcase. You hold on tightly, cursing under your breath. Whoever it is, he's got the cheek of the devil, fingers sliding inside the pocket of your suit. You struggle but there's no room to move, or even to turn round to identify the thief. The train's closer now, thank God. Two white lights blinking at you from the tunnel. The platform fills with a rush of engine noise and overheated air. You're safe again. The pickpocket has moved on to someone else, and the fat weight of your wallet is still there, snug against your ribcage. The train is yards away now, wheels hissing as it slows down. And that's when it happens. A hard thump between your shoulder-blades. You're too shocked to call out, too busy trying not to fall, grabbing at thin air.

No one tries to pull you back onto the platform. Perhaps they don't even see you pitching face first onto the tracks, as if you were diving into a swimming pool. Your briefcase flies over your shoulder, high above the commuters' heads. But you are not so lucky. The machine is eating you alive. For a few seconds the pain is unimaginable, your whole body electrified, every nerve ending shrieking the same message to your brain. And then you're calm. You don't lose consciousness, not even for a second. You hear every sound. The brakes squealing, metal gasping against metal as the wheels grind past your eyes. Your face presses against cold stones, the taste of engine oil filling your mouth. Somehow you must have survived, landed safely between the tracks. Laughter rises in your throat. You twist your head, but it's impossible to move, the black underbelly of the train pressing down on you. There's a glint of pale metal a few yards away, and for a second it doesn't make sense. When your eyes blink open again you see that it's your Rolex, still attached to your severed arm, sliced neatly at the shoulder. The fingers are twitching convulsively, grasping at something they can never have.

I

The foyer was heaving when I reached Guy's. A gaggle of new interns was being shown around, and I couldn't help pitying them. They were beginning their careers in the middle of the worst heat wave for fifty years, and the temperature was about to rise even higher. They had a year of hell to look forward to – sixteen-hour days of fretting over every diagnosis, with registrars bullying them at every turn. I forced myself to summon the lift. Even though I'd been using it every day, my claustrophobia was refusing to come under control. Jogging twenty-four flights of stairs to my department still seemed a far easier challenge.

Someone tapped me on my shoulder as I pressed the button. When I turned round, a young man was staring down at me. He was standing much too close, a flush of red across his cheekbones, hair shaved to a raw stubble. My mouth opened to say hello, but his name escaped me for a second.

'You don't even know who I am.' His breath smelled of cigarettes and last night's beer. 'I'm just a number to you, aren't I?'

'Of course I know you, Darren.' His probation officer had brought him to one of my anger management groups, and gradually he'd begun to join in, volunteering ideas without being asked.

'You cancelled my group, just like that.' His hands clapped

together like a book closing, inches from my face. 'No one even told me.'

'I'm sorry, you should have had a letter.'

'Who needs a letter? I haven't even got a fucking address.'

There was a mist of sweat on his forehead, eyes staring, as though he held me responsible for every bad thing he'd seen. And that's when I made my mistake. I took a step backwards to let him cool down.

'That's right,' he snapped. 'Walk away, you stuck-up bitch.'

Things went into slow motion after that. His arm coiled back, and his fist flew towards my face. I dodged just in time, because the first punch landed on my shoulder, then another on my ribcage, knocking me to the ground. When I looked up again, two interns were holding his arms, but the fight had already drained out of him. He was pale with shock, like a child waiting to be punished.

'Call the police,' one of the interns yelled at the receptionist.

'No need. It was a misunderstanding, wasn't it, Darren?' I struggled back onto my feet.

'What have I done?' He kept repeating the words to himself like a new mantra, his eyes screwed tightly shut.

'You can let go of him,' I told the two interns. 'You'll behave, won't you, Darren?'

He gave a miserable nod, and I made him sit down on one of the hard plastic chairs by the entrance. The receptionist was flicking through a magazine. Assaults on members of staff must have become so routine, she no longer batted an eyelid. Darren stared at the floor, his elbows propped on his knees.

'I never hit a woman before.' He dragged his sleeve across his face. 'You should let them put me away.'

'That wouldn't help, would it? But you've got to stop this. It can't happen again.'

His tears splashed on the tiled floor, and I rested my hand between his shoulder-blades.

'It's all right, I know you didn't mean it.'

'Nothing makes sense any more.' His voice had dropped to a whisper.

The pain in my side was still throbbing, but there was no sense of panic. This was nothing, compared to the things I'd already lived through.

'We'll help you,' I told him. 'Things will get better.'

He shook his head vehemently. 'I got the sack. I'll never find another job.'

'What were you doing?'

'Cleaning, in a bank. I was lucky to get it. No one gives work to ex-cons.'

'They will, if you keep trying.'

After a few minutes he seemed calmer. He waited in silence while I booked an emergency appointment with my boss the next morning – Hari has the ability to neutralise even the worst kinds of rage. Darren clutched his appointment card, but his gaze had slipped out of focus, as if he was having trouble seeing me properly. When I looked back he was still staring at me as I got into the lift.

I wanted to pull up my shirt to inspect the damage, but a gang of nurses had pressed in behind me, chattering gaily to each other. It was my ribs that hurt most, a hot burst of pain every time I breathed, and there was no chance of going home. Patients were booked at forty-five-minute intervals for the whole day, and most of them had waited months for an appointment.

My consulting room smelled of stale air, dust and cleaning fluid. The air conditioning had packed up just as summer came to the boil, but the maintenance team was still on strike. I opened the window and tried to catch my breath. Two hundred feet below me, London glittered. The Thames was binding south and north together, like a skein of dark brown thread. The city was a haze of sunlight and reflected glass – from this distance it was hard to believe it had run out of cash. I glanced around my room. Almost everything was waiting to be replaced, and my computer had developed a habit of withholding information. It occurred to me that a normal person would have been weeping buckets by now, releasing the shock of the attack in one quick outburst. The idea made me envious. My emotions were still as unpredictable as my computer, with broken connections and gaps in the circuitry. I gritted my teeth and got ready for the first appointment of the day.

Hari appeared at eleven o'clock. He looked as calm as always, beard neatly trimmed, wearing his immaculate saffron turban, eyes wide with concern.

'Why are you here? You should go home.'

'I'm okay, really.'

'No one's indestructible, Alice.'

I knew he was remembering my injuries after the Cross-bones case, and I wanted to tell him to stop fussing, but his kindness negates every argument.

'Can I get you anything?' he asked.

'Funding for my therapy groups, please. Or a lot more people are going to get hurt.'

Hari looked embarrassed. 'The trustees aren't listening. I've sent a complaint to the BPS.'

I shot him an ironic smile. There was nothing the British Psychological Society could do, because they didn't hold the purse strings. He patted my hand, then escaped back to his office.

By the time my last patient arrived, I was high on Nurofen and lack of oxygen. It didn't take long to diagnose her social phobia. Everyone and everything scared her – parties, strangers, walking through crowds. All she wanted was to barricade herself in an empty room where no one could reach her, for the rest of her days. But the session reminded me why I'd opted for psychology instead of medicine. Her troubles shrank as she voiced them, and by the end she looked relieved. I knew she'd respond well to rational-emotive therapy, because she was keen to learn techniques that would help her recover. I told her she'd need between ten and twelve sessions, and advised her to try exercise – yoga or t'ai chi. She still looked anxious as she prepared to leave. A world of uncontrollable noise was waiting outside, strangers barging past while she clung to the edges of buildings.

The thermometer in my room had reached thirty-two degrees, and the pain in my ribs felt like someone was beating them into shape with an invisible hammer. Someone knocked on the door while I was packing my briefcase.

'Come in,' I called.

My visitor was vaguely familiar, tall and heavily built, like a rugby player gone to seed. His suit hung from his wide shoulders, as though a bigger man had loaned it to him for the afternoon. But it was his eyes that gave him away, bright and obsessive, determined not to miss a trick.

'It's like a blast furnace in here, Alice.'

'It's never who I think it is.' I gaped at him. The shape of his face had changed completely, from a circle to an oval. 'You've been going to the gym, DCI Burns.'

'Tell me about it.' He pinched the baggy material of his jacket. 'This is my third new suit.'

It had been over a year since I'd worked as a consultant on the Crossbones case, helping him track down the serial killer who'd been targeting women in Southwark. Since then he'd shrunk from the kind of huge man that children jeer at in the street to a couple of stone overweight, and his terrible inch-thick glasses had been replaced by the thin-framed kind that journalists wear. Even his smile looked different. He rubbed a hand through his dark hair, embarrassed about being scrutinised.

'How much have you lost, Don?'

His shoulders jerked awkwardly. 'Five stone or thereabouts.'

I let out a gasp of amazement, my ribs protesting at the sudden movement. I kept trying to put my finger on something else that had changed – it looked like his confidence had deserted him.

'What have you been up to?' he asked.

'Research, mainly.' I pointed at my new book on the shelf, and he helped himself to a copy.

'*Treatment Options for Violent Personality Disorders*, by Dr Alice Quentin. Sounds like perfect bedtime reading.'

Burns's accent was exactly as I remembered it, still veering back and forth between Bermondsey and the Scottish lowlands, like the needle in a broken compass.

'But you're not here to borrow a book, are you?'

He turned to face me. 'I need your help. You're the only shrink I can work with, but I know the last time was tough.'

Tough was an understatement. I'd been in hospital for two weeks, recovering from a fractured skull. Since then I'd avoided working for the Met, just doing a handful of mental health assessments at police stations, and prison visits to diagnose suicide risks.

'What's happened this time, Don?'

'A bloke went under a train at King's Cross on Friday. Leo Gresham, a big investment guru in the City. Can I show you the CCTV?'

He pushed his memory stick into my computer, and grainy

black-and-white images trailed across the screen in slow motion. I had a bird's-eye view of a packed underground platform, more commuters piling in every second, pressing forwards as the train arrived. Then a man pitched face first onto the tracks, arms flailing. The last thing I saw was the pale sole of one of his shoes.

'My God.' I clapped my hand over my mouth.

It was impossible to tell who'd pushed him, but a man in a dark top was standing behind Gresham, his hood low over his face. When I looked again, he'd already vanished.

'It's the driver I pity.' Burns's sharp eyes observed me. 'I wouldn't fancy his nightmares.'

In spite of myself, I felt involved. You can't watch someone die like that without wanting to snatch them back onto the platform.

'Gresham lost an arm and both legs, he kept screaming that he was pushed,' Burns said. 'He survived for hours in intensive care.'

'I still don't see where I come in.'

'I want you to work with me. All the evidence is going into HOLMES 2, in case he does it again.'

'Aren't you jumping the gun? It's probably payback for a dodgy business deal, isn't it?'

'I'm not taking any chances. Gresham worked for a bank called the Angel Group. We found this in his pocket.'

Burns handed me a postcard, wrapped in a clear plastic bag. It was a close-up of an angel's face. Apart from a bloodstain smeared across her forehead, her features were perfect. Her pale eyes gazed at me calmly, as though she knew I could still be saved. The writing on the back explained that she was *An Angel in Green with a Vielle*, painted by a pupil of Leonardo da Vinci's, hanging in the National Gallery. My curiosity was growing – the killer would make a fascinating case study. I could imagine him browsing through the museum's gift shop for the loveliest image he could find.

'One calling card doesn't make a serial killer.' I passed it back to him.

'We found white feathers in his pocket too. The lab's checking them out.'

The strength of Burns's gaze was unsettling. It didn't let me forget all the times when he'd visited me in hospital. I used to wake in a panic and see him there in the half-dark, patient as a guard dog. He'd sit for hours by the window in my room without moving a muscle. It was hard to guess what had happened to him since then. His expression was so tense it looked as though he was hanging onto his nerve by a fingernail.

'Tell me the real reason you're here,' I said.

He shifted in his seat. 'They demoted me after Crossbones – the top brass said I mishandled the investigation. I got transferred to King's Cross two months ago. The team don't trust me, and the boss lady's watching me like a hawk.' He leant forwards, palms together like he was offering up a prayer. 'I can't do this without you, Alice.'

It didn't take a mind-reader to realise that emotional blackmail meant Burns was down to his last chance. One touch would have made him resonate like a violin string.

'Would I have access to all the evidence files?' I asked.

He nodded earnestly. This man was a far cry from the old Burns, working too hard but so disorganised that he forgot to pass on vital information. He seemed desperate to turn over a new leaf, and his gaze was starting to feel intrusive. It reminded me of Darren's stare, before he threw his punch.

'I'll let you know tomorrow, Don.' I glanced at the papers on my desk. 'I need to talk to my boss.'

Burns disappeared into the corridor and suddenly the heat felt unbearable. Even with the door wide open, it was difficult to breathe.

2

I inspected the bruise in the hall mirror. It had changed colour overnight to a vivid purple, six inches in diameter, and it hurt every time I moved. I pressed the wound gingerly. At least the rib felt intact – cracked rather than broken, so it would mend in days instead of weeks. The mark on my shoulder was less spectacular, a dull midnight blue. I emptied some ice cubes into a freezer bag then lay down on the sofa. The cold started to numb the pain immediately, and I concentrated on small mercies – if Darren had meant business, he could have beaten me to a pulp. With luck and a handful of painkillers, I'd get through the day.

A text arrived from Hari while the ice was taking effect, advising me to stay at home. I deleted the message immediately and forced myself to sit up. Hari had been a friend for years, but he still didn't understand that sick days weren't in my repertoire. I'd rather drag myself across hot coals than languish on the sofa, watching TV. I went into the kitchen and dumped the ice cubes in the sink. Through the wall I could hear my brother shuffling around in his room. Will was another good reason to haul myself into work. I couldn't face the morose silence while he stared out of the window. Although he'd never blamed me, his injuries were my fault. If I'd been smarter I could have prevented him falling from a third-floor window, the bones in his legs shattering as he hit the concrete. It wasn't surprising that the trauma had made his drug habit even harder to control.

A huddle of patients was waiting outside the therapy room when I got to work. Some came from the Probation Service, and others had been referred by their GPs, but everyone was there for the same reason. They were struggling to keep a lid on their rage. When I broke the news that there would be no more sessions, their reactions varied from outrage to resignation. But it was the rest of the week's groups that worried me more. They'd already been cancelled – I wouldn't even get the chance to say goodbye.

I took a walk round the quadrangle. Exercise has always been my preferred method for keeping rage under control. I hoped the stroll would clear my head, but the heat was already punishing. The hospital gardeners seemed to be sticking to the hosepipe ban, because the roses were struggling to bloom, and the lawn was a parched brown, aching for a sign of rain.

When I got back to the clinic I asked one of the receptionists if Darren had kept his appointment.

'He was a no-show, I'm afraid.' She looked apologetic, as if she was the reason he'd stayed away.

I was incandescent as I walked back to my office, ribs protesting with each step. Knowing Darren hadn't bothered to pitch up made me regret my decision. I should have let the police prosecute him for assault. It was a struggle to calm down in time for my next patient.

By six o'clock the temperature was tropical, my cheese plant withering before my eyes. Keeping the fan on full blast had no effect, apart from circulating stale air from one side of the room to the other. Normally I'd have pulled on my trainers and sprinted down the fire escape, but today a slow walk was the best I could hope for. The hospital foyer was almost empty, apart from a few visitors arriving with flowers and magazines, the last day-shift nurses racing for the Tube.

Commuters were flooding out of London Bridge station, shedding clothes as they walked – jackets, ties, cardigans, anything they could get away with. I had no choice but to limp behind them, a spasm of pain jolting through my chest with each footfall. By the time I reached the river I had to sit down. A cluster of tourists was blocking the walkway, taking snaps of each other, silhouetted against Tower Bridge. The last quarter of a mile took forever, dragging myself across the boardwalk at New Concordia Wharf. When I got to Providence Square I was ready to lie down in a darkened room.

A familiar sound greeted me from the hallway of my flat, a voice talking at full volume. It hadn't changed since we were at school, still husky and excitable, like she'd been gargling bourbon all afternoon.

'Al!' Lola flung her arms around me, then pulled a face. 'God, you look terrible. Are you okay?'

I kissed her then started to explain, but as usual Lola was too busy to listen. She was racing round the kitchen like a whirlwind, a clot of cheese sauce trapped in her long auburn curls, and she'd worked her usual magic on my brother. For once he was wearing clean clothes – a blue linen shirt and the new jeans I'd bought for him. She'd even made him wash his hair. I studied him from the corner of my eye. He was smiling at her, and his walking stick had been forgotten, propped against the wall. I made a mental note to buy Lola a bunch of flowers. She always brought gifts to keep Will entertained: a DVD of *The Motorcycle Diaries*, ingredients for pizza, even a battered Monopoly set she'd found in an Oxfam shop. I left them to it and ran myself a bath. It was a relief to slip into the warm water, rinsing the last few days from my skin. After twenty minutes the image of Darren lunging at me had almost soaked away. I rubbed arnica cream into my bruises then headed back to the kitchen.

Lola was scrubbing the sauce from her hair with a piece of paper towel. 'Shit, Will. We forgot the garlic bread. Whack it in the microwave, my friend.'

The kitchen looked like a bombsite, the floor littered with grated cheese, but it was impossible to resent Lola. There was no denting her *joie de vivre*.

'*Voilà!*' She pulled the pasta dish out of the oven in triumph.

Will was enjoying every moment. Normally he skulked in his room, refusing everything except sandwiches, but tonight he was almost his old self. It was easy to remember the way he used to be, before the drugs took hold. His whole body was angled towards Lola while she spooned pasta onto his plate.

'How's the show going?' he asked.

Lola's green eyes widened. 'The high kicks are killing me, and I'm the oldest girl in the chorus line.' She glared down at her mile-long legs as if they'd failed her in some way.

'Have you got a back-up plan?' I asked.

'Sort of. I'm working with a group of disabled kids in Hammersmith, helping them put on a talent contest. You should come over on Saturday, Al. You'd love it.' Lola leant across and stole some bread from my brother's plate. 'What have you been up to, Will?'

'Nothing, really. But I've joined the Cloud Appreciation Society. It's this website about different types of cloud.' His pale eyes flickered. 'And the thing is, we should study them more, because of the messages.'

'How do you mean?' Lola looked mystified.

'Each cloud holds a message. If you watch it long enough, you can decode it.' His expression was so earnest, he looked like a scientist reporting a key breakthrough.

'I'll have to give that a go.' Lola beamed at him, then helped herself to the rest of his garlic bread.

After dinner, Will returned to the sofa, and left us to the washing up.

'Christ,' she whispered. 'He's still got some pretty random ideas, hasn't he?'

'It's better than a few months ago. At least he can string sentences together.'

'I suppose so.' She stared at the bowl she was drying.

'You did well, Lo. He loves seeing you. That's the first proper conversation he's had in weeks.'

'And how are you doing?' She peered at me. 'Still working too hard, tragically celibate, and running marathons in your spare time?'

'Don't knock it. Soon I'll have legs like you.'

'What about blokes? Any hot dates lined up?'

'I told you, I'm taking a year off. My door is closed.'

She clapped her hands together. 'It's the summer, for fuck's sake. You're meant to be having fun.'

We'd reacted in opposite ways since the Crossbones case. Lola's injuries had been as bad as mine, but she'd never shown a moment's self-pity. She just clutched my hand when I tried to apologise, and told me to focus on the future. As soon as we were discharged from hospital, her pleasure principle went into overdrive. She dated as many men as possible, remaining a firm believer that love conquers all, despite getting her heart broken countless times. Sometimes I worried about the slump that would hit her if she ever slowed down. She accepted a hundred party invitations, while I stayed at home, writing books. There was no point in telling her that all I wanted was equilibrium. My nightmares came less often, but the idea of trusting someone was out of the question.

'This is a smokescreen, Lo. You've met someone, haven't you?'

Her grin widened. 'Maybe, maybe not.'

Lola spent the next fifteen minutes nagging me to search for the ideal man, but I was so grateful for her help that I kept my mouth shut, and nodded at appropriate intervals. Afterwards she curled up beside Will on the sofa, giggling helplessly at a repeat of *Rev*.

When I went to bed I noticed the light flashing on the answer-machine. The first message was from my mother. Her tone was so cool, it sounded like she'd spent the afternoon inhaling dry ice. When I pressed the button again, Burns's tone was anxious. He was reminding me about my visit to the police station on Pancras Way, even though he'd already sent me an email. There was a long pause after he stopped speaking, as though he expected to be let down. I deleted the messages immediately, but it didn't help. I stared at the ceiling for a long time before I fell asleep.

3

A young police officer collected me from reception the next morning. She asked me to wait in the corridor until the senior team called me into the meeting room, because Leo Gresham's investigation was the last item on their agenda. I noticed that she seemed relieved to be staying outside, and when the door swung open I understood why. The atmosphere was so tense you could have tied it between two skyscrapers and used it for a tightrope. The woman at the head of the table was in her mid-fifties, with deep lines etched across her forehead. Her face was free of make-up, framed by a shoulder-length frizz of grey curls. She didn't bother to crack a smile when she greeted me.

'Thanks for coming, Dr Quentin. I'm DSI Lorraine Brotherton.' Her voice was a low monotone, as if she was determined not to say anything memorable.

It took a while for everyone to introduce themselves, because there were at least a dozen people in the room. Pete Hancock, the senior crime scene officer, had thick black eyebrows which met in the middle, adding weight to his frown. A family liaison officer gave a brief smile, and the man sitting beside Burns turned out to be his deputy, DS Steve Taylor. He had a wide, ingratiating grin, and he looked more like a football pundit than a copper, keeping himself in trim, even though his glory days were over. His head was shaved to disguise his receding hairline and he was sporting a deep suntan. He seemed to be hanging on Brotherton's every word.

'DI Burns thinks the death at King's Cross might be the first in a series. I'm no great believer in gut instinct, but he's right to take it seriously. He'll be running the operational side of the investigation.' Her lips twitched as though she was trying not to laugh. 'You can give us your update now, Don.'

I was beginning to see why Burns had enlisted me. His deputy's body language spoke volumes, arms folded across his chest, eyes glazed. He was using every trick in the book to show that he didn't give a monkey's what his new boss had to say, and the rest of the room was following suit.

'The first hour after the attack doesn't give us much,' Burns said. 'The barriers at King's Cross closed five minutes after Gresham fell, but it was too late. Our man was already on the street. The CCTV caught him riding a bus, all the way to Putney. These are our last images before he slips off our radar.'

The blurred pictures Burns passed round showed a man of average build, shoulders hunched as he stepped off the bus. His hood was so low over his face that it cast an impenetrable shadow, like the Grim Reaper in a pantomime. I stared at the photos while Burns described the police work since the attack – dozens of witness interviews, lab analysis of Gresham's clothes, liaison work with his family. The exhibits officer pushed a grey plastic tray into the middle of the table. The contents of Gresham's pockets had been arranged like arte-facts in a museum: two white feathers, the angel postcard, a smart leather wallet, and a wad of blood-spattered bank notes, the stains dried to an earthen brown. His Rolex had survived without a scratch, still keeping perfect time.

Burns's talk confirmed my suspicion that he'd spent the past year transforming himself into someone else. In the old

days he'd have scribbled a few notes on the back of an envelope, relying on his deputy for support. But this time he'd
been systematic, making sure the evidence was logged. He
held up the postcard, so everyone could see the angel's face.

'The prints on this went through the box, with no matches,'
he said.

I had to wrack my brains to remember that 'the box' was
the Met's nickname for the Police National Computer. It held
the details of everyone who'd ever been cautioned or charged
with an offence.

'Any questions?' Burns asked.

'I still don't get why you think he'll do it again.' Taylor's
voice was a dull estuarine drone. 'Bankers aren't flavour of the
month, are they? Maybe Gresham lost someone a fortune. It
looks like a contract killing to me.'

Plenty of heads nodded vigorously, proving where their
loyalties lay.

'You could be right.' Burns kept his expression neutral. 'I
just want to make sure we've followed every lead.'

Brotherton raised her hand, like a teacher breaking up a
fight. 'What's your view, Dr Quentin?'

I glanced up from my notes. 'I'm still not clear that this
was a personal attack. But if it was, I'll need more information about Gresham's world to understand why he was
targeted.' My words stumbled as I glanced at the blank faces
around the table. 'In cases like this the killer's often fanta-
sised about throwing himself under a train, before pushing
his victim. It's likely he's being treated for mental illness, so
it would be good to check hospital records. His high-level
planning makes it more likely he'll try again. And there's a
reason why he chose a well-dressed, middle-aged, male
victim. Maybe he's got issues with his father, or with all
authority figures.'

Taylor smirked, like I'd told a lame joke, and the rest of the room gazed back at me, unblinking. The aggressive atmosphere was a surprise. Normally when I worked for the Met they treated me like a new kid at school, giving me time to learn their in-jokes and acronyms. But this team was different – hostility seemed to be woven into their DNA.

It was a relief when the meeting ended. Taylor paused as everyone filed out; he nodded in Brotherton's direction then hissed in my ear: 'You can see why she's called the Invisible Woman, can't you?'

Taylor left an unpleasant reek of aftershave when he walked away, but I could see what he meant. The DSI's clothes were nondescript, and her handshake was so insubstantial it felt like clutching at mist. I wondered how she'd reached the top of the tree. Maybe her anonymity was just an act; women who reach senior rank in the Met are either brilliant at their jobs or completely ruthless.

'You were involved in the Crossbones case, weren't you?' Her grey eyebrows shifted upwards by a millimetre.

'But I lived to tell the tale.'

'You were lucky, by all accounts.' She parted her grey fringe to observe me more closely. 'How much consultancy have you done for the Met?'

'I've advised on three major incidents, and carried out prison assessments for years.'

'What form will your work for us take?'

'Burns has asked me to work alongside him. I'll start by shadowing the visits to Gresham's family and contacts.'

Brotherton looked irritated. She obviously saw my presence as an unnecessary distraction. 'Let me have a copy of your Home Office licence by the end of the day, please, for my records.'

She melted back into the corridor's grey walls, and I

realised why the meeting had been so tense. Brotherton prided herself on her inscrutability. None of the team knew where the axe would fall, because it was impossible to guess what she was thinking. Maybe she was the reason why Burns had lost so much weight. Her air of secrecy would put anyone off their food.

4

Burns was flicking through a computer printout with a gloomy expression on his face, but the victim seemed determined to take a more positive view. A huge photo of Leo Gresham grinned down at me from the wall of the incident room, bald and avuncular, laughter lines creasing his eyes. Someone had parked a coffee machine directly under it, as though the team had chosen him as their favourite deity, making offerings of caffeine to keep him sweet. Burns was taking me to visit Gresham's family. I'd insisted on the meeting because, despite his obsession with serial killers, most murders were committed by someone close to home. After a few minutes Burns threw the report into a tray and grabbed his car keys.

'Come on then,' he muttered. 'Let's go up West, to see the merry widow.'

I watched him march away, struggling to believe he was the same man who used to drag himself around with so much difficulty. The interior of his Mondeo had been scrubbed to within an inch of its life. For once there were no crisp packets or chocolate wrappers strewn across the back seat.

I sniffed the air. 'You've given up the fags, haven't you?'

'Don't,' he moaned. 'I'm still grieving.'

The rush-hour traffic eased as we drove west, but Marylebone looked shabbier than ever. The streets seemed to be starving themselves: boarded-up cafés, bakeries and green-grocers on every corner.

'I should warn you, Marjorie Gresham's not the sweetest flower in the bunch,' Burns said.

'Grief does strange things to people.'

'Not to her. You'll see what I mean when we get there.'

We headed along Curzon Street into the heart of Mayfair. Bankers had been snapping up property there for a hundred years, and it was easy to imagine how a millionaire's wife would spend her days: strolling in St James's Park, a trip to the beauty salon, then the Royal Academy for a moment of culture. The car came to a halt outside a Georgian villa at the end of a cobbled mews.

'Prepare yourself for the dragon lady,' he whispered, pressing the doorbell.

The woman who greeted us bore a striking resemblance to Margaret Thatcher in her prime. Her hair was an immaculate blonde wave, which must have required considerable time, patience and hairspray. A Jack Russell appeared out of nowhere, snapping at our ankles.

'Quiet, Rollo,' she hissed. 'This is your final warning.' The dog scuttled away with a terrified look in his eye.

A marble sculpture filled one of the alcoves in Mrs Gresham's sitting room. It was an abstract nude, the stone so highly polished that I wanted to run my hand along its spine. Mrs Gresham lowered herself onto a settee cautiously. I guessed that she'd learned how to sit at finishing school, with her feet side by side, black dress smooth, so no creases would appear.

'Thanks for seeing me again,' Burns said. 'We've been looking at the circumstances around your husband's death.'

'I should hope so.' She nodded her head, but the blonde

wave stayed rigidly in place. 'My husband had no reason to take his own life. Leo never suffered from low spirits; he couldn't abide self-pity.'

'This must be terrible for you and your family,' I said quietly.

She softened for a moment, passing me a photo from her coffee table, in an elaborate silver frame. 'This is our son, James, and our granddaughters.'

'Pretty girls,' I murmured. 'What does your son do?'

'He's a GP, in Manchester.'

I studied James Gresham's face. He was doing his best to appear relaxed, but his three little girls looked downcast. Trips to Granny's house must have been an ordeal – always on their best behaviour, with no opportunity to watch TV or let off steam. I spotted another picture on the mantelpiece. It showed a dark-haired young man with an overstretched smile.

'Another son?' I asked.

'That's Stephen Rayner, Leo's deputy at the bank.' Her face brightened. 'He's been with Leo for years. We're very fond of him.' Her voice faltered as she caught herself referring to her husband in the present tense.

An invitation card was propped beside the picture, the letters embossed in gold. It was advertising a gala for financiers, on Friday evening.

'We've been going to the annual dinner for as long as I can remember.' She was still sitting bolt upright, as if she was aiming for a deportment prize.

'Just a couple more questions, Mrs Gresham,' said Burns. 'Do you know if your husband argued with anyone recently?'

She gave him a withering look. 'Of course he didn't. My husband advised banks all over the world on their investment policies. At the weekends he gardened, and on Sundays he went to church. He didn't have a single enemy.'

Burns looked chastened. 'He never fell out with anyone?'

'Envy. That's what killed my husband, Inspector.' She lifted her chin and stared at him. 'Young people today want everything on a plate. They won't work, but they expect all of life's luxuries.'

'I'm not with you.' He looked confused.

'Someone saw my husband, in his good suit and handmade shoes.' She spoke slowly, as though she was explaining something to a child. 'They can't bear anyone having more than them.'

Burns gave a polite nod, then rose to his feet. Rollo had learned his lesson by now. He observed us silently from the stairway, teeth bared. Just as we were leaving, Burns pulled something from his pocket.

'Would this picture have meant anything to your husband?' he asked.

It was a pristine version of the angel that had been found in his pocket. Mrs Gresham passed it back to Burns with a sour expression. 'My husband worked at the Angel Bank, Inspector, that's the only link you'll find. He had a strong faith, but he wasn't sentimental. Angels are best left to Sunday schools, aren't they?'

The door clicked shut the moment we turned away.

'Not the warmest reception I've had,' Burns murmured as we walked back to the car. 'She's got one hell of an art collection, though. That's a Brancusi in her hall and a Henry Moore by the window.'

'I didn't know you were an art lover.'

'We do have galleries in Scotland, you know.' He gave me a sideways look. 'Those pieces are worth a mint.'

The car was heading east, into less affluent territory. Prada and Gucci were giving way to Oasis and Miss Selfridge, and the summer crowds were out in force on the Strand. Young girls were ogling bikinis in the windows of Topshop, but money seemed to be thin on the ground. Hardly anyone was carrying shopping bags.

'We should go to that dinner at the Albion Club,' I said. 'I want to see how Gresham spent his downtime – I still need to figure out how his world operates.'

Burns nodded. 'I'll get it sorted.'

'What was the GP doing when his dad went under the train?'

'You're turning into a copper, Alice.' He gave a short laugh. 'He was at his surgery, his colleagues saw him.'

'Gresham wasn't getting his kicks at home, that's for sure. Have you checked his emails and his phone?'

'The IT guys are looking into it.'

It was eleven by the time Burns dropped me at work. The usual rush of stale air greeted me when I stepped into my consulting room. Almost before I could peel off my linen jacket, three depressives arrived in quick succession. Two were making a good recovery, but the other was refusing to take medication, convinced it played havoc with his mind. After twenty minutes of listening to his despair, my alarm bells were ringing. At the end of the session I asked him to reconsider, but he looked horrified, as though I'd advised him to go out and buy crack cocaine.

The lift didn't appeal when I left work. My painkillers were starting to wear off, and I couldn't face people pressing against me from all sides. The air conditioning kept me artificially cool as I made my way down the twenty-four flights, but outside it must have been forty degrees. A heat haze shimmered above the tarmac, the buildings across the street wavering like a mirage.

The front door was hanging wide open when I reached the flat. I stood on the threshold and called Will's name, but there was no reply. The door was still intact – at least the burglars had done a tidy job of picking the lock. I forced myself to march from room to room, but nothing had been taken. My pulse had almost returned to normal when I got back to the kitchen, and I remembered Will telling me he was going to his NA meeting. He must have forgotten to shut the door, happy to let any passing opportunist rob us blind. I closed my eyes and tried to imagine him sitting in a group, repeating the Narcotics Anonymous mantra: 'My name is Will and I'm a drug addict.' The picture refused to take shape, and when I opened my eyes again, my gaze fell on his VW van, hogging my parking space outside. Even though it was falling apart, he still saw it as a refuge. There was no point in nagging him to sell it before the council towed it away.

Will came home just after I finished dinner, and I was primed to deliver my lecture on home security. But he seemed in no mood to listen. He was clutching a slip of paper, a broad smile plastered across his face. He hobbled straight past me into his room – my stern advice would have to wait for another day. An hour later I heard him humming to himself; a contented sound, like a child discovering a brand-new toy. The scrap of orange paper lay on the hall table with his keys. It was an entrance pass to The Great Escape festival, with a phone number scrawled on the back. God knows who the number belonged to. I had visions of hippies lying on Brighton beach in a drug-addled haze – all the progress he'd made would vanish in the space of one weekend. My first instinct was to rip the ticket to shreds, but I forced myself to put it back.

When I got back to the living room, I saw the pile of reports on the table, and realised I'd forgotten to fax my licence to

Lorraine Brotherton. For some reason the thought cheered me up. It would be fascinating to see her reaction if someone stepped out of line. The shock might tear down her mantle of invisibility, just for a second or two.

5

By Thursday morning confidentiality had become a thing of the past. The air conditioning still wasn't working, and I couldn't shut the door in case my patients collapsed from asphyxiation. I tried to concentrate on my case notes, but when I heard a sound in the corridor, Darren was standing there. An odd, prickling feeling travelled across the back of my neck. I don't know why he unnerved me so much. It wasn't just the fact that he'd attacked me – there was something unpredictable about his body language, as if he could implode at any minute. He was having trouble meeting my eye, shifting his weight from foot to foot. His shaved hair was beginning to grow back, a few millimetres of black stubble blurring the outline of his skull. My finger hovered over the panic button under my desk.

'You're two days late, Darren. Dr Chadha was expecting you on Tuesday.'

'It's you I need to see,' he mumbled, 'to say thanks for not dobbing me in. I owe you one.'

'The only thing you owe me is to stop using your fists.'

He stared back at me with an odd, fixed gaze. 'You're different from the rest, aren't you?'

'How do you mean?'

'You did me a favour. I look after people like you.'

The smile had disappeared from Darren's face. He seemed to be growing more agitated, his mouth opening then closing again, as if the power of speech was deserting him. I was about to press the panic button when he crossed the room. I stood up to defend myself and time flicked into slow motion. It felt like I had hours to study the spider's web tattoo spinning across his neck. When his fingertips brushed my hand they felt unnaturally hot, and his face was so close, I could see the sharp line between his pupils and dark irises.

'Nothing's going to hurt you again,' he whispered, 'I promise.'

Darren disappeared as quickly as he'd arrived. My legs were still trembling, but the only thing he'd left behind was the smell of panic and unwashed clothes. I got the sense that he wanted my help, even if he was incapable of asking for it. The next step would be getting him to agree to a diagnostic meeting. I typed his name into my computer and scanned his record: Darren Campbell, twenty years old, unemployed. He was sent to a Roman Catholic children's home when he was nine, after his mother died. His father's identity was unknown. Then he'd spent a year in Feltham for assaulting someone outside a pub. The victim was in a coma for weeks, but Darren had shown no remorse. He claimed that the man had raped a girl he knew; he was only getting what he deserved.

I glanced at the bottom of the report. His address was the City YMCA – shorthand for no fixed abode. I could picture the building on Fann Street, close to Barbican Tube. A feature-less box of concrete, studded with minute windows, with no trees in sight. It was hard to imagine anyone flourishing there. I turned off my computer and stared out of the window. No wonder he was disturbed. His past had convinced him that the best way to deal with unfairness was to use his fists, and I could understand why. Watching Will suffering often left me desperate to punch a wall.

At lunchtime I dragged myself out of the building to a Turk-ish café on Borough High Street. Lola was there already, tucking into a plate of falafel. She had the sleek look of a pampered cat as she savoured each mouthful, and I felt glad I hadn't cancelled our lunch, even though I had a million things to do. Darren had cast a shadow over my morning, but he wasn't going to spoil my afternoon.

'You've got news, haven't you?'

'He's perfect, but he's a bit young.' She took a gulp of orange juice. 'He's nineteen.'

'Bloody hell, Lo. A teenager.'

She looked embarrassed for a second, then released a peal of laughter that bounced off the café walls. 'He's called Neal and he's adorable. Knowing my luck he'll dump me for a buxom sixteen-year-old.' She waxed lyrical about her toyboy, then turned her attention to the reasons why I was single. 'The trouble is, you've forgotten how to flirt, haven't you?'

'Honestly, Lo, I'm not even looking.'

'One smile and blokes are on their knees. Go on, try it on that waiter over there, before you lose your powers.'

I gave her an imploring look, but she wouldn't give up. 'The tall one by the door?'

'Give him the full force of your charm.'

Once I'd made eye contact the rest was easy, because he broke the ice and smiled first. For a moment the pain from my injury disappeared completely.

Lola patted my hand. 'That wasn't so tough, was it? I bet you've made his day.'

'Rubbish. He probably grins non-stop, to get bigger tips.'

She entertained me with details of her sex life, while I sipped my bitter Turkish coffee. At least she was happy. She was radiating so much contentment, it would have been churlish to rain on her parade. After half an hour I grabbed my bag to go back to work.

'Don't forget about Saturday, will you?' She eyed me expectantly.

I couldn't remember what I'd agreed to. 'Of course not.'

The waiter I'd practised my smile on beamed at me as I left. Maybe Lola was right. The last time I'd flirted with anyone was in the Dark Ages; it might be time to throw caution to the wind.

I spent the rest of the afternoon on autopilot, with rivulets of sweat running between my shoulder-blades. My last appointment was with a middle-aged man who'd been in pain since a car crash two years ago. His face was cadaverous, every bone visible under his skin, and his addiction to painkillers was making the problem worse. He seemed so desperate that I let his appointment overrun by fifteen minutes.

I was running late by the time the cab set off for the police station. Two things had been bothering me since I'd seen the CCTV film from King's Cross: the way Gresham's hands had scrabbled at thin air when he fell to his death, and the fact that Burns was so isolated. I felt duty bound not to let him down. Sunlight was still burning through the car window. It had been weeks since the last rainfall, and every time I turned the radio on, farmers were complaining about crop failure and reservoir levels at an all-time low. I peered at the river as we crossed London Bridge. The drought had made no difference. It was the same murky brown as always, churning with secrets.

DSI Brotherton was waiting for me in her office. She was wearing the generic black trouser suit owned by every professional female in the Western world, and even her accent was hard to pin down. It came from somewhere north of Watford, with just a hint of the Black Country.

'I didn't receive your licence, Dr Quentin.' She lowered her pen onto the table.

I handed over the envelope and she motioned for me to sit down. Her office was lined with colour-coded files, dating back to the Eighties. Her system looked so robust, she could have located anything within seconds. She filed my envelope in a cabinet and instantly seemed more relaxed. It must have been a relief to catalogue me, between all the other shrinks she'd employed over the decades. Brotherton peered at me through her curtain of grey curls.

'You know Don Burns well, don't you?'

'Not really. I've only worked with him once before.'

'But he trusts your judgement. He was adamant about using you, instead of a specialist from Scotland Yard.' The lines on her forehead deepened. 'Are you aware that Burns had quite a reputation at Southwark?'

I shook my head.

'He didn't follow procedures. I can't fault his commitment, but I won't tolerate that kind of approach here – I hope you'll reinforce that message for me.'

'Certainly. But wouldn't it have more impact if you warned him yourself?' I gazed back at her.

'I have, Dr Quentin. But policemen are lawbreakers by nature, and Burns is no exception. As far as he's concerned, I'm invisible.' Her lips trembled with amusement. She obviously knew about her nickname – maybe she'd coined it herself, to give weight to her reputation.

Brotherton ended our conversation by pressing a buzzer on the wall. A young man arrived in seconds, and he marched me along the corridor as if I was guilty of a grievous offence. When I got to the incident room, Taylor was swaggering around like he owned it, his tie hanging loose around his throat. I logged onto the nearest computer and scanned the evidence files. They'd doubled since the day before: dozens of interviews flooding into the system. Gresham's colleagues, friends from his church and golf club, had all given their opinions. I read a couple of interview forms but no one had reported a change in his behaviour. Taylor's sickly aftershave hit the back of my throat as soon as he sat down.

'Are you looking for Burns?' he asked.

I shook my head. 'I'm updating my report.'

'Forgive me for saying this, but you don't look much like a shrink to me.' His full-on eye contact was probably meant to be sexy.

'I know. Growing a beard's a struggle for me.'

The joke sailed straight past him and he carried on staring. 'You can always ask me for help. If anyone gives you a hard time, I'll deal with them.'

'I'll keep that in mind. Have you got some new information for me, DS Taylor?'

He grinned, then lounged back in his chair. 'I have, as a matter of fact. Gresham's deputy, Stephen Rayner, was off work the day his boss died. You should have a word with him.'

'Why?'

'Because he's a liar. He told his mates at the bank he's got a fiancée, but it's bollocks. She doesn't exist.'

'That doesn't make him a killer. Plenty of people hate admitting they're single.'

'He got cautioned for punching a colleague, years ago. The bloke can't control himself.' Taylor's expression hardened. 'He knows more than he's saying, I'd put money on it.'

Uncertainty didn't seem to feature in his emotional repertoire, so I didn't reply. I got the impression that trying to change Taylor's opinion should carry a health warning. It would be as risky as slipping your fingers between a pitbull's jaws.

6

Will was fast asleep on the sofa when I got back, oblivious to the sunlight flooding through the windows. I paused in the doorway to study him. At least he was beginning to look like my brother again, instead of a junkie who didn't care whether he took ketamine or crack. With my eyes half closed he looked like the golden boy he'd been at sixteen. His hair was exactly the same, thick and unruly, the colour of damp straw. But his features had changed almost beyond recognition. His eyes had settled deeper into their sockets, and his cheekbones were sharp-edged, jutting from his face like the angles of a picture frame. I had to remind myself how much progress he'd made. Six months ago the doctors thought his legs might never mend, but he was walking again and, if he chose to, he could follow a conversation from start to finish. It was hard to believe that he'd ever had a stellar career in finance. But when his bank heard about his bipolar disorder, they dropped him instantly, and none of his so-called friends had bothered to keep in contact. Their reaction had given me a biased view of financiers – I was convinced that most of them had hearts of stone.

There were no messages on the answer-machine in the hall, which always made me suspicious. Will often deleted them without telling me. Strangers whispering secrets seemed to be more than he could bear. I noticed the sound of water dripping when I walked towards the kitchen. The source was easy to find – the sink was overflowing, still loaded with last night's dishes. Will must have intended to wash up, then forgotten all about it. Luckily most of the water had drained down the overflow, but a puddle had collected beside the fridge. I cursed loudly, then hunted for the mop. Will was still out for the count when I finished rescuing the floor, and the exertion had made my ribs ache.

I stood by the bedroom mirror and pulled up my top. Half of my ribcage had become a rainbow, emanating from a black centre through shades of blue, to mottled red at the edges. But at least the inflammation was going down, and it was easier to breathe. I lay on the bed with an icepack over my sternum. When the phone woke me, I shivered; the cold had lowered my body temperature.

'You haven't forgotten about the bankers' do, have you?' Burns sounded even more uptight than before. 'I'll be round in half an hour. Put your glad rags on, Alice. The Champagne Charlies will be out in force.'

I hunted through my wardrobe for something suitable, feeling curious about the evening ahead, because Gresham's world was new territory. I'd never stood in a room full of millionaires before. It was a behaviourist's dream, and it had to beat an evening of crappy takeaway food, watching my brother doze on the settee. I put on some lipstick and squeezed into my only cocktail dress. It was a relic from a summer wedding, pale green silk, tight enough to accentuate every curve.

'Blimey.' Burns peered at me from the doorstep. 'You scrub up well.'

'Cheers, Don. You've got a real way with words.'

He'd unearthed a dinner jacket from somewhere, his bowtie slightly off kilter. I resisted the urge to reach up and straighten it for him. His profile had come into focus since he'd lost weight, with a newly defined jawline – Mrs Burns must have been thanking her lucky stars.

'Where is the Albion Club anyway?' I asked.

'St James's Park.' Burns's lip curled. 'It's the oldest gentlemen's club in town. You need serious cash to join, unless you're Prince Charles. It gives the banking boys a break from their wives. Women are barred most of the year.'

'You're kidding.'

He didn't seem to hear me. He was staring straight ahead, as though the killer might step into the road at any moment. 'Why are you so keen to go?'

'Everyone from the banking world will be there. A lot of them must have known Gresham,' I said.

'They won't tell us anything. They'll think we're journalists, sniffing for a story.'

When I glanced at Burns, his face was tense with anxiety, and I made an instant diagnosis. His shyness must have been crippling as a child. These days he was doing a good job of hiding it, but gatherings of strangers clearly filled him with dread.

The early-evening traffic brought the car to a halt at Piccadilly Circus. Gangs of teenagers were chatting on the steps of the Eros statue, oblivious to the traffic fumes. When we finally pulled up on St James's Square, a doorman rushed over to relieve Burns of his car keys, his jacket glittering with brocade. The Albion Club was a huge neoclassical eyesore. I spotted Richard Branson at the top of the stairs, a crowd of chinless wonders in tuxedos queuing behind him on a strip of red carpet. Several faces were instantly recognisable: Tory MPs, financial pundits and the governor of the Bank of England. In their shoes I'd have felt vulnerable. Given the state of the economy, a few unhinged members of the population must dream about strafing them with a machine gun.

'Not my cup of tea,' Burns muttered.

'Relax, Don. All you have to do is take a look around.'

The club's interior was even grander than its façade, the hallway lined with portraits of former members decked out in military regalia. Female guests were gathering in cliques, displaying the family heirlooms. Burns's eyes were fixed on the girl beside me; she was so encrusted with emeralds it was a wonder she could move.

'It's rude to stare,' I whispered. 'Let's split up. We'll see more that way.'

He vanished into the crowd, leaving me stranded in the middle of the room, as a waiter sailed by with a tray of champagne. Burns's shyness must have rubbed off on me because I'd been intending to drink orange juice, but I grabbed a glass and knocked back a large gulp.

'Steady, young lady, or you'll sleep through the speeches.'

The man peering down at me had a thin, expressive face. He was a little too tall, with curly chestnut brown hair and freckled skin stretched tight across his cheekbones. It was his smile that brought the whole ensemble together, snaggle-toothed and sincere. His voice was interesting too – it sounded permanently amused, and each word took ages to produce, as if his cheeks were packed with marbles.

'Ever been to Albie's before?' he asked.

'Never,' I replied.

'Andrew Piernan.' He held out a fragile, long-fingered hand. 'Delighted to make your acquaintance.' He leant closer to whisper in my ear. 'This lot are harmless, and don't worry, you're easily the prettiest girl here.'

Piernan was an impressive gossip. He had the lowdown on almost every guest. 'That guy's a shipping tycoon, between wives.' He nodded at an elderly man with a pronounced stoop. 'Rich as Croesus, and a rampant foot fetishist, by all accounts. If he asks for your shoe size you're in luck.'

44

I couldn't help giggling. He kept up a brilliant running commentary for the next twenty minutes, as though it was his job to keep me amused. His pale brown eyes flickered across my face, making sure my smile was intact. It was hard to guess his age. His curls made him look like a child, but his mouth was bracketed by deep lines. He could have been anywhere between thirty and forty-five.

On the other side of the room I spotted a man circulating from guest to guest, patting backs and flirting with every woman he passed. He was one of those men who don't follow the usual rules, like George Clooney or Clint Eastwood. A combination of good looks and brash confidence meant that women were turning round for a better look, even though he must have been in his sixties. His grey hair was glossy with health, and he had the weather-beaten tan that comes from years of tropical holidays.

'Who's that?' I asked.

'Max Kingsmith, head of the Angel Bank, and eternally young. He's got a new baby, believe it or not.' Piernan was standing close enough for me to count his freckles.

'How can a bank call itself angelic?' I asked.

'It was founded by a Quaker family. They used their profits to support the poor.'

'And now you lot squander them on Lamborghinis.'

'So young and yet so cynical.' His smile widened. 'But don't blame me. I'm a con artist, not a moneylender.'

'Who do you con?'

He wafted a thin hand at the crowd. 'This lot mainly. I've swindled millions out of them over the years.'

'Good for you. They probably deserve it.'

Piernan stared down at me. 'You're very forthright, aren't you?'

'Blunt, you mean.'

His eyes were fixed on my mouth, as though he was waiting for the next insult. I remembered Lola's advice about practising my flirting skills. This man seemed like the ideal target, because he was confident enough to walk up to a complete stranger, with nothing to recommend him except his Charlie Chaplin smile. But Burns was scowling on the other side of the room and I felt a pang of guilt. He held up his wrist and tapped his watch urgently, reminding me to get on with the task in hand.

'Did you know Leo Gresham?' I asked.

Piernan looked taken aback. 'Pretty well – our paths crossed at events like these. I have to go to a lot of mind-numbing fundraisers. What about you?'

I shook my head. 'What was he like?'

'Put it this way, the man certainly knew how to have a good time.' He watched me drain my glass of champagne. 'Another?'

'Better not. I'd hate to fall over before the food arrives.'

'Tell me about yourself.' He was observing me minutely. Maybe he'd never seen a woman in a cheap outfit, with a bag that failed to match her shoes.

'My name's Alice, my favourite colour's turquoise, and I'm a psychologist.'

'A shrink, in a room full of bankers?'

'It's a long story. I'd hate to bore you.'

'You couldn't.' He was standing so close that I could smell his aftershave, an odd blend of cinnamon and sandalwood. 'But I bet you've got a husband in the bar somewhere, cutting deals.'

'Wrong.' I smiled at him. 'The truth is, I'm a spy.'

The champagne was beginning to take hold, and after six months of avoiding men completely, the attention was going to my head. Piernan was about to ask me another question when a dinner gong clanged and an elderly woman seized my elbow. She propelled me towards the dining room, chattering loudly, as though we'd been friends for years. Piernan's eyes were trailing me when I glanced back. He'd been absorbed by a huddle of businessmen, and no doubt he was charming them too. I got the impression that he was on a mission to collect secrets from everyone in the room.

7

Every female guest was marching in the same direction, observing the club's tradition of seating ladies first. It felt like I'd arrived at Hogwarts as I gazed at the five-tier chandeliers, hovering over the dining tables. My companion was busy describing her ailments. Fortunately I didn't need to speak, because the list was so extensive: diabetes, rheumatism and gout. It made my bruises seem insignificant, and it gave me time to study the frescos in the dining hall. Huntsmen were galloping round the edges of the room, the fox's tail just visible between painted trees.

Burns was nowhere to be seen, and I was seated at a table full of elderly aristocrats. Their conversation fascinated me; they were bemoaning the increases in inheritance tax, the decline of Conservatism and the state of the Middle East. The menu was straight out of Mrs Beeton: potted shrimps under a thick layer of butter, then a plate of overcooked turbot. I asked the man to my right if he'd worked with Leo Gresham, but he looked straight through me.

'Nasty business,' he muttered. 'Pass the wine, can you?'

He seized the bottle, then turned his back on me, but the rest of my companions made an effort to be welcoming, even though they were twice my age. The woman sitting opposite looked bemused by the fact I was a psychologist. She told me about her mad uncle, who had enjoyed frolicking naked in his garden until he was carted away to an asylum. An endless succession of courses kept arriving: dishes of braised lamb, silver trays loaded with sliced beef and three new types of wine. My vision was beginning to blur, even though I'd paced myself, and I realised that the evening had been a wild-goose chase. The Albion Club had closed ranks. They had no intention of revealing their secrets to a pair of complete strangers. By the time the Eton Mess came, I was desperate for a strong cup of coffee. It crossed my mind to rush outside and flag down the nearest taxi. People were on their feet, networking before the speeches began. Andrew Piernan materialised while I was planning my escape.

'Fancy a tour of the building?'

I smiled at him and stood up, head spinning with wine. He put out a hand to steady me, then asked how I planned to spend the weekend. I told him about my promise to visit Lola at the Riverside Theatre. He gave me a wide, uneven smile and started to lead me through the crowd. But before we could go anywhere, Burns came racing towards us, listening avidly to his mobile phone.

'We need to leave, Alice,' he insisted.

I turned to Piernan. 'It's work, I'm afraid. I'll have to skip the tour.'

'Another time, I hope.' He gazed down at me then walked slowly away.

By now Burns was clutching my elbow, escorting me outside, like a vandal being taken to a holding cell. It was still so warm that it was difficult to breathe, the oxygen replaced by traffic fumes. The radio squawked loudly as soon as we set off. Scratchy voices were barking instructions at each other, and it was hard to know whether my discomfort was the result of worry, or too much booze. I clutched the edge of my seat, trying to control my nausea.

'What's happening?' I asked.

'The worst-case fucking scenario,' Burns muttered. 'He's done it again, just like I said. I'm taking you home before I go there.'

I shook my head. 'I need to come with you.'

He didn't bother to argue, keeping his attention on the road. We were racing along the Embankment past HMS *Wellington*, silver gun towers glittering in the floodlights. By the time we reached Cheapside there wasn't a soul around. The Square Mile would have been empty since six, every café locking its doors when the banks closed.

Burns parked by Gutter Lane. He took a deep breath, then shunted his glasses back onto the bridge of his nose. An ambulance, two squad cars, and a scene-of-crime van were there already, two coppers tying security tape across the mouth of the alley. Taylor strutted towards us. His gaze travelled across my body as he took in my cocktail dress. He gave Burns a curt nod when he finally eyeballed him.

'Having a night out, boss?' Taylor tagged the last word to the sentence like the world's slowest afterthought.

'We've been working,' Burns replied briskly. 'What have you got here?'

'A stabbing. He's a sick bastard, that's for sure.'

Pete Hancock made us put on protective suits before we could go any closer. I'd always hated the feel of them. The Tyvek fabric is so thin and scratchy, it's like wrapping yourself in greaseproof paper, your body heat slowly rising. It was hard to guess Hancock's state of mind, because his monobrow made him look permanently furious. He didn't bother to make conversation as he watched me replace my high heels with white plastic boots.

I followed Burns down the alleyway, between industrial rubbish bins with gaping lids. The smell was overpowering, a mixture of rancid beer, urine and rotting food. A paramedic was kneeling inside the inner cordon, blocking my view.

'Do you know what happened?' Burns was speaking in a stage whisper, as though he was afraid of waking the victim.

When the paramedic turned round, her skin was the colour of limestone. I realised the man's wounds must be horrific, because she'd have seen dozens of fatalities every year.

'It must have been quick,' she said. 'This much blood means the knife went through his heart.'

She scuttled back to the safety of her ambulance, and I caught sight of the man's body for the first time. He was lying in a wide circle of blood, with a black plastic bag over his face. A picture of an angel had been placed beside his head, her halo glittering as torchlight bounced from the walls. A handful of white feathers were scattered across the cobbles. The man was wearing dark trousers and a long-sleeved shirt. A wave of sickness rose in my chest. I wondered where he'd spent his last day. Working in an office, probably, fantasising about the weekend. His body disappeared from view as two uniforms pushed by. The photographer was already hard at work, taking pictures of the body from every conceivable angle. When the passageway cleared again, Burns was squatting down for a closer look, and voices were drifting from the street. The press had arrived, baying for information. Taylor trotted away to deal with them.

'Bloody ambulance chasers,' Burns mumbled. 'Looks like our man's having a laugh.'

'How do you mean?'

'He's left a bigger calling card, in case we missed the first one.'

He put on a pair of plastic gloves and picked up the card. It was larger than the one in Leo Gresham's pocket, and the image had been defaced. Thick lines had been drawn across her perfect Renaissance features, slicing them into sections. I stared down at the victim's body. There was a wound in the middle of his abdomen: a jagged cut, at least six inches long. I pressed the back of my hand across my mouth.

'Are you okay, Alice?'

'I've been better.'

'You don't have to stay. I'll get someone to take you home.'

I shook my head. It's always better to visit crime scenes, instead of working from photos. Sometimes the killer's escaped less than an hour before, and the details are so fresh, you're breathing the same air. You can inhale information that a photo could never give you. I'd already absorbed the care that had gone into staging the scene, the victim's arms arranged neatly at his sides, as if he'd made no attempt to struggle.

The pathologist arrived a few minutes later; a stout, middle-aged woman with a cheerful manner, determined not to let the horrors of her job ruin her evening. I waited outside the cordon with Burns to let her get on with it. By the time we returned she was removing the bag from the victim's head, so the photographer could take pictures. She eased the plastic back slowly, as though she was reluctant to cause more pain, and I forced myself to carry on looking. The man's face had been cut to pieces. His cheek had been sliced so savagely there was a hole beside his ear, exposing his teeth. A flap of skin lolled against his collarbone. The wounds on his forehead were so deep that the white bone of his skull was exposed. A hot rush of nausea surged in the back of my throat. I made it through the cordon, and stumbled a few more yards before retching behind a wheelie bin. At least Burns was polite enough not to comment when I tottered back down the alley.

I could have found a taxi, but I was too tired to refuse when Taylor offered me a lift home. My legs were starting to feel unsteady. Corpses have always unsettled me, unlike all the other students in my year at medical school. They loved dissections, humming contentedly as they sliced through human skin and bone as if they were carving the Christmas turkey. Despite the circumstances, Taylor seemed determined to be gallant, opening the passenger door with a flourish. His phone rang just as we were about to drive away, and he stood on the pavement to take the call. He spent several minutes reassuring someone that he'd be home soon.

'Third time tonight,' he moaned as he got back into the car. 'She hates letting me out of her sight.' We'd only been driving a hundred yards when he glanced in my direction. 'What about you? Someone waiting for you at home, is there?'

'Just my brother.'

I was too preoccupied to edit my reply, but I realised afterwards that I should have invented a boyfriend. Taylor gave me a meaningful smile, then talked about himself for the rest of the journey. I got the impression that he'd have carried on bigging himself up even if the car had been empty. He described his athletic prowess, explaining how well he'd done in his Sports Studies degree, collecting trophies for judo, football and diving. He'd won every prize under the sun. And it was the same with women – he could pick and choose. Only his career frustrated him.

'This is the third time I've been overlooked. They promised me the job, then Burns gets the push from Southwark, and I'm out of luck. It's unbelievable. The bloke's incompetent, so they give him to us.'

I didn't bother to correct him, because he wasn't listening. The expression on his face was the definition of heartbreak, and it seemed odd that he could obsess about himself while a man lay on the ground with his face in shreds. I wondered why promotion bothered him so much – it couldn't just be the money. Under all the bluster, his ego must be microscopic. It crossed my mind to tell him that a course of cognitive behavioural therapy would sort him out.

It was after two when Taylor finally drew up outside my building. 'Want some company?' he asked. 'You could make me a coffee.' His arm was poised across the back of my seat.

'I'll be fine, thanks.' I felt like reminding him about his long-suffering girlfriend, watching the clock at home. He shot me a look of disapproval, as though I'd refused the chance of a lifetime.

My reflection in the bathroom mirror proved how low Taylor set his standards. My chignon had collapsed, and lines of mascara were trailing down my cheeks. I scrubbed my face with soap and went straight to bed, but the day kept replaying itself. I tried not to think about the body on Gutter Lane, abandoned among the rubbish for the rats to find. The angels haunted me too: maybe the killer was an atheist, certain there would be no retribution for his attacks. The last face I saw belonged to my companion at the Albion Club. Andrew Piernan's gold-flecked eyes watched me as I fell asleep, focused as a bird of prey's.

8

The nightmares came back with a vengeance. Every time I closed my eyes, young girls were lying in front of me, their thin bodies covered in wounds. I had to crawl across them to reach the door. Under the palms of my hands I could feel their damp skin, the cold gloss of their hair. I woke up with an aching jaw, as though I'd spent the night gasping for air, and I knew I couldn't stay indoors. I would have to go running. Exercise is my only addiction, and I suppose I was bound to have one, because my family tree's littered with cravings: Will's need for stimulants, my father's alcoholism, my mother's love of control. Maybe I got off lightly – at least running's less harmful than gin or cigarettes or heroin. And it's the perfect antidote to thought. Whenever I want to indulge in a spot of avoidance, I reach for my trainers and let my worries drain through the soles of my feet. I knew it was a crazy idea to run with a soft-tissue injury, but it felt like I had no choice. A spasm of pain travelled across my chest with each footfall, but I had no intention of slowing down.

Tower Bridge was almost empty when I crossed the river. It was already so hot that the air tasted like it had been burned, a sour tang of petrol and smoke filling my mouth whenever I swallowed. Half a dozen cabin cruisers were tethered by the entrance to St Katharine Docks, mooring ropes stretched tight enough to snap. I ran north, skirting the edge of the City. Rows of brownstone buildings were minding their own business, windows shuttered, like closed eyes. When I reached Cornhill there was a cordon across the road, a cluster of police vans parked in the distance. Burns must have been blowing his budget on combing the area around Gutter Lane for evidence. I headed down Leadenhall Street, running through the narrow roads, until my hamstrings burned. Crowds of shoppers were flocking towards Borough Market as I crossed London Bridge, ready to pauper themselves for a bag of avocadoes.

My mobile was ringing on the hall table when I got home.

'You're still coming, aren't you?' Lola sounded about fifteen, worried I might abandon her.

Only Lola could drag me across town in the middle of a heat wave to admire her professional skills, followed by lunch in a café. After my shower I stepped into my thinnest sundress and a pair of ballet shoes. The journey took even longer than I'd expected, because of a signal failure at Paddington, but London Underground's security team had been hard at work since Leo Gresham's death. Posters were displayed on every platform, advising people to stand clear of the yellow line, and report suspicious behaviour. People were keeping their backs to the wall, eyeing the crowd for potential murderers. I glanced down at the headline in the *Independent*: ANOTHER MURDER IN THE CITY. One of last night's journalists had managed to get details of the attack on Gutter Lane: the victim was Jamie Wilcox, twenty-five years old, married with a baby. The story explained that he was a trainee trader at the Angel Bank and the links with Leo Gresham fell into place. They'd worked in the same building, so the two men would have known each other, by sight at least. There was a photo of Wilcox on his graduation day, round-faced and beaming with pride. He looked like my brother after he got his first job in the City. What kind of person could believe that killing such a young man put them on the side of the angels? Maybe the battle was simple, in his eyes – the haves would be defeated by the have-nots. He could be doing a reverse Dennis Nilsen, punishing society's high-flyers for their affluence. I stuffed the paper back into my bag.

I was seriously late when I finally reached the theatre. A crowd of thespians was standing in the foyer, shrieking at the tops of their voices. It reminded me that I would have been hopeless at drama school. Actors made wonderful friends, but their non-stop charisma would have exhausted me. I found Lola in the rehearsal room, helping a young girl in a wheelchair turn the pages of her script. She looked gorgeous as always, red hair scooped back from her face, showing off her mile-wide smile. About twenty kids were playing and teasing each other, with occasional acting exercises thrown in. Two young boys were dancing in their wheelchairs, manoeuvring so gracefully that the chairs seemed like extensions of their bodies. The room buzzed with excitement and noise.

After a few moments I realised that someone was staring at me.

I had to look twice to confirm that it was Andrew Piernan, and he was coming towards me, wearing the amused look that I remembered from the night before. His dinner suit had been replaced by jeans and a dark green shirt.

'Are you following me?' I asked.

'Of course. You said you'd be here, so I've been camping outside since dawn. But I do visit quite often, believe it or not.'

'My friend Lola twisted my arm.' I pointed her out. By now she was surrounded by small boys, capering in a circle, sticking out their tongues.

'I've met her. She must be hard to refuse.' Piernan carried on watching me, and I wished I was still wearing last night's shoes. He was so tall that I had to fling my head back to make conversation. 'Would you like to get some lunch? Or maybe you don't have time? We could just have coffee.'

'No.' I shook my head. 'Lunch would be fine.'

I gave Lola an apologetic look to let her know my plans had changed, but she gave me an excited thumbs-up. Obviously my flirting skills mattered more to her than sharing a sandwich.

Piernan managed to find a table in the bar with a view across the river, a row of Victorian warehouses lining the opposite bank.

'What's your connection with this place?' I asked.

'I fund-raise for them.' He laughed at the expression on my face. 'Why do you look so shocked?'

'You said you robbed people.'

'I do.' His skin stretched taut across his cheeks when he grinned. 'I work for a charity called the Ryland Foundation. It's named after Louisa Ryland, a Victorian philanthropist who gave most of her money away. We make companies hand over cash for good causes, but normally we use persuasion instead of guns.'

Piernan chatted to the waitress courteously when she took our order, and my image of him shifted. He could morph from public school clown to English gentleman and back again in seconds. His cut-glass accent fascinated me. I kept waiting for him to drop a consonant, but it never happened. He was like a newsreader from the 1940s, announcing victories and defeats in exactly the same tone. When the waitress disappeared he turned to face me again.

'This place works with people like my sister. That's why I got involved.'

'Your sister has a disability?'

Piernan hesitated. 'Eleanor has Asperger's. She's nearly thirty, but she's only just moved into supported housing.'

'Sounds like my brother.' The words popped out before I could stop them. Normally I never mentioned him, but Piernan's revelation had caught me off guard. I found myself talking about Will's bipolar disorder. I even explained about his injuries and learning to walk again.

'How terrible.' Piernan gave a sympathetic frown. 'One thing after another.'

We sat in silence for a minute, watching a barge fighting the tide, hauling itself past Hammersmith Bridge. It gave me time to observe him. His shirt had a wide, old-fashioned collar, and it looked as if he'd been faithful to his hairdresser for decades, the same fringe flopping in his eyes since he was a boy. He told me more about his sister. She'd never been to Paris, so he was planning a trip in a few weeks for her birthday. His face grew animated as he talked about the hotel, and a walk he'd planned through Montmartre. He seemed comfortable talking about anyone except himself.

'Are you a forensic psychologist?' he asked.

I nodded reluctantly. 'I'm licensed for it, but I prefer helping people while they're still alive.'

'Isn't there a morbid fascination?' He stifled a laugh. 'Putting all those twisted villains behind bars.'

'Sometimes it puts you off humankind altogether.'

'I'd love to hear more about it some time. I wanted to study psychology, but I ended up doing finance instead. A big mistake, probably.'

His eyes were a calm, golden brown as they observed me, and something twitched at the base of my stomach, like a string loosening. I rose to my feet in a hurry.

'I should go. It was good to bump into you again.' I made my getaway before he could reply.

The journey home was like descending into the jaws of hell. There was no sign of ventilation, not so much as a whisper of breeze, and I couldn't avoid thinking about Andrew Piernan. He'd given me no reason to run away, apart from the fact that I was starting to fancy him. There was no point in leading him on when there was nothing to offer. I was coping better than before, but I was still running on empty. The train burrowed under the belly of the city, jolting past Edgware Road, Baker Street and King's Cross, spitting people out and inhaling them again at every stop. The woman opposite me looked like an exotic flower. She was wearing a brightly patterned dress, but she was wilting in the heat, make-up trickling down her face. It was a relief to emerge into cleaner air. My phone vibrated in my pocket but I ignored it – Lola would be calling already, ravenous for gossip. All I wanted was to take a siesta, but a familiar car was parked by the entrance to my building, and by now it was too late to run away.

My mother was sitting in the kitchen, her jacket neatly folded on her lap, with a horrified expression on her face. Clearly she'd used her key to let herself in, then spent the last half-hour staring at the pile of dirty laundry waiting to be loaded into the washing machine. It was a typical piece of miscommunication. We'd been making an effort to meet more regularly, yet we always managed to wrong-foot each other. When I kissed her she smelled the same as always, a mixture of coffee, eau de cologne and rage.

'I didn't know you were coming, Mum.'

'Of course you did, darling. I left four messages.'

'You should have called my mobile.'

I cursed Will without moving my lips. He must have deleted the messages then forgotten to tell me. I glanced at my mother's clothes. She was wearing a crisp blue dress, a string of pearls nestling on her collarbone. Somehow she'd survived the journey from Blackheath in forty-degree heat without a single hair shifting out of place.

'I haven't seen Will today. Have you phoned him?' I asked.

'You know he never answers my calls.'

I sat beside her and tried Lola's smiling trick. 'We could go somewhere by ourselves, if you like.'

'Shouldn't you freshen up?'

'It's the weekend. I'm allowed to be scruffy.'

She sighed then gazed out of the window. 'He's still got that death-trap van.'

'I think he's scared to let it go.'

'Why?' My mother's voice was shrill with exasperation.

'He sleeps in it sometimes, when he's stressed.'

'You shouldn't allow it, Alice.' Her grey eyes darkened by several shades.

'He's thirty-six years old, Mum. I'm not his keeper.'

When we finally got outside, the walk along the river calmed her, and she told me about the holiday she was taking in Crete, with a friend from the library. It sounded like an endless slog around Minoan ruins, but it would suit her perfectly. It was hard to imagine my mother relaxing on a sun lounger, listening to the sea. She talked about her voluntary work too; one day a week for Help the Homeless, answering the phone. Maybe it appeased her guilt. Will had lived in his van for eight years but she'd never even offered him her spare room.

'I visited your father's grave on Monday.'

'Did you?' I was too stunned to offer an appropriate reply. Months had gone by since the last time she'd mentioned him.

'That rosebush I planted is doing well. It'll need pruning soon.'

I nodded. My father had never shown the slightest interest in gardening, unless she nagged him to mow the lawn; he was too busy getting pissed in the garage. My mother seemed to be on the verge of explaining something, but we arrived at the Design Museum before she could speak. We bought our tickets and stepped into a fantasy world. The exhibition was called Child's Play. Hundreds of Barbie dolls were trapped in a vat of transparent resin. Some of them had their arms raised, swimming frantically for the surface.

'Ridiculous,' my mother snorted. 'What on earth is that supposed to mean?'

I thought for a moment. 'That childhood memories are fixed, maybe? They can't be changed.'

My mother's frown deepened. She marched from one exhibit to the next, hardly glancing at the huge city made of Lego, suspended upside down from the ceiling. Afterwards I bought her an iced tea, but the museum had reinstated her bad mood. At least she found something to admire on the way back. Hanging baskets blossomed from every lamppost, filled with lobelia and trailing geraniums.

'Gorgeous,' she murmured. She'd saved her first smile of the day for a floral display.

There was still no sign of Will when we got back, so she smoothed her hair in the hall mirror and prepared to leave. She kissed the air directly beside my cheek, then stepped back to study my face.

'You look shattered, darling. Haven't you been sleeping?'

I gritted my teeth. The urge to tell her to fuck off was over-whelming. 'I'm fine, Mum, honestly.'

From the kitchen window I watched her return to her car. Her walk was the same as always, light-footed as a ballet dancer. She could have been forty, not sixty, completely care-free.

9

Burns was hard at work when I found him on Monday morning. His office was half the size of his old one at Southwark, as though the architecture had shrunk to match his stature. He was scribbling notes in the policy book. No doubt Brotherton had been breathing down his neck to keep it up to date. When he looked up from the pages, he studied me intently.

'Are you all right?' he asked.

'Of course I am. Why?'

'I should have taken you home. You didn't need to see all that first-hand.'

I could guess what he was thinking: he felt guilty for exposing me to yet another corpse. People handled me with kid gloves all the time when I got out of hospital. Friends spoke in whispers, and took me to see romances instead of thrillers at the cinema. The whole world seemed determined to smother me in tissue paper.

'It helps me to be there, Don. You know that.' I smiled at him. 'I'd like to see someone who can give me some background on the cards he's leaving.'

'An expert on angels? There can't be many of those around.'

I pulled a folder out of my bag. 'I've updated my report for you.'

'I'll get Steve. You can give us the headlines.'

I rolled my eyes at him. 'If you must.'

Burns suppressed a smile then disappeared. When Taylor

arrived he looked sulky, like a child disappointed by his birth-day presents. Maybe it rankled that his new boss had been right about Gresham's death being the first in a series, or he was still smarting from my rejection. He checked his watch pointedly as I listed the points in my report.

'The MO hasn't changed. He's still killing men, and leaving the same signature, but this time there was no spontaneity. Everything was stage-managed, with meticulous detail. Even the name of the street reinforces the message: Gutter Lane. An angel couldn't fall any lower. If a killer mutilates his victim's face that violently, it normally means he knows them. And he covered the wounds afterwards with the plastic hood. Maybe that's because he's ashamed, he couldn't bear to look at what he'd done. I think it's someone who's linked closely to the Angel Bank, or still has a job there. He's obsessed by the moral status of the place.'

'He could have good reason.' Burns peered at me over the top of his glasses. 'Their lawyers are stonewalling – we can't get access to their records. Who knows what kind of deals they're doing?'

My gaze drifted to the window as I tried to concentrate. 'He's got to be a Type A psychopath, super-bright, and comfortable wandering round the National Gallery, or read-ing his Bible stories. The images he leaves are some of the highest examples of Western art. He wants us to know how cultured he is. And he charmed his victim into following him down a dark alley in the middle of the night, which makes me even more sure that Wilcox knew him.'

Taylor gave an exaggerated yawn, as if my theories were a lullaby. I handed him a copy of my report and he marched out without saying goodbye.

Burns looked apologetic. 'Sorry about that. He's short on sleep.'

'And manners.'

I wondered how Taylor's girlfriend coped with his ego problem, while Burns got ready to leave. He stood by his desk patting the pockets of his jacket.

'What have I done with my phone?' he muttered.

I spotted it under a pile of forms and handed it to him. 'You've been losing plenty of stuff lately, haven't you?'

'More than I can afford.'

My comment was intended as a joke about his weight loss, but it seemed to hit a raw nerve. Burns crashed back into his chair, and when he started to talk again, his voice sounded like air gushing from a puncture.

'I've been losing things for years. The cardiologist said "drop the weight and quit the fags or you'll be dead at fifty", and now it feels like I'm running round in someone else's body. Then all the crap kicked in at work, and Julie left straight after. She couldn't handle it.' He gulped down a huge breath. 'She got the house, and the kids stay twice a week, if I'm lucky. I haven't slept properly in weeks.'

I was too shocked to reply. It was the first time I'd heard Burns speak about himself. His head was bowed, and he seemed to be struggling to keep it together. No wonder he was determined to hang onto his job. It must feel like the one thing he had left to lose. Only his machismo made him straighten back up. He polished his glasses frantically, before putting them on again.

'Sorry,' he muttered. 'Boys are told not to bleat about feelings where I come from.' He shuffled some papers into a folder, taking care to avoid eye contact.

'It's better out than in, Don.'

'Rubbish.' He gave a narrow smile. 'It's best kept under lock and key.'

'And that attitude is why Scottish men die young.'

Burns had promised to take me to meet some of Gresham's business contacts. The Angel Bank was being tight-lipped, so I was keen to meet anyone who was prepared to talk. So far Burns had been as good as his word, granting all my requests. I got the sense that he appreciated the company, because his colleagues had left him isolated. For the time being he was treating me like an honorary cop. The arrangement suited me, partly because I needed to know more about the world the victims inhabited, but also because I was worried about him. I watched him square his shoulders as we crossed the car park. His voice sounded calmer once he started driving.

'I saw the lad's widow, from Gutter Lane. She's in bits. Wilcox had only been at the Angel Bank a few months. Now she's stuck in a high rise on Commercial Road with a one-year-old kid, twenty grand's worth of debt, and a view of the railway.'

'Do you know what Wilcox was doing on Friday night?'

Burns's obsessive frown was back in place. 'He went to the Counting House after work, but the place was so rammed, the bar staff didn't see who was with him. The pathologist says there's no sign he tried to fight his attacker, but we'll have to wait for the PM.'

'Is there any news on Gresham?'

'The results came back from the UV test on his jacket. There was a trace of saliva on the back, but there's no DNA match on the database.'

I glanced across at him. 'Last time I saw Taylor, he had a bee in his bonnet about Gresham's deputy.'

'Stephen Rayner? Forget about it. Taylor's like a dog with a bone when he thinks he's onto something. We've got no evidence he's involved.'

'Does he have an alibi?'

Burns shook his head. 'He says he was at home on his own, both nights. Okay, he's a loner, but he's clean as a whistle. He got cautioned for punching someone in a pub fight when he was a youngster, but since then he's done an MA in Finance and worked his way up the ladder. He's not serial killer material, is he?'

I wanted to argue, but Burns was too morose for conversation as the car headed west. In less than twenty minutes we were passing through neighbourhoods with solid gold postcodes.

'Do all bankers live in Mayfair?' I asked.

'Looks like it, the lucky buggers. Nicole Morgan's place is out of this world. She does PR for the Angel Bank.'

The name rang a bell for some reason. Whoever Morgan was, she couldn't be short of a penny. Her home was a minute's walk from the designer shops on Bond Street, protected by a line of fir trees. A flash of turquoise glittered as we drove through the security gates. It was still so airless, I was fantasising about stripping off and diving into her pool. The house was an estate agent's dream, with rows of gleaming sash windows and a fuchsia-pink front door.

When Nicole Morgan appeared I did a double-take. I recognised her from breakfast TV. She had a regular slot, advising women how to run their lives. According to her it was possible to make cupcakes, have a great career and still find time to get your nails done. Her hair fell across her shoulders in immaculate dark brown waves, and she was wearing a Fifties-style summer dress, perfect for her hourglass figure. She treated Burns to a lingering smile, but her gaze was laser-sharp. I didn't even appear on her radar – clearly she had no time for other people's minions.

'Come through.'

She sashayed along the hallway to a conservatory lined with olive trees in granite pots. Her garden was so vast that no boundaries were visible. Two small boys were playing on the lawn with their nanny, and I wondered how frequently they got to see their mother. Morgan pressed a buzzer then turned to us.

'I'm afraid I haven't got long. A film crew's coming in half an hour.'

A man in black trousers and a crisp white shirt arrived with a jug of coffee. He struck me as the wrong physical type for a manservant, stocky and wide-shouldered as a bodybuilder. His expression was aloof, as if taking orders irked him, and it was obvious that he had the hots for his boss. His gaze stayed glued to her as he unloaded the cups and saucers onto the table.

'Thank you, Liam,' Morgan simpered. 'But could I have green tea, please?'

The butler gave her an adoring look then marched away.

'Leo Gresham was a close friend of yours, was he, Mrs Morgan?' Burns asked.

She widened her eyes, lips pouting. 'This is confidential, isn't it? No leaking anything to the press?'

I couldn't help staring. Flirts have always fascinated me – she seemed determined to get a sexual response, but Burns was refusing to comply.

'Of course,' he said calmly. 'This is a police investigation.'

Her teasing manner cooled for a second. 'I've known Leo forever. His house is a stone's throw from here. He made a pass at me donkey's years ago, but he was a complete gentleman when I turned him down. We've worked together for five years at the Angel Group. He was head of investments, and they're PR clients of mine. I can't imagine who'd want to hurt him.' Her hands fluttered, demonstrating her expensive manicure. 'The bank let a few people go last year, but that's no reason to kill someone, is it?'

'Only if you've got a family to feed,' Burns mumbled. 'Could anyone in particular be holding a grudge?'

'One of Leo's girlfriends, I suppose. He had plenty of admirers.' She giggled. 'His wife didn't have a clue. I'd have been wondering about all his business trips.'

'How do you know what he was up to?' Burns asked.

'He told me he kept a laptop at work, so he could arrange things without Marjorie finding out.'

The butler arrived with Morgan's tea. 'That took a while, Liam. I thought you'd forgotten me.'

'Can't get the staff,' Burns said as the man hurried away.

'Oh, he doesn't work for me, at least not any more. Liam was my personal trainer, but now he's my husband.'

Burns's neutral expression didn't flicker, but I wondered what he was thinking. Maybe he hadn't met many men who lived in thrall to their wives.

'Time's up I'm afraid.' Morgan looked regretful. Perhaps flirting with a gruff policeman was more fun than a film crew invading her home. 'I'm glad you stopped by, Inspector. Leo was an old charmer, I still can't believe it.'

There was a quaver in Morgan's voice, and I thought her emotions might be defeating her, but her eye make-up stayed intact. Evidently it would take more than the death of a close friend to reduce her to tears. Burns looked stunned when we reached the car.

'The poor sod, running round like a slave whenever she rings her little bell.'

'Maybe he enjoys it,' I replied. 'He's passive and she's active. The ideal match. She's right about the bank's ex-employees though. Plenty of them must be nursing grievances.'

Burns nodded. 'The bank are still stalling on handing over their employment records. If it carries on like this we'll need SOCA to get involved.'

'Who're SOCA?'

'The Serious Organised Crime Agency, commonly known

as the heavy mob. They can open any door they like, if there's enough evidence.'

When I closed the car door, Burns pulled away in a hurry, like he was performing an acceleration test for *Top Gear*. His emotional outburst at the station already seemed as unlikely as something I'd witnessed in a dream.

10

Bette Davis was glaring at me like I'd stolen her one chance of happiness. She was dressed in a lavish, bright red ball-gown, screaming abuse into her fiancé's face. It was a relief to mute the sound when the phone rang. I recognised Lola's giggle immediately.

'I saw you flirting in the café, you reprobate.'

'It's called having a conversation, Lo. Grown-ups do it all the time.'

'My arse. When are you seeing him again?'

'I didn't give him my number.'

'Are you mad? The man's perfect for you.'

I didn't reply, because no reason on earth would have satisfied her. If I admitted that I fancied him, but he'd arrived too soon, she'd have grabbed me by the scruff of my neck and delivered me to his front door.

'Jesus,' Lola moaned. 'You'll die in a bedsit, surrounded by cats.'

Bette Davis looked keen to join the tirade, her expression even more hostile than before. I reminded Lola that she'd agreed to bring her toyboy out for a drink the next evening. My friend Yvette would be coming along too. I wanted to ask her a few questions, because she knew everything there was to know about the banking world. By the time Lola said goodbye, the excitement had drained from her voice. She seemed convinced that my romantic prospects had fallen to zero.

When the film finished I behaved virtuously for the rest of the afternoon, collecting Will's dirty clothes from the floor in his room, cursing quietly to myself. A full ashtray was balanced precariously on the windowsill, used crockery piled by his bed. It was hard to remember the man who made his guests take their shoes off before admitting them to his Pimlico flat. Before his breakdown he could spend hours trawling Bond Street for a shirt in exactly the right shade of blue. Maybe the old Will still existed in a parallel world, holding down his big-money job and taking models to Annabel's.

I heard his key in the lock as I loaded the washing machine. He looked so relaxed I couldn't bring myself to tell him off.

'I went to the market, Al.' He beamed at me as he dumped a carrier bag full of vegetables on the counter. 'I'll make us a risotto.'

It was a struggle not to look amazed. 'Brilliant. I'm just getting in the bath.'

The lavender oil gradually soaked into my pores. The details I'd heard about Jamie Wilcox were still bothering me. His son was too young to understand that his dad would never come home. It seemed incredible that Wilcox hadn't even made it to his twenty-sixth birthday. I sat up and watched the bathwater disappear down the plughole. At least Will was making progress. A few days ago he could hardly drag himself off the settee, but now he was going out more, and keeping himself busy. Eventually I forced myself to get dry.

Will was hard at work in the kitchen. It was a miracle to see him cooking a meal by himself, for the first time in months, but his heels were clicking on the lino as he passed me the dish, making the whole table quiver. He delivered his bomb-shell before I'd eaten my first mouthful.

'I'll be leaving soon, Al.' His pale eyes glittered. 'I'm going to Brighton, then I'll move on.'

'Move on where?'

'I don't know yet. The clouds showed me I'd start travelling again; all I had to do was meet the right people.' His face was open as a child's, confident that his fate was written in the sky.

'Who are these friends, Will? How long have you known them?'

'A month or so, they're from my NA group.'

'That's not long. You don't need to rush, do you?'

My brother's smile switched off, like a light bulb shattering. 'I knew you'd be like this. Why don't you want me to have fun?'

'I do. But you don't have to burn your bridges, that's all.'

'That's crap.' His expression was turning vicious. 'Some bridges need to go up in flames.'

'Okay,' I said quietly. 'I'm just suggesting you take your time.'

'Stop controlling me, Al.' His voice had risen to a shout. Then he leant over, his face a few inches from mine. 'Your trouble is, you wouldn't know happiness if it smacked you in the face.'

Will reached out to grab his stick, knocking his glass of water to the floor. The shattering sound was followed by the slam of the front door. Maybe I should have chased after him, but anger had paralysed me. I'd spent years carrying him through crisis after crisis, yet he'd flung everything back in my face. It made me realise how people commit acts of violence; the mist that drops down before you stab or shoot someone. All I could do was wait for it to pass, which gave me time to take a long hard look at myself. It worried me that my anger could still erupt at any minute. How could I help my patients when it was so hard to govern my emotions? Months of worrying about Will and going back to work before I was fully recovered had taken their toll. Most of the time I felt like an automaton, my emotions so blunted it was hard to empathise. I hadn't shed a tear since my release from hospital, but on the few occasions when my feelings surfaced, they were too powerful to contain. I drew in a deep breath and did my best not to panic.

The evening sun was still glowing, but it felt like the walls of the flat were closing in on me, so I hauled my bike downstairs without thinking of a destination. My muscles were fuelled with enough nervous energy to race to Dover and back without stopping. I headed west towards the City. The Square Mile's an ideal place to cycle at night, because it's a ghost town. Three hundred thousand workers flood in every day, but hardly anyone lives there. Streets lined with banks and insurance offices hold their breath, until the rush hour starts their lifeblood pumping again. The Bank of England looked like a fortress, guarded by huge pillars – men in grey suits must have spent the weekend hunkered inside, arguing over the state of the economy. Every street name was advertising its wares: Ropemaker Street, Cloak Lane, Milk Street. Four hundred years ago, people would have known exactly where to buy what they needed, and the walk across town would have taken fifteen minutes. Now the urban sprawl had swallowed so many villages, the same journey would last for days.

I turned right on Princes Street, then carried on to Angel Court. The passageway opened onto a deserted square, and the bank was lit up, pale as a ghost against the darkness. Two life-sized angels were guarding the entrance. I leant my bike against the wall to study them more closely. Their stone faces were impassive, features softened by decades of rain. They looked as though they'd been uprooted from the gardens of a nunnery – relics from a time of greater benevolence, when building societies helped savers, instead of turning a profit for their shareholders. Gresham would have walked between the

angels a thousand times without stopping to ask for a bene-
diction, but Wilcox was still new enough to be impressed by
the Angel Bank's façade. I felt certain that the clean exterior
was only skin deep. Will's experience had convinced me that
there was a shortage of humanity in the banking world. No
one cared if you quit your job, so long as the money kept rolling in. I wondered how many people had even noticed Jamie
Wilcox's absence. A few miles away, his fiancée would be in
meltdown, while her son slept in his cot.

I turned my bike around, but I couldn't face going home to
scrape Will's congealing risotto into the bin. Flashes of anger
kept threatening to overwhelm me. Was I meant to be over-
joyed that he'd found some other junkies to hook up with?
Jamie Wilcox's face had been so badly mutilated, they'd
advised his wife not to identify him. His future had been stolen
from him, yet Will seemed happy to abandon his in a single
weekend. I set off again, standing on my pedals, racing in
circles through the empty streets.

I I

Dr Paul Gillick looked nothing like an expert on angels. I'd been expecting a thin-faced ascetic with a page-boy haircut, but he was a dead ringer for Santa Claus. He must have been close to seventy, with a thick white beard and a gentle smile. His office was in the basement at the National Gallery, but it had a celestial atmosphere, with hundreds of cherubim and seraphim covering the wall by his desk. Their round eyes fixed on me as I sat down. A committed atheist would have lasted thirty seconds before running screaming from the room.

'I need a crash course on angels, please,' I said.

He smiled at me. 'How much do you already know?'

'Very little, I'm afraid.'

He folded his hands across his ample stomach. 'They're a bit weighed down with social meaning, unfortunately. We call people angelic when they're pure and unselfish, but in mythology they're a mixed bunch.' Dr Gillick glanced at me, as though he was afraid of dashing my hopes. 'There's a hierarchy of nine different kinds of angel. It goes all the way from the lowest hand-servants, up to the archangels, like Michael and Gabriel, and that's where the problem starts.'

'The problem?'

'According to the Bible, God defeated one of the archangels in a battle and he was banished from heaven, taking a third of the angels with him. He and his followers became the fallen third.'

'You're talking about Satan?'

Dr Gillick smiled. 'I prefer to think of him as a former angel.'

'But the rest are sent to do good, aren't they?'

He shook his head. 'Not always. You've heard of avenging angels, haven't you? They can start fires, release clouds of locusts on unbelievers, hand out all sorts of terrible punishments. They wreak havoc, basically.' Dr Gillick looked apologetic, as if he was accountable for the angels' poor behaviour.

'Why would a killer be obsessed with them?'

He stared into the distance, fingers buried in his beard. 'Because no human can win a fight against an angel. You could say they're the original superheroes.'

'Like Batman and Superman?'

'Exactly. They can fly, but they can pass as ordinary mortals, and they punish wrongdoers.'

I handed Gillick the images that had been left at the crime scenes and he peered down at them.

'At least he's got taste,' he murmured to himself. '*An Angel in Green* was painted by a pupil of Leonardo's. Renaissance beauty doesn't get much lovelier, does it?' He shifted his attention to the second picture and frowned. 'Now this is a different style altogether. It's a close-up of an angel's face, from a bigger painting by Guercino, done more than a century later.'

He showed me an illustration in a book on his desk. The picture was of two angels, looking down at the dead Christ. One of them was gazing at his wounds, as if she was trying to make sense of his death, but the other was inconsolable, eyes hidden by his bunched hands.

'You can feel their despair, can't you?' Gillick glanced up at me.

I stared down at the two pictures the killer had left behind. The angel in green was an image of submission, head bowed over her violin, playing music to please her God. But the angels who stood beside Christ's body seemed far more human. They looked like servants, dressed in rough clothes, with their sleeves rolled up, weeping for their dead master. I kept trying to analyse what the paintings told me about the mindset of the killer; he'd chosen an image of devotion, then one of grief. Maybe he'd been a loyal servant, but he'd been let down. Everything he believed in had been stripped away.

Gillick helped me for a while longer, running through a whistle-stop tour of religious iconography. I was about to thank him and leave when he rose from his chair.

'Let me show you something by Spinello before you go,' he said.

I followed him up four flights of stairs, and a painting of a battle scene stopped me in my tracks. A gang of angels was terrorising a crowd, daggers and spears raised above their heads. Black wings protruded from their shoulders, but the most disturbing thing was the ethereal calmness on their faces as they slaughtered their victims. At any minute it looked as if they might fly out of the canvas and hack us to death.

'That's the avenging angels, casting Lucifer's followers from heaven.' Gillick's Santa Claus smile slipped from his face. 'Enough to give you nightmares, aren't they?'

Angels buzzed around my head while my bus headed south. Their perfect, expressionless faces floated in front of me, and it was easy to see why an intellectual killer could become obsessed. Their complexity was fascinating. They were capable of the most extreme forms of violence, yet they could show mercy and tenderness. Maybe the killer saw himself in the same role, handing out rough justice to every sinner who crossed his path, but treating his family with angelic kindness.

My mind switched back to humans as soon as I reached Guy's. One of the clinic's receptionists beckoned me to her desk, with a sour expression on her face. She informed me that a patient of mine had been causing havoc. He'd demanded to see me, and when she told him I was unavailable, he'd yelled abuse into her face.

'Was it Darren Campbell?'

'That's the one.' She looked disapproving, as if I was a parent who let my kids riot in public.

'If he comes back, can you book him a diagnostic with Dr Chadha, please?'

She pressed her lips together, as if she was sucking a boiled sweet, then carried on tapping notes into her computer.

My consulting room felt like a sauna. I threw open the window, then sat down to check my email. Hari had copied an incident report to the trustees, recording Darren's assault – concrete proof that cancelling the anger management groups had been a mistake. I was tempted to rush up to the executive suite to show them my bruises. The phone rang at lunchtime while I was fiddling with the air-conditioning unit, and Burns launched straight into the middle of a conversation.

'Jamie Wilcox's toxicology results came back,' he said. 'There was enough Rohypnol in his system to kill a horse.'

It interested me that the killer had given him a lethal dose of the date-rape drug before the attack. It would have rendered Wilcox unconscious. Perhaps he was too squeamish to watch his victims suffer.

'And the bank finally handed over Gresham's laptop. They seem to think it'll keep us off their backs.' Burns gave a low whistle. 'Seeing is believing. Orgies, cocaine, mistresses. No wonder he didn't want the missus finding it.'

Mrs Gresham would hate seeing her husband fall from his pedestal. Maybe the iron mask would drop for a moment, like Thatcher on the night of the long knives. Then I remembered the picture of Stephen Rayner, gazing at his boss in wonder.

'I need to pay his deputy a visit,' I said.

'Why? Taylor's been hounding him non-stop. We'll get sued at this rate.'

'Humour me, Don. He worked alongside Gresham for years. I need to know if he saw changes in his state of mind.'

He grumbled reluctantly. 'How was the angel bloke?'

'Interesting. They're a lot more vicious than I realised. Our man probably thinks he's on a holy crusade.'

'Fantastic,' Burns groaned. 'The God squad are always the worst.'

I walked to London Bridge station when work finished, and Leo Gresham came to mind as I stood on the platform. I closed my eyes and pictured him falling, his shoulder hitting the cold metal of the track, a few seconds of terror before the agony began. By the time I opened my eyes again, my train had vanished. Who in their right mind would think that showing so little mercy gave them moral authority? It had to be someone who was in excruciating pain themselves. When the next train arrived, I steadied my nerves and climbed on board.

My mood had improved by the time I reached Bank. The pavements had been absorbing heat all day, and now they were releasing it, like a network of giant radiators. Crowds of girls had swapped their suits for tiny backless dresses, chatting as they sauntered down the street. Yvette was waiting for me outside the Counting House. Her appearance hadn't changed since she left her job as Human Resources Manager at Guy's to earn three times as much in the City. Her fashion sense was still outrageous; she was wearing a shocking pink dress, her hair braided in cornrows to show off her high cheekbones. She gave me a hug and kissed me on both cheeks.

'Do we have to go in there?' she asked. 'The place'll be heaving with idiots.'

I nodded. 'It's a work thing, I'm studying their behaviour.'

'You never give up, do you?' She grinned at me and rolled her eyes.

I glanced at the pub's exterior. It was showing off its history as a Victorian building society, with a row of arched windows and an austere granite façade. The entire banking fraternity seemed to be holding a meeting inside, a mass of pinstriped backs gathered by the bar.

'Look and learn, Al,' Yvette whispered. 'These are the guys who brought the country to its knees.'

When she left me to hunt for a table, her dress was the only splash of brightness I could see. Almost every other punter was male, under thirty, bouncing with ambition and testosterone. The man ahead of me was ordering the world's most complicated drinks: gin slings and super-dry martinis, and the barman looked desperate to go home. At least the queue gave me time to admire the building. It was a shame the City boys had commandeered the place. Evening light was flooding through a glass-domed cupola, and a row of mahogany booths lined one of the walls, like confessional boxes. Debtors must have hidden there a hundred years ago, whispering secrets to their financial advisers. Yvette waved at me from the mezzanine, but it took a while to push my way up the stairs.

'These guys are acting like they never saw a black girl before.' Yvette glanced across at a table full of young businessmen. 'One just offered to take me home.'

The place was a sea of identical pastel shirts, silk ties and Eton haircuts. Women were still in the minority, but at least more were sprinkled through the crowd than there had been a few years ago. The markets must have had a good day, because the roar of conversation was deafening. Cockney accents mixed with genteel Home Counties. Clearly the City didn't care where you hailed from, if you could turn a profit. It was a struggle to hear Yvette's voice. She was telling me she'd found a better job, at a multinational bank.

'I'll have underlings to do my photocopying.' She looked pleased with herself.

'Tell me what makes bankers tick, Yvette.'

She sucked in her cheeks. 'Imagine a world where nothing exists except money. The milk of human kindness dried up years ago, and all that matters is buying yourself a top-class boob job, owning a Ferrari, and grinding your colleagues' faces in the dirt with the heel of your Italian shoe. Every man, woman and child who visits the City ends up getting corrupted, including me. I've been spending money like water.'

'The clichés are all true, then?' The disgust on her face made me laugh.

'Seriously, these people have calculators for souls.'

'Why work for them, if you despise them so much?'

'The world's not perfect, Al. I'm putting my niece through medical school in Ghana – no one else can.' Her tiredness displayed itself briefly, then slipped back behind her grin. 'And I've got my shopping habit to maintain.'

'Can you do some digging for me? I need to find out about the Angel Bank.'

'I'll see what I can do – I know someone who used to work there.' She held up her hands as if I was throwing things at her. 'Now give me the gossip about Lola's new man.'

'He's jailbait, by all accounts. Tonight's the big night.'

Yvette was busy scanning the crowd on the floor below. 'Bloody hell. She's a lucky, lucky girl.'

I caught sight of Lola's flame-red hair immediately. The young boy standing beside her had borrowed his face from a Greek statue, with full lips and wide blue eyes, blond curls spilling across his forehead. When they arrived at our table, even his smile was an advert for high-class dentistry. I couldn't help wondering if Lola minded barmaids asking for his ID every time he bought a drink. But Neal turned out to be good company, and he could handle being teased. He told us that he was studying music and acting at the Guildhall. He'd met Lola two months ago at a party, and no, the age gap didn't bother him one iota.

'No one mentioned it,' Yvette protested.

He hooted with laughter. 'But you were dying to, weren't you? It's the elephant in the room.'

I could see why Lola had chosen him. Star quality exuded from every pore, but it wouldn't have worked for me. Waking up next to a face without a single wrinkle would have been too daunting.

'You owe me a favour, Al.' Lola's eyes narrowed when she finally sat down. 'I gave Andrew Piernan your number.'

'Jesus, Lo,' I spluttered. 'You could have asked.'

'She's crazy.' Lola turned to Yvette. 'This lovely bloke's after her, and she's running a marathon in the wrong direction.'

Yvette rubbed her hands together. 'Send him my way. I'm auditioning for husband number two.'

The rest of the evening turned out to be the best fun I'd had all year. After a few drinks our mental ages descended rapidly, until we were telling embarrassing stories about each other to keep Neal amused. The place was beginning to empty when I saw a young girl loading glasses onto a tray at the end of the bar. I knew Burns would be outraged, but I couldn't resist the temptation. She carried on working when I approached her.

'I know it's a long shot,' I said. 'But do you remember this bloke?'

She peered at my photo of Jamie Wilcox. Thick lines of kohl were blurring her eyes, and she was wearing a shapeless black dress. She must have made a strategic decision to hide her attractiveness, to stop punters hitting on her.

'He's the one that died, isn't he?' She had a faint Eastern European accent.

'That's right. He was here on Friday.'

She looked around anxiously. Her boss probably sacked waitresses who fraternised too much. 'He came in about six, with some friends. They left him to finish his drink.'

'And you remember him?'

She blushed. 'He was polite – not like the rest. This blonde girl was all over him for a while, then she left.'

'Is that unusual?'

'Not really. Plenty of girls come here looking for business.' She glanced at me. 'He left a few minutes after her. The strange thing is, he was staggering, but he'd only had a few beers.'

A red-faced man strutted over and snapped his fingers, inches from the girl's face. 'Another round, love. Quick as you can.'

The girl's face tensed as she served him, and I didn't blame her. The punters' endless rudeness was enough to grind anyone down. When I thanked her and dropped a ten-pound note on her tray, her face lit up. No doubt the City slickers forgot to tip her, even though she was on minimum wage.

At midnight I poured myself into a taxi, navigating unsteadily up the stairs to my flat. My bedroom tipped from side to side, and the ceiling lamp swung around my head in uneven circles.

'I'm too old for this,' I groaned.

Sleep was out of the question, because my brother came back soon after me. I could hear his voice, loud and excitable, burbling through the wall. It sounded like he was having a party in his room; four or five different voices all talking at once, with an occasional screech of high-pitched laughter. God knows what they were chatting about in the middle of the night. Cloud systems, drugs, or The Great Escape. I felt like barging into his room and telling his hangers-on to get out. Anger fizzed inside my chest like a chemical experiment. Who would feed him if he took to the streets again? And what would happen when winter came? I pictured him huddled under a blanket as the snow fell, then I stuck my fingers in my ears and did my best to pass out.

12

To say that I felt the worse for wear in the morning is an under-statement. The shower was deafening, and standing up felt like hauling my body through quicksand. The heat was unforgiving when I got outside, sunlight reflecting from every surface, making my head pound. Burns had left a mysterious phone message, asking me to visit one of Gresham's secret haunts. The invitation was too intriguing to refuse, but the rush-hour traffic turned my journey through the Chelsea heartlands into a nightmare. Crowds of women were racing into Mulberry, as if their lives depended on locating the perfect holdall. They looked like members of the same family, complexions glowing from expensive facials, with identical honey-coloured hair. It reminded me that my trip to the salon was long overdue.

Burns had reached Knightsbridge before me. His car was parked outside an elegant townhouse on Raphael Street, and he was checking his phone messages. It was clear that Gresham's secret acquaintance was prosperous. The building was at the centre of London's swankiest postcodes, a two-minute stroll from Hyde Park.

'Late night?' Burns inspected me over the top of his glasses.

'Don't ask. Who're we seeing?'

'Gresham's favourite girl, Poppy Beckwith. He sent her hundreds of emails.' He gave a wry smile. 'I've dealt with her before. Her family are loaded, but she fell out with them. She's been on the game since she left school.'

I felt curious as I followed Burns to the door. Whoever lived there was paying their concierge handsomely, because every inch of paintwork gleamed. We climbed to the top floor and the woman who greeted us was tall and slim, a swathe of black hair almost reaching her waist. She had one of those delicate, symmetrical faces that photographs perfectly from any angle. You could have hung her upside down for days and she'd still have looked beautiful. She ignored Burns but shook my hand, as if she was offering a partial truce.

'This is the worst time to call. I'm just on my way out.' Her voice was the product of elocution lessons, or a good public school, roughened by years of cigarettes. She was wearing a dark pink silk dress, held together by a narrow cord. Her whole outfit looked in danger of falling to the ground at any second.

I stood by the window of her living room. The view stretched past the boats drifting on the Serpentine all the way to Hyde Park Corner. By the time I turned round, Beckwith had perched on a red chaise longue, keeping a watchful eye on Burns. Footsteps pounded across the floor in the adjoining room and her shoulders twitched. She was so jumpy that I realised smoking was just one of her addictions. I couldn't help pitying her. Despite all her luxuries, she seemed to be suffering as badly as the girls who touted for business in the pubs on Marylebone Road.

'How's life been treating you, Poppy?' Burns asked.

'Brilliantly, thanks. Recessions don't touch me.'

I glanced around the room. It was too glitzy for me, but I could see that it had style. A gold silk throw hung over one of the settees, two scarlet rugs almost covering the white floorboards. And there were some well-judged touches of kitsch – a gorgeous female nude filled the wall over the fireplace, modestly keeping her back to us.

'It's me, in case you're wondering.' Beckwith stared directly into my eyes, challenging me to criticise her.

'Beautiful,' I said, returning her gaze. 'The whole flat is.'

She looked smug, as though she'd been proved right about something fundamental.

'We're not here to admire the decor, Poppy.' Burns thumbed through his notebook. 'It's your dead boyfriend I want to hear about.'

'Don't,' Beckwith said quietly. 'Leo was one of my favourites. He took me to the best restaurants and spoiled me rotten. Everything you could want from a sugar daddy.' Her laughter petered out instantly. 'He was generous to everyone.'

'Did he pay for this lot?'

Beckwith's eyebrows shot up. 'You're joking. The flat's mine, lock, stock and barrel.'

'You're joking. You were in Holloway on drug charges last time I saw you.'

'That was six years ago.' She glared at him, but the silence soon defeated her. 'I've turned my life round since then, not that it's any of your business.'

Burns held his tongue, but his patience seemed to be wearing thin. Poppy had the opposite effect on me – I could have listened to her all day. Her voice was a refined growl like Marianne Faithfull's.

Beckwith transferred her gaze to me. 'My clients are millionaires. One guy even paid me to sail round the Caribbean with him. He proposed when we got back, but I refused. I need my independence too badly.'

Burns sighed loudly. 'You still haven't told us anything about Gresham, Poppy.'

'Maybe I don't want to.' She stared back at him.

The floor shuddered and a huge, bald-headed man emerged from the room next door. She must have been feeding him a diet of anabolic steroids. When he scowled at Burns he looked like a Rottweiler that had been chained up for days, half crazy with rage and hunger. Beckwith didn't bother to turn round. She just held up the palm of her hand, and after a few seconds he slunk back through the door, in search of his kennel.

'Who's the charming new boyfriend?' Burns asked.

'That's my assistant.' She gave her sweetest smile. 'But it's you I'm worried about, Don. I've never seen you so uptight. Isn't Mrs Burns looking after you? I'm free on Tuesday mornings, you know. My best clients are from the Met.'

His frown deepened. 'Just give us the information, Poppy. We haven't got all day.'

'Leo was sweeter than you, that's for sure. There was a romantic side to him. He sent me enough roses on my birthday to fill a bathtub.'

'How long did you know him?' I asked.

'Two years. I checked my appointments book when I heard the news.'

I could imagine Beckwith scratching Gresham's name from her client list, then poring over her schedule, making sure the cash flow never dried up. It was hard to guess her age, but she was probably on the wrong side of thirty. Small lines were appearing at the corners of her eyes. Perhaps she lay awake on her rare nights alone, wondering how long before the next girl stole her crown.

Burns laid a photo on the coffee table. 'Ever seen him before?'

'He's cute.' She paused for a second. 'You can send him my way.'

He stuffed the picture back into his pocket. 'Too late. He was murdered on Friday night.'

'That's a shame.' Beckwith blinked rapidly then checked her watch. 'I have to go. A client's waiting for me at The

Dorchester. I can't say I'm thrilled – all he ever wants is a striptease and a blowjob. No imagination at all.'

Burns's look of outrage was still in place when we got outside.

'You're not keen on her, are you?' I said.

'It's not that.' He shook his head. 'She could have anything, and that's what she's choosing.' He stared at Poppy's building like it was the worst possible destination.

My car felt like a pressure cooker as I followed Burns back to the station. I could understand his frustration. Poppy had everything going for her: looks, privilege, taste – yet she was risking her life every day. Maybe she was capable of venting her destructive impulse on her clients too. But I sensed that she was too controlled to act like Aileen Wuornos, savaging the men who used her. She was taking drugs to keep her emotions in check, rather than letting them break her.

When we got back to the station, Steve Taylor was already in the Invisible Woman's office. He was sitting so close to her, it looked like he was planning to climb onto her knee. Other members of the team were filing in with gloomy expressions on their faces. The group seemed united in their dislike of Burns, and happy to bad-mouth colleagues behind their backs. I had a strong suspicion that Brotherton liked it that way. She never revealed her loyalties, encouraging competition through divide and rule.

Photos of Jamie Wilcox were scattered across the table, and one of them caught my eye. He was the spitting image of my brother in his twenties, with the same dark blond hair and tennis player's physique, unshakeable confidence written across his face. I remembered the painting beside Wilcox's body, showing the angels weeping in despair. Maybe he'd been a casualty of war, as the killer worked his way through the ranks to more powerful targets at the bank? When I looked up again, Taylor was handing the action book to the Invisible Woman.

'The incident room's running like a Swiss clock, ma'am.' He beamed at her like she was his new infatuation.

Burns talked through Jamie Wilcox's toxicology results, and mentioned that he'd been seen with a blonde woman at the Counting House. I was grateful that he didn't mention my unauthorised visit – Brotherton wouldn't have been impressed by my off-the-record chat with the Latvian waitress.

'Someone gave Wilcox a massive dose of Rohypnol before he died,' Burns said. 'At least ten milligrams.'

Taylor's mouth dropped open. 'You think some blonde slipped him a Mickey Finn, then led him to the killer?'

'It's possible. So far the only link between Gresham and Wilcox is the Angel Bank, but they're not co-operating. Their lawyers have delayed access to their records on the grounds of confidentiality, but we've had a tip-off from an anonymous caller. She said they've been breaking trading laws for years. SOCA are interviewing them today.'

Brotherton's cool eyes observed him as he spoke. It was impossible to tell whether she was taking sides in Taylor's campaign, but the conflict seemed to be weighing on Burns. He walked with me to the exit without saying a word.

'I'm sure this is personal,' I said. 'If someone wanted to destroy the bank's reputation, they wouldn't be killing people, they'd be writing letters to the Financial Services Authority. It's someone who hates the place so much, they want to lock everyone inside, then burn the place down.'

Burns looked morose as he squinted into the sun.

'How long do you reckon this heat can keep up?' I asked.

'God knows. Give me a bit of sleet any day.' He gave me a half-hearted smile as he said goodbye.

*   *   *

My consulting room was close to boiling point that afternoon. One session ended abruptly, because a patient passed out from heat exhaustion. I had to ask a nurse to help me lift her into the corridor and wait for her to come round. My mobile buzzed in my pocket just as I was packing up for the day. It was a voicemail that I hadn't received, because my phone had been switched off. I recognised Andrew Piernan's charming, upper-class drawl immediately. He was inviting me to dinner the next evening. There was a slight tremor in his voice and I couldn't decide what to do. He was great company, but the idea of a date sent a surge of panic through my nervous system. I should have called him immediately and said no, but I decided to give myself some thinking time. Until I'd come up with an answer, my only option was to lie low and pretend his message had never reached me.

13

I phoned Piernan from a French café on Tooley Street the next morning. Almost every table was full of couples eating croissants and drinking café au lait. Maybe I was hoping for safety in numbers when I gave him the bad news. He sounded as relaxed as ever when he picked up the phone. I wondered if I'd misjudged him; perhaps he took a different woman to Chez Bruce every night of the week.

'I'm busy tonight, I'm afraid.'

'Doing what, may I ask?' My excuse seemed to amuse him.

'Running. I'm training for the London marathon.'

'Good.' He didn't seem fazed that his invitation had been turned down flat. 'I could use some exercise.'

Anxiety fizzed inside my chest when I rang off. Somehow he'd scuppered my plan to delete his number and get on with my life. I knocked back the dregs of my coffee and wondered how it had happened. Freud was right about one thing: mistakes are just another way of getting what we want. Despite my nerves, I was already looking forward to seeing him again.

A copy of yesterday's *Metro* was lying on the back seat when I hailed a cab. The headline blared from the front page as the driver battled with the traffic. ANGEL KILLER STILL AT LARGE! I was surprised by how much information the police had released about the two attacks, including the killer's fixation with angels. Maybe Burns was hoping someone would read the story and remember a friend's interest in the winged messengers. The only detail he'd held back was the feathers left at the murder scenes. I flicked through the rest of the paper, but it contained very little information, apart from pictures of celebrities' botched plastic surgery, and yet another footballer who'd cheated on his wife.

Stephen Rayner's flat was in an upmarket area, close to Old Street station, with window-boxes blossoming above art galleries and upmarket delis. I scanned the street for Burns's Mondeo, but Taylor hailed me from the pavement opposite. He looked different in the harsh sunlight. Deep lines were carved around his eyes and his skin looked desiccated. Maybe he lay in his garden every weekend, soaking up the rays. It was a struggle to fight my dislike. Taylor was exactly the kind of macho man I'd crossed the street to avoid, ever since one put me in hospital.

'I was expecting Burns,' I said.

'You struck lucky and got me instead.' His smile had been replaced by a sneer. 'You can do the talking, I'm looking forward to seeing you in action.'

I ignored him and walked up the steps to Rayner's apartment. It was over an estate agent's – every morning he'd be woken to the clamour of phones ringing; a constant reminder that the city was nothing more than an assortment of properties, waiting to be resold. When the door finally opened, Rayner's appearance surprised me. He'd been off work with stress since his boss died, but I'd never seen anyone more pristine. The creases in the sleeves of his shirt were knife-sharp, and it was hard to believe he'd ever experienced a five-o'clock shadow. But there was something unsettling about his face. His features seemed too large for his face to accommodate: bulging eyes, his nose a broad pink slab, and a wide, thin-lipped mouth.

He led us into his living room. A whole wall was covered in

unframed photographs, pinned so closely together they were overlapping. Dozens of strangers gazed down at me, and a series of landscapes showed a hillside turning pink as the sun rose.

'Did you take these?' I asked. 'They're amazing.'

His mouth gaped open. 'What is this? I've had the bad cop so now I get the good cop. Is that it?'

'I'm a psychologist. I'm just helping the police with the investigation.'

'They've already been here three times. They won't leave me alone.' He threw an angry glance at Taylor, who was studying his notebook.

'I don't want to put you under any more pressure, but I need to know why the police cautioned you ten years ago.'

His cheeks flushed a vivid red. 'That was fifteen years ago, before I started at the Angel. I had a few drinks after work and someone insulted me.'

'What did he say?'

'He said gay men disgusted him.' Rayner looked so furious that I wondered if Taylor was right about his violent tendencies. 'Banking's full of Oxbridge idiots stabbing each other in the back. It's like football or the army – no one's openly gay. You've got to boast about your wife and your lovely kids if you want to get on. Leo was the only one to accept me; everyone else makes me feel like my face doesn't fit.'

Nothing about Rayner's face seemed to fit when I glanced at him again. His mouth was quivering with distress, bulbous eyes shiny with tears. Maybe his need for acceptance explained why he'd invented a fantasy life, including a devoted fiancee.

'I'm sorry to keep pressing you, but the bank's blocking our requests for information. Can you tell me if there's anyone Leo was afraid of at work?'

'I don't think so,' he said hesitantly. 'Except the boss, of course. Even Leo tried not to get on the wrong side of him.'

'Max Kingsmith?' I remembered the svelte grey-haired man, schmoozing people at the Albion Club.

He nodded. 'Even the directors have to watch their step. His temper's unbelievable. Leo was one of the few people who could handle him.'

'I can see how much you miss Leo,' I said. 'Apart from his wife, you were one of the people he trusted most. Can you think of anyone else the police should be talking to?'

His face crumpled, and I got the sense that he was holding something back; either too cautious or too afraid to explain. His body language had been tense since we arrived, and he was struggling to meet my eye. The long pauses between his statements made me sure he was plucking up courage to share something. I glanced again at the wall of photos – some had obviously been taken in the local parks. He'd captured every detail: flowers, statues, old men asleep on benches, even the rubbish littering the grass. But it was the portraits that interested me. Most people's faces showed surprise or anger, as though he'd stolen their images, without seeking permission. Rayner's voyeurism interested me, but his personality struck me as too passive for violence. When I looked at him again, he was doing his best to pull himself together.

'There's one person you should see,' he said. 'Lawrence Fairfield knows everything about the Angel. That's why they got rid of him.'

Out of the corner of my eye I saw Taylor scribbling the name in his book. I waited for Rayner to explain, but he was still too distressed to speak. On the way out I noticed a Nikon lying on the hall table, a set of lenses lined up beside it. Maybe he harboured fantasies about escaping from banking and joining the photo team at the *National Geographic*.

Taylor's swagger was less pronounced when we got outside. Rayner's homosexuality seemed to have scrambled his brain temporarily.

'Christ, what a freak. You wouldn't want him running a scout group.' His sneer deepened. 'I wouldn't mind swapping jobs with you, though. All you have to do is ask questions, then let us do the dirty work.'

He strutted back to his car without offering me a lift. There was no doubt in my mind that his aggression posed more of a threat to the general public than the man I'd interviewed. I thought about Stephen Rayner as I reached Leicester Square. Few people would take two weeks off work when their boss died, no matter how close they'd been. He was doing his best to present an immaculate image to the world, but he was near to breaking point. It seemed hard to believe that a gay man could still feel intimidated in the twenty-first century. Banking sounded like the opposite of the NHS. I was lucky to work for an organisation where everyone went out of their way to be politically correct.

Rayner soon slipped from my mind as I rushed to my meeting with the hospital trustees. The executive suite gave no clues that the place was low on funds – plush carpet and floral displays everywhere you looked. I paused on the landing to admire the skyline. It rose and fell like spikes on a cardiogram: Centre Point, The Pinnacle and The Shard soaring effort- lessly into the sky. A row of blank-faced suits stared back at me when I reached the boardroom. I explained the reasons why they should fund the anger management groups: follow- up studies showed a reduction in domestic violence, and ex-prisoners were fifty per cent less likely to reoffend. No one batted an eyelid, and the chief executive marched me to the door as soon as I'd finished.

'Thank you, Dr Quentin, you're very passionate about your cause.' He didn't bother to crack a smile as he nodded goodbye.

I was seething when I got outside – my time would have been spent more usefully shrieking into a paper bag. I forced myself through the afternoon's duties with gritted teeth.

At five o'clock I put on my running gear and sprinted down the fire escape. When I reached the ground floor I was glad I'd taken the stairs, because Darren was hanging around by the lifts. His jeans and T-shirt looked so crumpled he must have been wearing them for days, but it was his body language that worried me, alert and watchful as a guardsman, and I knew he was waiting for me. Maybe no one else had given him the benefit of the doubt. I should have run back upstairs and told Hari about his vigil, but the idea exhausted me. I've always resisted giving in to paranoia about my safety, so I jogged towards the station without looking back.

Commuters were packed into the Tube compartment like fish in a drag net. When I finally reached the escalator at Warren Street, everyone was staring upwards expectantly, longing for a glimpse of the sky. My heart lifted as I reached Regent's Park and started to jog. It's my favourite of all London's parks – so big that it's a world in itself, with enough attractions to keep you entertained for weeks: a boating lake, a mosque, a theatre, cafés. It even has its own zoo, with cages full of sad-eyed orang-utans. Perhaps Stephen Rayner was a regular visitor, taking photos to keep his stress at bay. It was easy to spot other would-be marathon runners. The punishing heat hadn't broken their training schedule, and they'd invested in the best trainers they could afford. The woman in front of me was setting a brisk pace, so I followed her, admiring the mansions on Cumberland Terrace. They must have been built two hundred years ago, for the landed gentry. It was hard to imagine who owned them now. Only oligarchs and supermodels would have the right cash flow.

Andrew Piernan was sitting on a bench beside Clarence Gate, wearing a dark blue tracksuit, and he fell into step without saying a word, thin shoulders rising and falling steadily. I felt guilty for assuming that he never took exercise. He looked completely at ease, and he had the right physique for distance running – wiry and long-limbed, no excess weight to carry.

'You've done this before, haven't you?' I asked.

'Couple of times a week. Not here, though. I run in the City.' He nodded at my backpack. 'Let me carry that.'

I shook my head. 'I'm fine, thanks.'

'Of course. You're superwoman, how could I forget?'

I gave him an old-fashioned look and we ran on in silence. The fact that he was relaxed enough to tease me meant I didn't have to worry. It didn't matter that my ponytail had collapsed, and patches of sweat were soaking through my T-shirt, while he ran effortlessly.

'Want to go faster for the last mile?' I asked. Sprinting at the end of each run was one of my strategies to improve my speed.

He smiled back at me, then cut left along the Broad Walk. People were relaxing on the grass, a young couple sitting under a chestnut tree, giving each other mouth-to-mouth resuscitation. Piernan was sprinting so fast that my wounded ribs ached and my lungs heaved with effort. The late-afternoon sun was still dazzling when we reached the café.

'You're quick.' He grinned at me. 'You'll do that marathon in no time.'

'If I survive,' I gasped.

I left him queuing for drinks while I splashed cold water across the back of my neck in the toilets. When I blotted my face with a paper towel, I noticed that I looked surprised. The shock of discovering that Piernan could outpace me was still registering. He was pouring mineral water into ice-filled glasses when I got outside. His hands looked fragile, knuckles white under his freckled skin.

'How long have you been running?' I asked.

'Forever. It was the one thing I enjoyed at school.'

'Let me guess, you went to Eton, right?'

Piernan laughed. 'You think I'm a cliché, don't you? A posh twit with oodles of money and no sense.'

'The jury's out. For all I know you're on Jobseeker's Allowance.'

'I bet you went to some nice girls' grammar, followed by three years of mayhem at Cambridge.'

'God, no. A grotty comprehensive in Charlton, then London for my degree.'

Piernan's expression hardened suddenly, and he was silent for a while before he spoke again. 'You're quite wrong about me, you know. I'm from a privileged background, but it doesn't interest me.' His voice petered out. 'I've always worked hard, partly for my sister.'

The attendants were collecting the last fares of the day on the boating lake, and Piernan still looked angry, the muscles tight around his mouth. It was a trait I recognised in myself – rage bubbling out of nowhere, requiring constant effort to keep it in check. Maybe he was sick of being reminded about his silver spoon, or his sister's condition made him feel guilty. It took a while for him to talk easily again, the tension gradually lifting from his face. He told me that he'd grown up in a country house that his family had owned for generations. It took ten minutes to walk from his bedroom to the kitchen, which was hidden in the basement.

'It was like Downton Abbey, but with fewer scandals,' he said. 'They had to sell it in the end. They live much more modestly now.'

The café had emptied since we'd arrived. The waitress was starting to clear away noisily, stacking chairs on tables. Piernan leant forwards in his seat.

'The thing is, you're not really looking for a relationship, are you?' His light brown eyes were studying me. 'Is that because of something in the past?'

'Probably. The last time wasn't much fun.'

'You could set the pace, you know. I can be surprisingly patient. You might even get to like me.'

'Stranger things have happened, I suppose.' I smiled back at him.

He handed me his card with a grave smile. 'If you want to meet up again, text me, or send me an email.'

'Thank you.' I put the card in my rucksack. 'Time I was going.'

I set off across the grass, and when I glanced back, he was still sitting there, surrounded by empty tables. I waited for a bus on Euston Road and thought about his offer. Normally the men I ended up with were brash, confident and determined to take charge. Piernan had been shrewd to offer me the driving seat, because it made me keen to see him again. I studied the delicate blue lettering on his card, then looked out of the window and did my best to forget him.

14

Marimba music woke me before the alarm. I thought I'd woken up in Havana, until I remembered I'd changed my ring tone. I hauled myself upright and rubbed the sleep from my eyes. It was six thirty, and a man's voice was babbling too fast to make sense. It took me a while to realise that it was Steve Taylor.

'I hope I'm not disturbing your beauty sleep.' I could picture him leering into his phone. There was a buzz of voices, then a door slamming somewhere nearby. 'Brotherton wants you at the hospital, quick as you can.'

I let out a string of curses then got dressed and jogged to my car. The river was already glittering with sunlight, boats motionless on the tide. Going to work so early felt unnatural, like the start of a nightmare, but the press had beaten me to it. A crowd of journalists and photographers were loitering by the entrance doors, clutching cameras and cigarettes. I picked up my pace when I saw Dean Simons. He was a freelance hack who touted nonsense to the tabloids, and he'd made my life hell after the Crossbones case, doorstepping me for weeks, begging for an interview. It had taken two solicitor's letters to make him slink back into the shadows, but he'd exacted his revenge. He wrote a story that was full of fabricated quotes, insinuating that I'd been so broken by my ordeal that I'd never work again. I'd decided not to sue, but the sight of him still made my skin crawl. He looked the same as ever. An overweight, red-faced, fifty-year-old with dirty grey hair, trying to hide his beer belly inside a tight leather jacket. A look of excitement crossed his face when he saw me, like he'd spotted a long-lost friend.

'I'm still waiting for that exclusive, Alice. Come and chat on the way out.'

A chorus of shutters snapped at me as I hurried past. When I found Burns he was standing outside Marshall Ward, looking sheepish, as though he regretted getting me involved.

'Nicole Morgan was attacked last night,' he explained. 'Brotherton wanted you here before the press briefing.'

'What happened?'

'She went to a meeting at one of the banks. He attacked her by her car.' Burns was leading me up the stairs, pacing so fast I could hardly keep up.

'And it's definitely our man?'

He stopped to pass me a crumpled piece of A4 wrapped in an evidence bag. The garish colours looked like an image from a stained-glass window. It was a different type of angel this time, downloaded from the internet, a crude contrast to the serene Renaissance faces from the previous attacks. I stared at the image in surprise.

'He's changed his signature,' I said.

'No feathers this time either. A car frightened him off before he could finish her. Nicole can't tell us much else – he got her from behind.'

The changes to the killer's signature were beginning to make me wonder whether Morgan's attacker had been a copycat.

I used my pass key to unlock an office nearby and he followed me inside.

'Was it a knife attack?' I asked.

Burns pulled some Polaroid photos from his pocket

reluctantly and handed them to me. I studied each one, then closed my eyes. Nicole Morgan's attacker had gone for maximum damage. The first concern would be her kids; they would need counselling to help them accept the change. It looked as if a plastic surgeon had made a series of catastrophic errors. A knife wound had extended her mouth by several inches, but the left side of her face had taken the brunt of it. It was sliced cleanly in two, so badly lacerated that the flesh had collapsed. A deep vertical cut ran from her hairline, through her eyelid, and her cheek. The blood loss would have been terrifying, and so would the pain. With any luck the doctors had given her enough morphine to knock her out.

'Where's her husband?' I asked.

'Out there. He's been with her all night.'

Through the glass window I caught sight of Liam Morgan, still dressed in his manservant's uniform of black trousers and white shirt. His sleeves were rolled back, revealing a blur of military tattoos. He was too preoccupied to notice me staring. His face was tense with misery, and I could hear him negotiating Nicole's transfer to a private hospital on his mobile, his voice cracking with strain.

'What time does the plastic surgeon arrive?' he asked.

I felt like telling him to protect her from more pain. No surgeon in the world could disguise those wounds. But that was the downside of being Helen of Troy. The TV shows would drop her, unless someone performed a surgical miracle.

Lorraine Brotherton appeared while Burns was giving me the details, with Taylor following in her wake. She was so thin, her grey suit made her look as insubstantial as a wisp of smoke, but her frown lines had deepened overnight, and it was clear she was in no mood for small talk. The four of us were acting like warring factions eyeballing each other across the table, failing to achieve a truce.

'This happened right in the middle of our demographic,' Brotherton snapped. 'Who's responsible for the street patrols?' Her glare alternated between Taylor and Burns.

'He is, ma'am.' Taylor lounged back in his chair.

'What went wrong, Don?' She gave him the full force of her glare.

'We're been covering the Square Mile with thirty extra uniforms, and another twenty on the streets round the Angel Bank. That's the policy we agreed.'

'Our policy screwed up then, didn't it? Nicole Morgan's celebrity has changed the game – the media will be round us like flies. I've got a press conference in twenty minutes. You need to brief me.'

Burns was refusing to look apologetic. 'We want to hear from anyone who was on Staining Lane, around 10 p.m. The SOCOs say there are bike tracks at the scene.'

'A motorbike?' Brotherton sounded incredulous.

He shook his head. 'Pushbike. It looks like our man's following the mayor's advice and using pedal power.'

My image of the murderer was starting to fragment. It was hard to picture someone calmly putting on his bike helmet then cycling off to commit murder.

'He's not stupid, is he?' Taylor said. 'Those streets are a labyrinth. A bike's his best bet.'

'What do you think, Dr Quentin?' Brotherton asked. Her gaze was so chilly, it took me a moment to gather my thoughts.

'His MO's changed. This is his first female victim, and he's getting less squeamish. He went for maximum pain, instead of sedating her, or pushing her under a train and walking away before the first scream. Even the calling card's different, and there were no feathers.'

Taylor looked outraged. 'You're saying it's a copycat?'

'It's possible. Or two people could be working together. But if it's the same killer, he was much less organised – he might be starting to break down.'

Brotherton gave me a curt nod, then turned her attention to Burns and Taylor. She drew herself up in her chair and peered at them through her grey curls. Her voice was slow and deliberate, as though she'd audited every word.

'A celebrity was maimed last night, right under your noses. What have you been doing? You're meant to be senior officers, running a double murder investigation. If I hear any more gossip about sparring, or failing to follow procedure, one of you will collect your P45. Do I make myself clear?'

Taylor's head wagged violently, like a nodding dog on the dashboard of a speeding car. I could understand Brotherton's anger. She was about to become famous for all the wrong reasons, stepping out from her smoke and mirrors to appear on millions of TV screens. Taylor broke the silence as soon as she left.

'What a bitch,' he sighed, polishing the crown of his head with both hands.

'If you hate her so much, why brown-nose her every day?' The contempt in Burns's voice lowered the room temperature by several degrees. It was the first time I'd seen him riled since the start of the investigation. It was a relief when he followed me into the corridor instead of letting the disagreement turn into a slanging match.

I arrived at my consulting room an hour before my first appointment. Burns had given me the most recent printout from HOLMES. It was several inches thick, with dozens of pages of work-flow analysis and evidence management to skim through before I reached the Dynamic Reasoning

Report, which was frustratingly brief. The system had picked up just one parallel, to a serial killing case in Brixton over a decade ago, but the attacker was already behind bars. I grabbed a highlighter and got to work. The killer's motivation must be hidden somewhere inside the ream of paper, and keeping busy would help me forget what I'd seen. But Nicole Morgan's wounds came back to haunt me when I put down my pen. The plastic surgeon had an impossible job to perform – he'd need a yard of surgical twine to mend her heart-shaped face.

15

A surprise was waiting for me when I turned on my computer. I was already feeling queasy from lack of sleep, and the first email I opened didn't help. It was from Darren, and the message consisted of just five words. YOU CAN RELY ON ME. My heart twitched uncomfortably in my chest. The font size was huge, each letter at least an inch tall, the equivalent of standing in front of me, screaming at the top of his voice. It crossed my mind to harangue the receptionists, but I knew it wasn't their fault. There were half a dozen websites where he could have found my work email address. I looked up the details for Darren's YMCA and left a voicemail asking the manager to contact me. His probation officer wasn't answering her phone either. I wrestled with the window, gasping for fresh air. A helicopter was hovering over the tip of The Shard, giving its passengers the perfect photo opportunity. I felt like beckoning them to land on the hospital roof. Maybe a tour of the building's failing resources would give them an attack of philanthropy.

The day went by too quickly, with hardly any intervals between patients. At five thirty I went looking for Hari, hoping to share my worries about Darren, but his secretary said he was meeting the trustees, so I locked my office door and set off. The street was crammed with stationary cars, drivers revving their engines impatiently. The air felt sticky with heat and bad humour.

My brother was shuffling around in his room when I got back. Normally I would have made him a cup of tea, but we hadn't spoken since he'd slammed out of the flat. I went into the bathroom and turned the shower to full blast. The jet of water was strong enough to hurt. It felt like a masseur was standing behind me, pummelling the tension from my muscles.

Will was frozen in the middle of his room when I came out, clutching a handful of CDs.

'You look busy,' I said.

'I'm packing some of my stuff.' He made no attempt to return my smile.

I wanted to tell him to forget about leaving and wait until he was well, but I bit my tongue. 'Do you need a hand?'

He looked at me in surprise. 'You can do the books, if you want.'

It was a struggle to pick my way between piles of clothes, newspapers and dirty coffee cups. I found a cardboard box then scooped a handful of paperbacks from the shelf. Will was standing completely still, gazing around the room.

'I should get rid of all this crap. It's only weighing me down.' He held my gaze, waiting for me to protest. 'We're going to Brighton in my friend's car; there won't be any room for it anyway.'

'Where does your friend live?' I stacked more books into the box, lining up the spines.

'Whitecross Street,' he said. 'He's there now, waiting for me.'

He turned on his heel and disappeared out of the front door. I stood there clutching his copy of *The Rough Guide to Mexico*. Whitecross Street was a place I always avoided at night; a bleak row of council flats, every ground-floor window protected by a metal grille. The tenants must have grown tired of bricks being hurled into their living rooms.

I could have sat down in the middle of Will's debris and howled, but I made myself stick on a CD, and the music worked wonders. It's hard to feel miserable with Bill Withers belting out 'Lovely Day' at full volume. I spent an hour doing therapeutic cleaning, scouring the sink to within an inch of its life. By the time I'd finished, the kitchen was immaculate and I was starving. I melted some butter in a pan and fried three eggs, sandwiching them between doorsteps of white bread, loaded with ketchup.

All the fat and cholesterol I'd consumed had given me an unexpected surge of energy, and my mood was beginning to lift, so I texted Piernan before I got cold feet, asking if he was free the next evening. He replied immediately, inviting me to a private view. I put on some lipstick, then lugged my bike downstairs to meet Lola, feeling oddly pleased with myself.

It took ten minutes to cycle along Tooley Street, the air still solid with heat and exhaust fumes. Lola was waiting outside the Market Porter, sipping a glass of Pimm's. Her friend Craig was standing beside her, two inches of dark roots visible in his long blond hair. He blinked at me through layers of expertly applied mascara. Lola went to drama school with Craig, sharing flats and misadventures. He made a living as a cabaret performer, and his relationship with Lola was like a chemical experiment. It either burned with adoration, or fizzled into despair. When we went inside, the Greek god was setting up microphones on a small stage.

'I didn't know Neal was in a band. What are they called?' I asked.

'The Jack Pescod trio,' Lola beamed. 'They're heavenly.'

She was right about the music. Normally I'm allergic to jazz, but this was in a different league. The trumpet hovered above the piano's melody, pulsing and washing over me, like the sea at ebb-tide.

Lola was gazing at me expectantly, and I could tell she was planning an interrogation, so I headed her off at the pass.

'How's love's young dream?' I asked.

'Amazing. He says I'm his soul mate.'

'What goes up must come down,' Craig muttered.

'Cynicism's so unattractive, darling,' Lola rebuked him. 'Don't yield to it.'

'The rest of us call it realism, sweetie.' He turned his cornflower-blue gaze in my direction. 'You wouldn't go for a juvenile, would you?'

'Probably not. But only because it would make me feel ancient.'

Lola's green eyes snapped open. 'What's happening with Andrew? I think he's adorable. He's got that posh charm, like Hugh Grant in *Notting Hill*.'

'Don't get your hopes up, Lo. It's too soon after the last disaster.'

'But you're seeing him again, aren't you?' she ploughed on.

'Tomorrow.'

The subject of romance was finally dropped because Yvette had arrived. She'd poured herself into a skin-tight orange dress, and I saw a man by the bar do a complete 360-degree turn to watch her sashay through the crowd. When she reached our table, she pulled a piece of paper from her bag.

'There you go,' she said. 'The salaries of every employee at the Angel Bank.'

'Who stole this for you?'

'I shouldn't tell you.' Yvette seemed to be relishing her Mata Hari moment. 'My friend Vanessa took a risk getting it. I've no idea how they're paying those wages in a recession.'

Craig and Lola were still bickering about relationships, while I stared at the figures. The traders' bonuses were eye-watering – even the lowest payout was enough to buy a penthouse suite in my building.

Yvette peered over my shoulder. 'They're fighting for the biggest prizes in the City. I wouldn't want to be around on bonus advisory day.'

'Too much machismo?'

'Worse than that – they'd be tearing each other limb from limb.' The smile slipped from her face. 'You should let it drop, Al.'

'In case I end up in a concrete shroud?'

'Vanessa says she'll talk to you, but I think you're crazy. It could get both of you in trouble.'

'You're serious, aren't you?'

'Too right I am. When there's that much cash at stake, people don't play by the rules.'

I shook my head. 'It's a personal vendetta, not some mafia-style corporate feud.'

Yvette looked unconvinced. It took half an hour and two large gin and tonics to calm her down, before I could say goodbye.

My pulse was racing from the cycle ride when I got home, so I switched on the TV. I had to blink twice before my eyes accepted that the woman standing on the hospital steps was Lorraine Brotherton. She was surrounded by a sea of report-ers, with dozens of microphones aimed at her, and she'd transformed herself for the cameras. Her grey hair had been swept back, and she was wearing lipstick and eye make-up. She looked more than capable of keeping Taylor in his place, explaining that dozens of extra officers were working round the clock on the Angel case. The camera panned across mounds of flowers and cards, propped against the hospital gates, wishing Nicole Morgan a speedy recovery. But when

Brotherton reappeared, she was working too hard to convey her message. She tried to explain that the situation was under control, but she was staring at the camera without blinking, as though a gunman was forcing her to read a statement she didn't believe.

16

I felt a pang of envy as I walked to work on Saturday. A woman was sunbathing on a bench, legs stretched in front of her, taking in the view. In an ideal world I'd be the one watching the river ebb downstream, but there was no wriggling out of it. A skeleton team had to keep the department open each weekend to deal with emergencies. When I reached Great Maze Pond the media circus was still camped in front of the hospital, so I skirted round Newcomen Street to the back entrance, keen to avoid another clash with Dean Simons. I thought about Nicole Morgan as I climbed the stairs. I'd treated a man once who'd lost most of his face in a horrific car accident. It was months before he could confront a mirror, and it would be even harder for someone like Nicole, a recognised beauty, whose looks had helped her become a celebrity.

I spent the day catching up on the paperwork I'd neglected since the investigation began. The thermometer in my room was edging past thirty-three degrees by the time I escaped, and I stood under the air-conditioning vent in the stairwell, letting cold air chill the back of my neck. By the time I'd jogged down four flights I was picking up speed. But when the next corner came, I had to slam on the brakes, because an obstacle was blocking my way. Darren was sitting in the middle of the stairs. It crossed my mind to vault over him and keep running. All I could hear was the echo of my own breathing. No one would disturb us, because the fire exit was only used by a few renegade nurses, desperate for a fag. I glanced over my shoulder, but the concrete stairs looked unforgiving. Darren seemed more confused than last time. The hood of his grey top was half covering his face, and his lips were moving constantly, without producing a sound.

'I want you to do something for me, Darren. Come up to the clinic. I'll fix another appointment for you, with Dr Chadha.'

His gaze shifted back into focus, as if he was waking from a long sleep. 'It's you I need to see, not him.' His hands jittered across the concrete, and I knew he was losing control.

'This way,' I said quietly. 'Follow me.'

I started to walk back up the stairs, ignoring my impulse to run, and Darren trailed behind me. When I glanced back, his expression was flickering between anger and fear. Maybe they were the only feelings he could access, his emotional range even narrower than mine. I tried to suppress my anxiety, because I knew it would prevent me helping him. He seemed calmer by the time we reached my floor, standing quietly by the reception desk when I handed him his appointment card.

'Promise you won't miss it this time.' He nodded his head, but wouldn't meet my eye. 'You can go home now, Darren.'

He took a long time to leave. Maybe that was because he had no home to go to, just a room at the YMCA, shared with a dozen strangers. My heartbeat gradually steadied itself, but the urge to fly had deserted me. When I opened the door to the fire exit for the second time, I took each flight at a steady pace.

Someone had left a newspaper on a bench in the quadrangle. 'HOTTEST JULY ON RECORD', the front page announced. The picture showed hundreds of people frolicking in the grubby waters of the Serpentine, like it was the Côte d'Azur. By the time I reached the river, the idea of ripping off my clothes and diving in seemed appealing. I leant on the railing and watched the tide roll past. The shore was an expanse of black silt, littered with broken glass and McDonald's wrappers. No doubt dozens of poisons were lurking there: Weil's disease, salmonella, maybe even a touch of Hepatitis B. I sat at a table outside Browns and ordered an orange juice loaded with ice. When I opened the paper, another headline caught my eye: NICOLE MORGAN IN SAVAGE ATTACK. Morgan's friends in PR had rallied to her rescue. The picture showed her in a glamorous dress, before the attack took place, and the article described her brave determination not to let her injuries ruin her career. A woman at the table opposite was reading the same story, completely immersed. There was a tense expression on her face, as though she'd discovered her name was next on the Angel Killer's list. I reached for my phone and called Piernan.

'Not you, pestering me again.' I could hear him suppressing a laugh, as though I was a constant source of entertainment. 'You're coming to the gallery tonight, are you?'

'Will there be lots of anorexic women in black dresses?'

'Of course. It's a private view, what do you expect?'

'I'll wear something colourful, then.'

'Good for you. It's the weekend, let's go crazy and break the rules.'

I finished my drink and sauntered home, but by eight o'clock my anxiety levels were rising, and a headache was pulsing behind my left eye. I kept trying to convince myself it wasn't a date, just a trip to an art gallery with a new friend, but it didn't work. The mirror in my bedroom showed a scrawny woman in a yellow dress, in dire need of a holiday. I pinned my hair into a chignon and forced myself out of the front door.

The bus delivered me to Cork Street quarter of an hour late. I used to love browsing through the galleries when I first moved into town. They seemed like the height of sophistication. I was convinced that all of the city's beautiful people inhabited the narrow gap between Bond Street and Soho, spending their days shopping for exquisite clothes on South Molton Street. I saw them differently these days. They were still beautiful, and they haunted the same bars, but they didn't intimidate me any more.

By now the Bruton Gallery was heaving with patrons. The men looked well fed and prosperous, but the women were taking tiny sips from their wine glasses, monitoring each calorie. Piernan was already there, studying his catalogue, linen suit hanging from his slim frame. He looked relieved to see me, and for a second I thought he might kiss my cheek, but he drew back at the last minute. He was standing so close, I could see the flecks of gold round his pupils.

'What's your verdict on the paintings?' I asked.

'I haven't got a clue, to be honest. I only brought you here to impress you with my highbrow interests.'

'Except you're not interested, are you?'

His curly hair fell across his forehead as he grinned. 'I made them do a charity auction recently, so I had to show willing.'

An elderly man bustled over with his hand outstretched, and it was clear from his manner that he was the owner. A pink handkerchief lolled from his top pocket like an extra tongue. 'You must be the famous Alice – I've heard all about you.' When he finally released my hand, he gave Piernan a knowing smile, then turned away to flatter someone else.

Piernan looked embarrassed. 'Shall we take a look around, so you can see the extent of my ignorance?'

I admired a brightly coloured butterfly, trapped in a small frame. But a throng had gathered by a line of prints on the opposite wall. Rows of dollars were lying side by side, picked out in neon pink and green.

'They're all the same,' I commented. 'Are they Warhols?'

He checked his catalogue and nodded. 'You won't believe what they're worth.'

'How much?'

'A few hundred thousand each.'

'That's obscene.' My headache stepped up a gear. The wine must have gone to my head, because normally I don't make judgements about how people choose to spend their money.

'Is something wrong, Alice?' Piernan asked.

I turned to him. 'Where do I start? There's no money for my anger management groups. Kids in this city are getting rickets from malnourishment, and bankers help no one but themselves. It's unbelievable that people are blowing that much on a piece of paper.'

Piernan gaped at me. 'That's the longest speech I've heard you make.'

'Sorry.' I gave a shaky laugh. 'I think the police work's getting to me.'

'You're right about the finance world. It started to sicken me too – that's why I got out.'

'You must know people at the Angel Bank, don't you?' I asked.

'Quite a few. I worked there years ago, selling bonds.'

'You didn't tell me.'

Piernan shrugged his shoulders. 'I had friends there, but it made me decide to do something different with my life.'

He looked so uncomfortable that I realised he was only giving me a fraction of the story.

'It's a conspiracy of silence,' I said. 'There's something wrong with the culture there. It's driven someone over the edge.'

His eyebrows shot up. 'It must have changed since my day. It was competitive, but people weren't slitting each other's throats.'

I wanted to ask more questions, but he steered the conversation to lighter subjects, and after a few minutes he went to get us more wine. Discomfort was still bubbling in my chest. Maybe it was because it was so easy to imagine sleeping with him, after months of waking up alone, because he was so flattering and funny. But what would happen in the morning? The trapped feeling would come back, and I'd wake up gasping for breath. The people around me were starting to blur around the edges, and Piernan had been cornered by the gallery owner, on the far side of the room. The woman beside me was trying to persuade her husband to buy a pair of prints, for their living room. The expression on her face was petulant, like a child demanding more pocket money.

'One's enough,' he replied firmly. 'They could go down as well as up.' His mouth twisted into an ugly line as he fought to win the argument.

Everywhere I looked, people were poring over their catalogues, doing mental sums. Things got easier when Piernan came back. We found a quiet corner, and he was so entertaining, it was easy to ignore the frenzy of consumption in the background. The owner was rushing around, sticking red dots onto frames. Piernan asked me about the cuts at work, then he entertained me with stories about a pompous acquaintance of his, who managed to upset everyone he knew. Time passed so quickly that it was midnight by the time I checked my watch.

'When are we meeting again?' He gazed down at me.

'Can I call you?'

'Of course.' His mouth twitched with amusement. 'After you've checked your hectic schedule.'

He flagged down a cab for me, and I was about to say goodbye when he passed something through the open window.

'For you, Alice. A token of my esteem.' His madcap grin was the last thing I saw as the car pulled away.

When I lifted the brown paper, my breath caught in my throat. The butterfly I'd admired was trapped inside the package. Its wings were a gorgeous, vivid turquoise, and Andy Warhol's signature was scribbled in the corner of the frame.

17

When I was twelve years old my boyfriend gave me a present. It was Duran Duran's newest album, and I wanted it with all my heart, but I handed it straight back. Maybe I already knew that gifts can be bribes, or burdens, or apologies. But at least it went to a good home. He gave the CD to Heather Marks from year eight, the same day I chucked him.

I pressed my hands over my eyes, and when I opened them again, the butterfly was still sitting on the hall table. I turned my back on it and hunted for my running shoes.

There was no sign yet of the usual crowd of Sunday dog walkers when I reached Butler's Wharf. I kept my thoughts to a minimum, watching the sun pooling on the black surface of the river. Sooner or later I would have to confront Piernan, but I was determined not to spoil my run with worrying. I chased along Pickford's Wharf until my lungs burned. By the time I reached the Tate Modern I had to squat for a few moments, heaving for breath. A few couples were crossing the pedestrian bridge to St Paul's. It looked too fragile to support them, metal wires stretched taut as a cat's cradle. I took my time running home, listening to my iPod. Gladys Knight was lamenting that it had been a rainy night in Georgia, but in London the sky was still pure azure. The weather seemed to be stuck in a permanent loop, every morning just as irritatingly perfect as the one before.

Will was in his bedroom when I got back, hurling CDs into a bin bag. The plastic cases shattered loudly as they hit the floor.

'What are you doing?' I asked.

'Clearing this lot.' He carried on destroying his music collection, without bothering to look up. 'I'm taking my junk down to the bins.'

'Right,' I tried to speak calmly. 'Are you keeping anything?'

'Just the stuff I need.' He pointed at a small pile of belongings. All I could see was a pair of canvas shoes, a yellow T-shirt with Club Ibiza printed on it, his wallet, a bar of soap, and his passport.

'Is that all?'

'The rest's too heavy to carry.'

'Okay,' I replied calmly. 'Do you want some coffee?'

'I'll take another load down first.'

I waited until the door clicked shut, then ran back into his room to hunt for his laptop, and the speakers that had cost him a fortune. They were in a tea crate, heaving with photo albums and his entire vinyl collection. It was the records that upset me most. Ten years ago I'd stood beside him, scouring the stalls at Greenwich Market for vintage David Bowie. I crammed armfuls of his belongings under my bed and in my wardrobe, hoping he wouldn't notice. When I looked out of the window he was standing on the pavement, calmly abandoning everything he owned. The huge communal bin was already half full of clothes, books and the wooden sculptures he'd shipped back from Bali.

Will looked tired when he came back up the stairs, sweat dripping from his face. I watched him from the corner of my eye as he stuffed the rest of his shirts and jackets into a plastic sack. He was barefoot and his shorts were coming adrift at the seams, legs sliced apart by livid scars. Once the bag was full, he wrenched his T-shirt over his head, used it to wipe his face, then dropped it into the sack. Maybe I should have tried to stop him, but there was no point. He would only yell at me if I got in his way. It was impossible to imagine myself in his place. I'd have fought tooth and nail to rescue my photos and letters if the flat went up in flames.

It was a relief when the doorbell rang. It was bound to be Lola arriving for her weekend coffee. With any luck she could perform her usual magic and calm Will down. But when I opened the door my mother was standing there, wearing her favourite outraged expression and a dark green dress without a single crease.

'Didn't you get my messages? I must have left half a dozen.'

'You should have called my mobile, Mum.'

She pursed her mouth, unwilling to concede the point. I was about to advise her to jump straight back into her lemon-scented Nissan, but it was too late. She barged past me, just as Will emerged from his room. At least I had a ringside seat for the showdown. My brother had avoided her for the last six months. Maybe he listened to my phone messages to find out when she would visit, giving himself time to escape. He was clutching a bin bag against his chest. My mother eyed his bare torso and dirty feet with distaste.

'There you are, William.' Her voice was cool enough to refreeze the polar seas. 'What on earth are you doing?'

'Nothing,' he mumbled, 'just clearing out my stuff.'

Her expression softened. 'Well, that's good, isn't it? Always best to be neat and tidy. Let's see how you're doing.'

My mother stood in the doorway, scanning the overflowing ashtrays, abandoned clothes and empty wine bottles. She let her mouth hang open for a few seconds, too stunned to speak. It was me she turned to when she finally came round.

'How did you let this happen, Alice?'

I considered reeling off the history of my efforts to make Will take his lithium and see different doctors, but none of it would have been good enough. She glared at me, as though I'd failed a crucial exam.

'Leave her alone.' Will dumped his bin bag on the ground. 'Al's been amazing. She's let me stay here for months.'

My mother shook her head. 'You don't understand, darling. Someone should take care of you, because you're not yourself, are you?' Her voice had the sing-song tone that people use to placate bad-tempered toddlers. She walked towards him and I held my breath, knowing exactly what would happen next. One more step and he'd throw her across the room.

'You're the one who doesn't get it.' Will held out the palm of his hand, level with her face. But suddenly his shoulders dropped and his breathing steadied itself. 'Look through the window, Mum,' he said calmly. 'What can you see?'

'Very little,' she snapped. 'A few buildings, and your dreadful van.'

'You're not looking hard enough.' He pointed at the only cloud in the sky, so thin it was almost invisible. 'What about that?'

'For goodness' sake,' my mother complained. 'This is ridiculous.'

'If you've got any sense you'll watch that cloud, until you understand what it means.'

He backed away and, after a few seconds, the front door slammed shut. I don't know whether my mother took his advice, because I went into the kitchen to give her a minute alone. When I glanced out of the window, Will was hobbling along the pavement, empty-handed. He would draw plenty of curious stares as he limped through the streets, barefoot and half naked, covered in scars.

It's possible that my mother shed a tear, because she disappeared into the bathroom. By the time she came out again she'd powdered her nose and fixed the damage to her eye make-up. I poured some coffee and noticed that the usual look of disapproval was missing from her face. Her expression was completely blank.

'It doesn't make sense,' she murmured. 'Everything I did was to protect you both.'

'I know, Mum.'

I gritted my teeth, trying not to remember the sound of my father's footsteps when he rampaged through the house, looking for someone to hurt. That was the closest I'd come to forgiveness. But afterwards she pretended nothing had happened. She told me about her holiday plans, drank one more Americano, and for the first time in years actually made contact with my cheek when she kissed me goodbye. From the window I watched her gleaming silver car edge past Will's van, wondering why I never told her anything about my life. Maybe the world wouldn't end if I opened up to her occasionally. I stared down at my brother's belongings in the bin, tempted to add the Warhol butterfly to the pile. Part of me envied his ability to scrap everything and start again, no matter how crazy it seemed. My mother used a similar tactic. She battened down the hatches and kept the past rigidly under control. I would have loved to wipe my recent history, but neither technique appealed to me.

18

It takes a strong constitution to give a speech to a roomful of coppers. I'd dressed carefully for the event, in trousers and a high-necked top, in spite of the heat. Experience had taught me that revealing even an inch of flesh could be disastrous. Burns had given his team a three-line whip, so the incident room was packed, but the only smile I could see belonged to a dead man. Leo Gresham's photo beamed down benevolently while I switched on my laptop. Steve Taylor was sitting beside Brotherton, smirking in the front row, like a sixth former who'd shaved his head for a prank. I hit the return button on my computer and a map of the City appeared on the wall. When the room fell silent, I knew I had approximately twenty seconds to win their attention.

'Everyone loves bankers, don't they? Those generous people who invest our cash and never take anything for themselves.' There were a few hoots of derision. 'But this campaign isn't being carried out by some group that hates every banker on planet earth. If it was, they'd have published their manifesto by now. It's much more specific.' I pointed at the red dots on the map, marking King's Cross, Gutter Street and Staining Lane. 'The victims were all attacked close to the Angel Bank, and we know about their commitments to the place. Gresham ran their investments, Nicole Morgan spends one day a week doing their PR, and Jamie Wilcox was a trainee.'

I touched the computer key again and three angel paintings appeared behind me.

'You could be literal about his calling card, and say that the angels only tell us where the victims worked, but I think he's enjoying the symbolism – he's taking the moral high ground, because something about the bank disgusts him. It could be the name, because it implies the place is sacred. And the feathers are another way of showing us how much he despises his victims; conscientious objectors had them stuffed through their letterboxes as a sign of cowardice. They tell us something else as well – he's got time on his hands to plan the details. He's unemployed, or he's got a private income, spending days following his victims and working out their patterns. He could be so highly functional that the people nearest him don't have a clue what he's up to. He carries out his attacks at night then sneaks home again, and his family are none the wiser. Killers like this are often brilliant at compartmentalising. They can be good parents and partners, and still go out and commit acts like these. I think he's probably a graduate, with a high IQ. He's happy browsing in the National Gallery, informed about culture, with a religious upbringing. It's likely he's been treated for a mental illness, and he may have made suicide attempts.'

Some old-timers were refusing to meet my eye, but most of the room seemed to be listening, some new recruits diligently scribbling notes.

'You'll get copies of my report today, but one thing we have to keep in mind is that the MO and the signature in Nicole Morgan's attack were different from the first two. That's rare. Serial killers normally get more violent with each attack, but the MO hardly ever changes. Nicole was his first female victim, he was less decisive, and he left a new calling card. That suggests you could be looking for a copycat.' There were some grunts of disgust from the back of the room, then a ripple of heads shaking. 'Both attackers know about pain. When the attacks are this violent, the killer's normally getting even for his own trauma – sexual abuse, or the kind of mental suffering that makes people kill themselves. The main difference is that the killer tries to avoid watching his victims' pain, but the copycat wanted to see Nicole Morgan in agony.' I paused to scan the room. 'Any questions, before I let you get on?'

A young man put up his hand. Under the strip-lights his skin was a raw, glistening red.

'That's just guesswork, isn't it? What makes your guess better than mine?'

Taylor's smirk grew even more pronounced. It didn't take a Nobel Prize to work out who'd planted the question. I smiled at the young man before giving my reply.

'Psychology's not a precise science, we all know that. But it's based on the evidence you give me. Every report you put through the system adds to my profile. For example, you interviewed dozens of commuters at King's Cross. Five of them saw Leo Gresham's killer walking away, and their descriptions help explain his mindset. He walked decisively, pushing through the crowd, and he never looked back. He had no desire to gloat, or to hear Gresham's screams, but he wasn't afraid. His actions were planned and clinical. He'd probably visualised every stage of the attack. Those five interviews form a composite picture, don't they?' I held the young man's gaze then smiled again. 'I've worked on three major incidents so far, and I keep getting asked back, so I must be doing something right.'

He looked deflated. Maybe he'd been expecting some verbal sparring, to inflate his standing in front of his mates. There were no more questions. Either the team was too stunned by the idea of the Angel Killer roaming the streets with a copycat trailing him, or they were tired of listening to my psychological jargon. Most of them looked relieved when Burns got to his feet and started passing out orders, even though there were no definite leads. He took command of the room easily. His stature helped, and his deep voice bouncing off the walls. He explained that the Serious Organised Crime Agency had applied for a licence to seize the bank's records. The managers must have seen the writing on the wall, because they had agreed to provide lists of past and present employees.

It was ten o'clock by the time we got into Burns's car, to go to the Angel Bank. His scowl indicated that their endless stonewalling was starting to get to him.

'I want you to figure them out for me, Alice. I need to know what they're hiding. So far they haven't given an inch.'

'I'll do my best,' I replied.

Burns gave me more details about Leo Gresham's secret lifestyle on the way. It sounded like one long jamboree of expensive hotels, champagne and escorts. Jamie Wilcox had been his direct opposite. He'd done heroic amounts of overtime in a warehouse while he studied, to support his wife and son. There was still no news about the mystery blonde at the Counting House. Half a dozen prostitutes worked the place, but none would admit to meeting Wilcox on the night he died. I told Burns about my visit to Rayner's flat but he didn't react. Maybe he'd grown so tired of Taylor's obsession that he was sick of hearing about him.

The traffic was getting worse, and Burns was too focused on the road to make conversation, so I sat back and watched the city drift by. A heat haze was already floating above the pavement as we reached the financial district. Businessmen were striding to their next meetings as if the fate of the world economy rested on their shoulders. Their uniforms were gradually adapting to modern times; pinstripes replaced by Armani and Paul Smith, but they must have been sweltering inside their suits. The women seemed determined to look elegant at any cost, hobbling along the pavement in killer heels.

We turned left into Angel Court and the narrow cul-de-sac looked different in sunlight. The bank was much taller than the surrounding buildings, and its white fascia was a stark contrast to its grubby Victorian neighbours. The marble angels observed us calmly as we walked through the doors.

'This lot don't really call themselves angels, do they?' I asked.

'I'm afraid so, yeah.' Burns looked appalled. 'They're on a mission to rescue your finances.'

The chequered floor of the foyer was so clean it glittered. An army of janitors must have slaved over it at dawn, scouring and polishing. I'd never visited a private bank before. It was a far cry from my branch of the Co-op on Cornhill, with its harassed tellers, hiding behind bulletproof glass. I kept looking for evidence that staff were receiving huge bonuses, but the atmosphere seemed low-key. The traders must be hidden on another floor, Jaguars parked discreetly behind the building. There wasn't a counter in sight, but occasionally a black-suited executive whisked some clients up the marble stairs. Burns was speaking to a young woman, who looked like she was enjoying the most riveting conversation of her life. I thumbed through a brochure. It claimed that the Angel Bank enjoyed a golden reputation. It was one of the oldest banks in London, and a percentage of its profits went to charities. It supported disabled children, and helped the unemployed to retrain. Soft-focus pictures showed a gang of kids dressed as angels playing in tree houses, having the time of their lives. I noticed the Ryland Foundation logo at the bottom of the page and wondered if Piernan had visited the place recently.

'They're waiting for us in the boardroom.' Burns looked anxious when he trotted towards me, as though he'd been summoned to see Alan Sugar.

Two men were sitting at the end of an oval table, chairs so close together their heads were almost touching. I recognised one of them immediately from the Albion Club. Max Kingsmith's tan had grown even darker. Maybe he'd just returned from a holiday in Barbados, or he'd spent the morning playing golf. Up close it was clear that he was trying too hard to maintain his good looks. He was in his sixties, but his smile was too flawless to be real.

'You didn't say you were bringing an assistant, Inspector.' Kingsmith appraised me carefully, like an item of furniture waiting to be auctioned.

'Dr Quentin's helping us with the investigation,' Burns explained.

Kingsmith's smouldering glance was obviously meant to send my pulse into a racing gallop. 'Forgive me, Dr Quentin. We're more security conscious than normal, as you can imagine.' He was doing his best impersonation of George Clooney, but his accent was resolutely British. His eyes were hard to categorise, hovering somewhere between grey and green. It seemed odd that his confidence was undamaged by SOCA's investigation. He looked determined not to appear cowed.

The other man stood up to introduce himself. 'Henrik Freiberg,' he said quietly. 'It's good of you to come.'

Freiberg was polite and apologetic, with the sloped shoulders of a man who spent too long at his desk. His grey hair was in need of a cut, and he was wearing heavy tortoiseshell glasses. His suit was so old-fashioned that he looked more like a history teacher than a banker.

The two men gazed expectantly at Burns while he made his request. 'We still need access to all of your client records.'

Kingsmith looked exasperated. 'We've given you details of every single member of staff. Our clients won't let us release their financial information. I've already told you that.'

'You must be worried by all the negative press you're getting. The sooner you hand over the information, the sooner we can leave you alone. We're only doing this to keep you and your employees safe,' Burns said.

'I doubt whether you're capable,' he sneered. 'You didn't stop Nicole getting attacked.'

'My officers are working round the clock.' Burns seemed to be struggling to stay calm. 'We need to find out about anyone with a grudge – ex-employees, or customers with grievances.'

'We pride ourselves on looking after our staff and our clients, Inspector.' Kingsmith's tone had turned icy.

I wondered if he knew that staff members like Stephen Rayner felt compelled to lie about their sexuality. Certainly he didn't come over as someone you could reveal your secrets to. He could switch his charisma on and off at will, like Nicole Morgan. I decided to see how he'd react to a direct confrontation.

'But some of your staff must feel the pressure,' I said. 'You pay the highest bonuses in the City.'

Kingsmith's stare was needle-sharp. 'We never publish salary details. I'd like to know who told you that.'

I gave him a pleasant smile, which seemed to disarm him. When the discussion continued he vented his aggression on Burns instead, until Freiberg placed a restraining hand on his forearm.

'These people are trying to help, Max.' Freiberg reminded me of a prefect, confronting the school's worst bully.

I glanced around the boardroom, while Burns tried to persuade Kingsmith to open his records. The bank's Quaker founders gazed down from oil paintings on the walls, dressed in black frock coats, expecting us to part with vast sums of money. When the meeting ended, Henrik Freiberg showed us to the door, speaking in a low voice.

'You'll have to forgive Max. He's got a new baby; he doesn't need any more stress.'

I smiled at him as I said goodbye. Maybe Kingsmith's wife was the reason for his Peter Pan complex. He was trapped in a cycle of marrying young, childbearing women, to hold back the clock.

'That didn't help much, did it?' Burns came to a halt on the pavement. 'Let's hope Lawrence Fairfield gives us the real picture tomorrow. What did you make of them?'

'The top man's a classic case of narcissistic personality disorder.'

'He's vain, you mean?'

I shook my head. 'Kingsmith's built his own universe, and everyone has to obey his rules.'

'I can think of easier ways to describe him. How much did you say he earned last year?'

'Fifteen million basic, and more in bonuses.'

His expression was a blend of envy and disgust. 'They say money corrupts, don't they? The killer could be anyone inside the Square Mile.'

Burns offered me a lift, but I chose to walk instead. Ten minutes of radiation would do me good, even though I'd forgotten my sun block. The light was so intense that the pavement shone, railings glittering like quicksilver. I thought about Kingsmith, with his chilly, indeterminate eyes. There was something threatening about him. Or maybe I'd treated too many narcissists in my time. Their world view was brutal but simple – nothing mattered to them, except their own wants and needs.

19

Will was still AWOL the next morning, and Piernan hadn't returned my call. The butterfly shimmered at me every time I walked past. I almost felt grateful that Burns was an early riser. When I peered out of my bedroom window he was leaning against his car, tapping out a tune on the roof with the fingers of both hands. He pulled the passenger door open for me without saying a word. He looked like he'd been awake for days, his stubble gradually turning into a beard.

'You've been overdoing it,' I said.

'I'll take a week off when we catch him.'

If the driver in front had taken her foot off the gas, he'd have carried on regardless, leaving tyre tracks on the roof. There was no point in advising him to rest, so I kept quiet as we drove through the hinterlands of Battersea and Wandsworth. The council estates were looking sorry for themselves. I wouldn't have fancied raising a family there, looking down on rusting cars, and the rats nesting in the rubbish. I occupied myself with inspecting the CDs in his glove compartment.

'James Blunt?' I asked.

'Not guilty. The one thing Julie left me, bless her.'

'But Nina Simone's yours, and Gil Scott-Heron?'

'Yup.'

'I'm impressed.'

'Thank God.' Burns pretended to wipe his brow. 'The relief's overwhelming.'

By now we were pulling into the prison car park. I'd visited Wormwood Scrubs dozens of times to carry out assessments, without ever really noticing it. For some reason the huge scale of the building was easy to ignore, its drab façade eclipsed by the gleaming bricks of Queen Charlotte's Hospital next door. Rows of barred windows blinked down at us as we approached the entrance.

'How many inmates have they got?' I asked.

'Thirteen hundred.' Burns fiddled in his pocket for his ID. 'And they're the lucky ones. It's a fuck of a sight better than Brixton.'

It was hard to understand why anyone would feel fortunate to serve time at the Scrubs. The quadrangle looked as if it had been doused with Agent Orange, not a flower or a tree in sight, and the corridors were worse. If the prisoners ever got the chance to draw or paint, no sign of their efforts was on display. The air tasted like it had been boiled several times. We sat in the crowded waiting area, the young girl beside us struggling to keep her toddler under control. He kept tugging at her hand, telling her it was time to go home. Judging by her expression, she was in complete agreement, but loyalty was forcing her to stay.

'What job did Fairfield do at the Angel?' I asked.

'He was a director for years, until they let him go. He's done a year for insider dealing. They're letting him out in two weeks.'

Eventually a poker-faced guard marched us back across the quadrangle, without saying a word. I didn't blame him. If I worked there I'd have fallen headlong into clinical depression too. But at first sight the man waiting for us in the interview room appeared to be thriving on prison life. He looked about forty-five, skin glowing, only a few strands of grey visible in his thick brown hair. Even his prison uniform of blue sweatpants and a shapeless T-shirt couldn't dent his self-confidence. He sprang to his feet as we entered the room and extended his hand. At first I thought he was high on the prospect of being released, but his eyes gave him away. They had a glassy sheen, pupils dilated a few millimetres too wide.

'Lawrence Fairfield,' he purred, 'delighted to meet you.' His voice was smooth enough for late-night radio, loaded with false bonhomie.

He listened carefully while Burns explained the purpose of our visit. His sympathetic frown when he heard about Leo Gresham's death lasted for a nanosecond.

'I read about it. How sad for his family.'

'You've heard about Nicole Morgan too?' I asked.

His jollity disappeared. 'Poor girl. That lovely face of hers.'

'Can you think of anyone who hates the Angel Bank enough to do this?' Burns asked.

'Pretty much everyone who works there, especially the trainees. The top guys love tormenting them.' He lounged in his chair, as though the Scrubs was a much more civilised environment. 'I wouldn't mind shooting a few people there myself.'

'Meaning what?' Burns glanced up from his notebook.

'They destroyed my reputation. I've blown everything to clear my name, but mud sticks, doesn't it?' His confidence wavered for a moment. 'I'll never work again.'

Burns folded his arms. 'But it's not you, is it, Mr Fairfield? Unless you're managing your hit men from in here.'

'That would be tricky. I get one phone card a week, so my lawyer can tell me about my house being repossessed. If you ask me, there are plenty of people who'd love to take a pop at Max Kingsmith.' His mouth curled into a sneer. 'But at least he doesn't pretend to be a nice guy. I played golf with Leo the day I was arrested and he didn't say a dickie bird, even though he knew I was being set up.'

'The bank won't give us access to their records.' Burns studied him over the top of his glasses. 'Why do you think that is?'

A broad smile spread across Fairfield's face. 'All money's filthy, Inspector. Ninety per cent of tenners have been up someone's nose, haven't they?' His words were slightly slurred. 'They'll have shredded the evidence by now, but they've got clients in Iran and Syria. That's where you should be looking.'

'What do you mean?' Burns stared at him with distaste.

'I don't have to spell it out, do I? Henrik and Nicole are the only decent people there. Nicole's a sweetheart, but she's out of her depth, and it's a mystery how Henrik ended up in finance. He should be doing social work.'

I pictured Henrik Freiberg's apologetic smile and ill-fitting suit, his shoulders stooped by other people's burdens.

Fairfield seemed happy to scribble down a list of employees who had left the Angel Bank under a cloud, but he drew the line at providing written information about illegal trading. Maybe he was afraid of another spell in prison. When we stood up to leave, he reached out to shake my hand.

'I could tell you secrets about the Angel Bank that would make your hair curl. Come and see me when I get out.' His vacant eyes lingered on my face, and it was a relief to escape into the corridor.

'God almighty,' Burns murmured. 'What did he have for breakfast?'

'Cannabis resin, probably, or a couple of lorazepam.'

He shook his head. 'That's prison for you. They go in clean as a whistle and come out grubby as fuck.'

Thinking about Fairfield's drug habit made me remember Jamie Wilcox, his blood loaded with Rohypnol when he died. The anaesthetic had been the killer's one gesture of mercy. I stared at the wall ahead, gathering my thoughts.

'There's no way this is political,' I murmured.

'It could be.' Burns looked across at me. 'For all we know, the bank's been laundering money for arms dealers.'

I shook my head. 'It's about morality. He thinks anyone who works at the Angel is corrupt. He believes it's his duty to hand out punishments.'

Burns seemed to be on information overload. He dropped onto a bench in the quadrangle and studied the list Fairfield had given him. A few grey faces peered down from the windows above, and I wondered how many hours the inmates spent locked inside. Within a week I'd have been like Fairfield, gulping Xanax like they were going out of fashion. I looked up at the mildewed walls towering over us. The place must have been built around the same time as the Bank of England, but for the opposite purpose. This fortress was designed to lock danger safely inside its walls.

'Someone's trying to dismantle the Angel Bank's kingdom, piece by piece,' I said.

Burns polished his glasses on his sleeve. 'You think that's how they see it?'

'It's not the money they hate, it's the people. If the killer wanted to rip the finance system apart, he'd be dropping bombs on Threadneedle Street.'

'And Kingsmith's the top man.'

A chorus of wolf whistles drifted down from the barred windows, but Burns was oblivious. He was so preoccupied that his gaze had slipped out of focus. Eventually he stuffed the sheet of paper back into his pocket, and dragged himself to his feet.

20

The next morning there was a note from Will on the kitchen table. It told me that he'd left for Brighton, his door key abandoned beside the scrap of paper. I can't explain why I was so upset. Maybe it was because he hadn't bothered to say goodbye, or because my first reaction was relief. Will's problems had been mine for so long, I couldn't remember being free of worry. I peered into his bedroom and found it completely empty, apart from a few items of furniture. But when I went into the bathroom to get ready for work, the first thing I saw was his medication: lithium and chlorpromazine in a row of plastic containers on the top shelf of the cabinet. He'd forgotten everything he needed to stay on an even keel. My first instinct was to jump into my car and head for Brighton, but another part of me felt overcome by relief that I was no longer responsible for him. My phone rang just as I was about to leave, and Piernan's voice sounded as breezy as ever.

'Sorry I've been incommunicado. I had three events back to back, a logistical nightmare.'

'I was calling about your present. I can't accept it, Andrew, I'm sorry.'

He laughed quietly. 'Why? Doesn't it match your wallpaper?'

'It's too valuable. You should sell it for one of your good causes.'

There was a shocked silence. 'It was free, Alice. I told Giles you liked it and he gave it to me for nothing. He gets a cut from our charity auctions at the gallery – I'm one of his best customers.'

I couldn't think of a reply. The gift still felt complicated, even though no money had changed hands. It crossed my mind that a normal person might just say thank you, and accept his claim that there were no strings attached.

'Look, Alice, we're meeting tonight, aren't we? Let's talk then.'

By the time I reached Kensington I'd put the butterfly from my mind, and Steve Taylor was standing at the end of Marloes Road, topping up his tan. He looked even more thrilled with himself than normal.

'The boss lady's got Burns in for a mauling,' he said, grinning widely. 'Between you and me, his days are numbered.'

'That's your opinion, is it?'

'The bloke's not up to it. She needs someone who's on the ball. I mean, the Crossbones case was a real cock-up, wasn't it?'

I held my breath and counted to ten. Taylor had been doing his research, and no doubt he was rushing into Brotherton's office constantly, feeding her misinformation. As we walked towards the hospital, he carried on explaining why he was uniquely suited to do Burns's job. All the DSI had to do was wake up and smell the coffee.

I tuned him out and prepared myself to see Nicole Morgan. She'd requested a meeting with me, because she hoped to remember more details to help the investigation – but I had misgivings. The attack had happened too recently. People bury memories for good reasons. Dragging them into the daylight can be dangerous; it's best to let them drift to the surface in their own time.

The press were thronging on the steps outside the Cromwell. I kept my head down, but Dean Simons had already spotted me.

'I've written a story for you, Alice,' he yelled. 'Give my best to Nicole.' His face was ruddy from booze or sunburn, his clothes so creased he must have slept in his car.

Taylor shot me a look of disgust. 'One of your mates from the last case, is he?'

I did my best to ignore him as I marched up the steps. Nicole Morgan had chosen one of the most exclusive hospitals in London for her plastic surgery. The Cromwell was more like a deluxe hotel than a hospital. Patients could visit the cinema or beauty salon, then take a dip in the pool. When we arrived at Morgan's suite, two uniforms were standing sentry. They nodded Taylor through immediately, but one of them kept me waiting forever, studying my ID card. Maybe he'd been told to keep a look out for small blonde assassins masquerading as psychologists.

Morgan had made a remarkable recovery since her attack; she was sitting in an armchair, issuing orders into her Black-Berry. Most of her face was obscured by dressings, but her dark hair was carefully styled, nails newly manicured. Taylor receded into the background, happy to let me do all the work. A cameraman was setting up equipment in the corner.

'They're filming you?' I asked in amazement.

'Channel 5's doing a series about my recovery. They've even got the gory bits, in the operating theatre.'

I couldn't help staring. Indomitability has always fascinated me – there's something impressive about people who refuse to lie down. But the reason behind Morgan's request for a meeting was becoming crystal clear. An interview with a shrink while she struggled heroically to remember her attacker would make brilliant TV. It might even help her become a national treasure. I noticed that her speech was still shallow and rasping, her voice box bruised from the attack.

'I'm afraid the camera has to go.'

Morgan looked outraged. 'Why? The viewers can't miss this. It's part of my story.'

'You'll need privacy, if you want to remember who attacked you.'

'Of course I do.' Her one visible eye flashed at me.

The cameraman argued long and hard before finally agreeing to leave. Morgan's behaviour changed instantly. Her radiance faded by fifty per cent, like swapping a flashlight for a low-energy light bulb; but at least she was still willing to talk.

'The Angel Killer's got to be an insider,' she told me.

'You think so?'

'Of course.' The bandages shifted around her throat when she nodded. 'Jobs in finance are like gold dust. There are dozens of people out there, nursing grudges, and I bet Leo trod on some heads to get to the top.'

I got the impression that self-preservation was driving her desire to remember, and I couldn't blame her. She must have been afraid her attacker might return to finish the job. It was fifteen minutes before she started to relax.

'What's the last thing you remember before the attack?' I asked.

'Talking to Liam on my phone. He told me not to walk to the car by myself. I'd parked a few minutes away, on Staining Lane. It was eleven by then.'

'And what did you say?'

'I told him to get a grip.' Morgan looked irritated by her husband's concern, even though he'd been proved right. 'Let's just get on with it, shall we?'

I nodded. 'You can stop at any time, but I want you to try and tell me what your senses were picking up as you walked to the car. Everything you saw and smelled and heard.'

Morgan took my instruction at face value, relaxing in her chair, as though she was hypnotising herself. My concern intensified. Very few victims are strong enough to relive such a brutal attack so soon afterwards.

'Some friends were getting into a taxi, then Liam called. I didn't think it was risky – the street was well lit and there was no one around. I was carrying my jacket because it was still so hot. I had to look in my bag for my keys.' Her voice stalled, like she'd run out of air.

'Don't push yourself too hard, Nicole. Stop there, if you prefer.'

'He grabbed me from behind, and that's when I saw the knife. I tried to scream but no sound came out. He was dragging me between the buildings.' Morgan's hands clenched into fists. 'I can't remember anything after that.'

'Did you hear him speak? Sometimes people remember a few words, or the person's accent.'

Morgan sat bolt upright, taking short, panicked breaths. She looked terrified, as if the worst part of her ordeal had come back to her.

'It's okay,' I said quietly. 'It's best to wait until you're ready. You can talk about it then.'

Morgan's husband appeared with a huge gift-wrapped package as we got up to leave. His face wore the overstretched smile people always adopt when calamity strikes. It's a combination of shock and the need to convince everyone that you're coping.

'It's from Max and Sophie,' he said brightly.

The hamper from Nicole's boss brought our meeting to an end, and I was glad to see she'd calmed down enough to coo over the luxury chocolates and toiletries. The camera was already rolling again.

Liam Morgan showed us out, and I couldn't help wondering why she'd chosen him; he was as thickset as a weightlifter, an ugly knot of veins bulging over his collarbone. Maybe she saw him as her protector, loyal and unquestioningly devoted, but it wouldn't have worked for me. Apart from his cropped blond hair, he was a dead ringer for the thug Poppy Beckwith paid to guard her door. I hung back to talk to him while Taylor paced away down the corridor.

'How are you coping with all this?' I asked.

He squared his shoulders. 'Water off a duck's back.' His accent had a hard-edged northern twang.

'Really?' It was hard to tell whether he was being ironic, but the alarm bells in my head were as loud as klaxons.

'Twelve years in the army. This doesn't even compare.'

'But it's different when it's someone you love, isn't it?'

'Nicole's a fighter. She'll come up smiling.' His hard-man mask didn't even twitch.

I made a mental note to call Burns as soon as I got back to my office. If he wasn't investigating Liam Morgan already, then he should be. Either Morgan was completely desensitised or still in shock. He didn't seem to care that it would be a year, at least, before his wife could manage even the ghost of a smile.

21

A miracle happened the next day. The trustees did a U-turn and agreed to fund my anger management groups for the next two years. Hari was peering into his filing cabinet when I burst into his office. He looked unruffled as always, as though he'd spent the last hour meditating. I wanted to fling my arms round him, but it would have disturbed his perfect calm.

'How did you manage it?' I asked. 'They couldn't care less when I saw them.'

'It's a mystery. Those guys never justify anything.' Hari's slow smile gradually opened to its fullest extent. 'How are you doing? I haven't seen you all week.'

'Pretty good, except I've got an unwelcome admirer.'

He gazed back at me. 'A touch of De Clérambault's?'

'It's probably just a slamming case of loneliness.'

'We're talking about Darren Campbell, the one who hit you?'

'That's him.'

'Have you called his probation officer?'

'She hasn't got back to me yet. I've booked you to do a diagnostic. Can you tell me how it goes?'

'Of course.' Hari's calm eyes assessed me. He seemed to be fighting his temptation to offer me advice.

The air-conditioning unit had finally been fixed, but it had developed an ominous rattle. I was so elated that I ignored it, even though the noise loudened to a full-blown scream. By the time I left, it sounded like the brass section of an orchestra was tuning up in the room next door. It felt wonderful to escape the cacophony, but I stepped outside into a solid wall of heat.

My bus slogged west through Kensington Gore, giving me time to admire the architecture. The Regency villas in Holland Park looked glorious in the warm evening light, dripping with wedding cake stucco. I don't know why I was so excited about seeing Piernan again. Maybe it was the fact that he came from a secret world. I'd grown up in the dull middle-class suburbs, while he'd been raised by a nanny, on a country estate. His childhood sounded like a series of *Upstairs Downstairs*. Or perhaps it was much simpler than that. I couldn't stop thinking about him. I walked from the bus stop to a garden square in Notting Hill, and a tall, well-dressed man was waiting under a London plane tree, grinning at me. I had to blink several times before I realised that it was Andrew.

'You look amazing,' he said, as I walked towards him.

'That's an overstatement.' My outfit was incredibly simple – a black sleeveless dress, high heels and my favourite silver jewellery.

'I was worried about you on Friday, you didn't seem yourself.'

'The private view made me a bit queasy, that's all. I can't believe anyone could blow half a million on a piece of paper.' I glanced around the square. The houses were perfectly conserved, with glossy black railings marking out their empires. 'Is this where you live?'

'God, no. I'd need a fatter bank balance. It's Max Kingsmith's birthday party. It's a bit of a duty call. Do you mind if we pop in, just for an hour?'

I was so surprised that it took me a moment to remember

that he'd worked at the Angel. I wondered what kind of welcome I'd receive from his old boss. Burns wouldn't approve, but it was the ideal opportunity to look behind the scenes of the Angel Bank's empire.

The party was already in full swing. The Kingsmiths' house was large enough to occupy almost an entire side of the square, and clusters of people were hanging around in the hallway, clutching glasses of punch. It made me realise how small the banking world must be. Most of the guests from the Albion Club were there, including the girl who'd been weighed down by emeralds. She'd swapped them for a diamond pendant tonight, large enough to bring a tear to Elizabeth Taylor's eye. A tall, dark-haired woman was striding along the hall towards us. Her baby was clinging to her shoulder, but she managed to greet us warmly, even though the child was yelling at the top of her voice. Max Kingsmith was surrounded by admirers, lapping up the adulation like an ageing film star. His face tensed when he saw me, then transformed into a lingering smile. His wife was still waiting by my side.

'Can I get you a drink?' she asked. 'My name's Sophie, by the way.'

I smiled at her. 'I'd love one, please.'

I followed her through the crowd, and when I looked back Andrew had been trapped by a red-faced man with a loud, overbearing voice. Sophie's kitchen was almost empty, apart from a clique of dedicated boozers who'd set up camp by the drinks table, where a waiter was patiently doling out champagne. They didn't bat an eyelid when they saw her, and I wondered if they knew she was the host's wife. They'd come to placate her husband – no one else mattered. But at least Kingsmith had provided her with a state-of-the-art kitchen. It looked like a set for *House and Home*, with glass work surfaces and sofas to lounge on. The baby stopped bawling as soon as

Sophie put her back in her Moses basket. She must have been five or six months old.

'Thank God for that. You weigh a tonne, Molly,' she told her daughter as she rubbed her back.

I watched Sophie collect a glass of wine for me from a passing tray. I'd been expecting a fragile blonde with cut-glass cheekbones. She was beautifully dressed in a long, dark blue dress, but she looked too robust for a trophy wife, her hair cropped into a short bob. She had the broad-shouldered physique of a serious swimmer, and there must have been a yawning thirty-year gap between her and her husband. She looked surprised when I told her how I'd met him.

'This can't be an easy time for you,' I commented.

She perched on a stool opposite. 'It's worse for Max. He worked with Leo since the year dot.'

'And you knew him socially?'

She nodded. 'I know everyone at the bank. They have so many lunches and dinners.'

Maybe I imagined it, but I thought she flinched. Her social duties must have been overwhelming, with a new baby to care for. 'Does Max talk about what's been happening?'

'He prefers to play eighteen holes if something's getting him down.' Her smile dimmed for a second.

'Are you a golfer too?'

'God, no, I'm hopeless,' she said, laughing. 'I used to be an interior designer. That's how I met Max – the charm offensive started when I walked through the door.'

She would have done a roaring trade as a designer, listening politely to her clients, keen not to challenge their taste. But it was harder to understand why she'd settled for someone old enough to be her father. She didn't seem the type to target someone for their money. Maybe she'd found some good in him that was invisible to the naked eye. We chatted for the next twenty minutes, and it turned out that we had a lot in common. She was a south Londoner too, and she'd lived in a flat a few streets from mine before she got married. I got the impression that she could happily have ignored the party and talked to me for the rest of the evening.

'Do you have kids?' Sophie's hazel eyes fixed on me.

'Not yet. But one day, maybe.' I was tempted to admit that procreation wasn't high on my agenda, given my family's gene pool, but when I glanced at her again she was on the edge of tears.

'You should.' Her lower lip trembled as she spoke. 'It doesn't matter how bad things get. They make everything worthwhile.'

She leant over to pick up her daughter, but she'd given me a split-second insight into the state of her marriage, and it made me want to slap Kingsmith's face. Not that it would have made any difference. Narcissists don't change. No matter what happens, they're always sublimely convinced that the universe exists to serve their needs.

I noticed a row of maps hanging in the corner, clipped to a metal wire, like photos hung out to dry. Small yellow islands were scattered on an expanse of turquoise.

'Are those maps of the Seychelles?' I asked.

'The Maldives. We went there on honeymoon. It was unbelievable; we just sunbathed, and sailed from island to island. We didn't see anyone for weeks.' Her face relaxed into a smile.

'Was Max married before?' I asked.

'Twice. He says I'm his third time lucky.' She was still staring at the maps. 'We swam for hours every day over there. I still try to get to the pool, when Mum can look after Molly. But, to be honest, I haven't done much since all this began.'

'At least your mum's nearby.'

'Very near,' she said, nodding at a tall, grey-haired woman

who was talking politely to the men by the drinks table. 'She's living with us at the moment.'

'It must be good to have an extra pair of hands,' I commented.

'I'd sink without her. I just wish Max could spend more time here. He's always done crazy hours – I'm working on him to retire, but it's a hopeless cause.'

I rummaged in my bag for my card, to give her my phone number and address. 'Give me a call if you fancy a coffee some time.'

'Or we could go to a pub.' Sophie's face lit up, as though it had been months since her last night on the town. She studied the card carefully before slipping it into the pocket of her dress.

Sophie's mother crossed the room just as I was about to search for Andrew. She told me her name was Louise, and I noticed that she had the same broad shoulders and strong bone structure as her daughter. She gave Sophie a concerned look as she reached out to take Molly.

'People have been asking for you, darling.'

Sophie seemed reluctant to part with her daughter, but after a moment she hurried away. Her mother was wearing a green linen dress, with no jewellery apart from a small gold crucifix. I guessed that Louise was around sixty, straight-backed and fit-looking, as if she'd enjoyed a lifetime of outdoor pursuits.

'Would you like to see the garden?' she asked.

'I'd love some fresh air.'

'Could you hold Molly while I open the door?'

The baby's eyes were closed, and she was a warm, relaxed weight in the crook of my arm. Her dark eyelashes fluttered against her cheek, as if she was in the middle of a dream. I held my breath as I carried her across the lawn to a wooden bench.

'I'm not used to all this commotion,' Louise said. 'I'd just retired to Cornwall when Molly was born.'

'You must miss the sea.'

She nodded vigorously. 'I miss the countryside too, but I can't leave.'

'You're staying indefinitely?'

'Sophie wants me here till the end of the year. She spends too much time on her own.' A cloud of anger passed across her face.

I was surprised that she let her dislike for her son-in-law surface in front of a complete stranger. Her anger must be bubbling so powerfully, she couldn't suppress it. And I didn't blame her. She'd have seen her daughter's distress every day, while Kingsmith carried on with his business, ignoring his wife's needs. I chatted with Louise for a while longer, and she told me that she'd bought her cottage in St Ives five years ago, but her husband had died before they could move in. I got the sense that she disliked London intensely, but her sense of duty made it impossible to leave. She gave me the same hesitant smile as her daughter when I finally left her to look for Andrew.

The volume of the music had grown louder, and girls were dancing in the hall, Pimm's slopping from their glasses onto the parquet floor. Kingsmith was flirting with a well-preserved woman in a plunging red dress, but he turned in my direction when he spotted me.

'I hope my wife's been looking after you, Dr Quentin,' he said.

'She introduced me to Molly.'

He brushed the comment aside. 'Working with the police must be tiresome, mustn't it? They're a complete waste of time. I've had to get a licence so we can use our own security.'

Kingsmith was standing uncomfortably close, and I felt like telling him that the police would be more effective if he gave them the information he was hiding. But he'd already changed the topic, and my suspicions were confirmed. The only narrative that interested him was his own. He launched into his life story: four years at Oxford, a decade on Wall Street, then back to the small world of the UK to run the Angel Bank. There was something oddly mesmerising about him, despite his egotism. The colour of his eyes was impossible to judge. They changed from grey to green at five-minute intervals, according to his mood. I was so busy studying them that I didn't notice Sophie approaching until it was too late. She was watching us and I felt mortified – she must have been sick of women gazing into her husband's eyes. I took a rapid step backwards and it was a relief when Andrew appeared, with the red-faced man still chattering in his ear.

He exhaled loudly when we got outside. 'Sorry about that. It would have been rude not to show my face.'

'Their marriage is rocky, isn't it?'

'Really?' He looked at me in surprise. 'I hoped Max might finally be settling down.'

'I doubt it. His wife's drafted her mum in for support.'

'Five minutes in a crowded room and you've psychoanalysed everyone.' He grinned at me then glanced at his watch. 'Have you eaten yet?'

We ended up at Le Pont de la Tour. Piernan rested his feet on the railing, completely at ease, and I decided to tackle him about the butterfly.

'You shouldn't have given it to me, you know.'

'I told you, it didn't cost a thing.'

'That's not the point.'

He turned to study me. 'Don't tell me you're one of those people who never accepts anything, just in case it turns out to be a bribe.'

I drew in a sharp breath. 'Something like that, maybe.'

'I'm not trying to buy you, Alice. You'll have to trust me on that, won't you?'

A flash of anger passed across his face. It reminded me of the rage I'd seen in Regent's Park. He must have learned to conceal his temper years ago, so hardly anyone would know it existed. It was a few minutes before he could talk freely again. He told me about the fundraisers he'd organised: a charity lunch, a dinner and an auction of promises. I couldn't help wondering what he was avoiding by working so hard. When I told him that the funding for my therapy groups had been extended, he looked pleased but not surprised. Maybe financial miracles happened to him all the time. He poured me another glass of wine after we'd eaten, and something he'd said at the Albion Club came back to me.

'Tell me what it was like, working at the Angel Bank,' I said.

He shook his head. 'You're an enigma, Alice.'

'I don't mean to be.'

'I know. That makes it easier to bear.' He looked out across the river. 'I'm just research for you, aren't I?'

'Not at all. I just wondered how you found it.'

'I hated it, to be honest. But I didn't fall out with anyone – the Angel Bank's still my biggest donor. The place suited Gresham perfectly. He loved what money could buy, and he had a limitless appetite for pleasure – a true hedonist. Max Kingsmith looks on me as a friend, but he's got a vicious reputation. He can break anyone who crosses him.'

I wanted to ask more questions, but it was clear Andrew had nothing else to say on the matter, so I stopped probing, and his good humour soon returned. He told a couple of unrepeatable stories about a politician and three female secretaries from his campaign office, which made me laugh so much I could hardly breathe. I asked for the bill and paid my half, then got up to leave. It surprised me that he rose to his feet too. When I looked down, his fingers had closed around my hand. He leant across the table and kissed me hard on the mouth. I was so startled that I kissed him back. Afterwards I stared at him in amazement.

'Sorry. That was flagrant rule-breaking, wasn't it?' He gave me an apologetic grin. 'Blame it on the lateness of the hour.'

He offered to walk me home, but I made an excuse and hurried back along the boardwalk. It was hard to decide whether the churning feeling in my stomach was excitement or terror. I stopped by Cherry Garden Pier to catch my breath. The tide was going out at an alarming rate, exposing miles of black riverbank, thick with carrier bags and Styrofoam cups. The river was a useless hiding place. Everything the city abandoned came back to haunt it on the next tide.

22

By the next morning I was headline news. I stopped to buy a paper at the newsagent in Shad Thames and leafed through the pages of the *Express*. The journalists were still having a field day at Nicole Morgan's expense. A photographer had caught her in hospital, looking frail, still wreathed in bandages. Dean Simon's story about me was printed on page twelve. ALICE IN MURDERLAND was the best headline he could come up with, and the photo showed me hiding behind my sunglasses, refusing to smile. He'd dredged up every detail of the Crossbones case, with photos of all the victims, guaranteed to make their families grieve all over again. But the thing that made me angriest was his reference to Will. My eyes dropped to the story's last sentence: 'Given that mental illness runs in Dr Alice Quentin's family, is she the right psychologist to help the Met track down the Angel Killer?' It was lucky for Simons that he wasn't standing next to me: the urge to punch his lights out would have been over-powering.

A young black man in an ill-fitting suit was standing by the entrance doors when I got to work. He walked up and introduced himself, and I didn't stop to question how he knew me. Sam Adebayo looked too young to be the deputy manager at the YMCA, but the job must have been taking its toll, because his hair was turning pure white at the temples, even though his face was unlined. We found a seat in the gardens, surrounded by a wilderness of parched flowerbeds. Adebayo started talking as soon as we sat down. He seemed relieved to get his concerns about Darren off his chest.

'He was keeping out of trouble, more or less. Then the wheels came off the bus when he lost his job. The routine was his lifeline. We couldn't get through to him after that. The other guys complained about him talking all night, keeping them awake. Maybe that's why he left.'

'He doesn't stay with you any more?'

Adebayo shook his head regretfully. 'But that's not the reason why I'm here. Darren's got a photo of you on his phone, that's how I recognised you.' His words tumbled out in a rush. 'He's got this thing about protecting people. He liked this girl who worked on our reception desk, but she couldn't handle it. She resigned after a few months.'

My brain was scrambling to remember the information from Darren's file. The only thing I could recall was that he'd gone to jail for attacking a man who'd raped a friend of his. Adebayo's face was still tense with concern.

'Can you tell me why you're so worried about Darren?'

'This is a big city, Dr Quentin.' His eyes lingered on my face. 'He's a genuine lost soul.'

'I think he'll contact you again. Could you call me, next time you see him?'

Adebayo took my card then said goodbye. He covered the ground slowly when he walked away. Either he was a young man carrying a heavy burden, or he was much older than he appeared.

I spent the rest of the morning keeping busy. There was no point in worrying about Darren until Hari had finished his assessment. I contacted the estates office and rebooked the therapy room for my anger management classes, and at three o'clock one of the receptionists called to say that a man was waiting for me in the foyer. I thought Sam Adebayo might have returned, to share some more of his concerns, but Burns was waiting by the revolving doors with an unusually solemn look on his face.

'It's bad news, isn't it?'

He nodded. 'Remember our mate from Wormwood Scrubs? He was found dead in his cell this morning.'

I stared back at him, waiting for him to explain.

'His wife was divorcing him,' he said. 'His body's in the mortuary, but she's not prepared to identify him.'

Burns's skin had developed a greyish tinge. It was clear that he wanted me along for moral support, and I didn't have the heart to refuse. If no one from work was prepared to accompany him, his isolation was even worse than I'd realised.

'The perfect end to a summer afternoon,' I sighed.

Normally I avoided going anywhere near the mortuary because it gives me the creeps. There's a secretive look about its shuttered windows, permanently closed to protect the dead from prying eyes. Sometimes there are a dozen bodies waiting for burial, and more in the cold room. Corpses wait in the deep freeze for years if the cause of death is unknown. Burns must have requested that Fairfield's body be kept there, because it was close to Pancras Way, and it would be easier for him to attend the post mortem. I kept thinking about Fairfield. Maybe his wife's desertion was the reason why he'd relied so heavily on drugs. They must have eased the pain of watching everything slip through his grasp.

'Come on then,' I said. 'Let's do it, if we have to.'

The chill hit me as soon as we stepped inside. The temperature plummeted from blazing heat to a cool twenty-two degrees, and goose-bumps prickled across the back of my neck. A supervisor admitted us to room one, then beat a hasty retreat. I didn't blame him. It was hard to see why anyone would choose to work there, surrounded by cadavers. But at least you'd be your own boss; no one to complain if you belted out Nirvana all afternoon. I studied names listed on the wall then pulled out the metal drawer. A blast of freezing air hit my face and Burns stared down at the grey body-bag.

'Ready?' he asked.

I watched him tug the zip open, but I wasn't prepared for the look on Fairfield's face. His bulging eyes stared straight up at me, the whites clotted with broken capillaries. None of the prison guards had shown enough decency to close them for him. His skin was pale green under the strip-lights, and trails of saliva had dried on his cheeks. He must have been frothing at the mouth when he died. I peered down to take a better look, and inhaled a sharp reek of formaldehyde. I glanced across at Burns, in time to see him falter. There was a loud thud as he hit the ground. By the time I reached him, he was doing his best to sit up.

'Stay where you are for a minute,' I told him.

Burns had lost his glasses when he fell, and he looked like a younger brother of himself a year ago, worn out by the fight to hold his world together. I almost touched his face to comfort him, but he was already coming round. By now he was struggling to sit up and I helped him back onto his feet.

'When's the last time you ate something?' I asked.

'Fuck knows,' he mumbled. 'Last night probably.'

'Do you want to sit outside?'

The pugnacious look was already back on his face. 'Don't be daft. Let's get it over with.'

We stood side by side, and I reached down and closed Fairfield's eyes. His skin felt spongy and unnaturally cold under the palm of my hand. There were no wounds on his body, but his hands and mouth were a bluish white, his chest and abdomen covered in a network of scratches.

'How do you think he died?' Burns asked.

'I'm a shrink, not a pathologist, Don.' I looked down at Fairfield again and tried to remember the facts from my time at medical school. 'Maybe he swallowed poison. That would explain the foaming mouth. A big dose of toxins makes your skin itch, and it can stop your heart.'

'Poor sod,' he replied. 'What a way to go.'

'Don't quote me, Don. You need to wait for the PM.'

The colour returned to Burns's cheeks when we got outside, and by the time he'd eaten a sandwich in the canteen, he could give me more details.

'An envelope arrived at the Scrubs today, with feathers and an angel inside, bringing tidings of comfort and joy.'

He passed me a postcard wrapped in clear plastic. It was another beautiful Renaissance portrait. The killer had reverted to the same signature he'd used with Gresham and Wilcox. The archangel looked like a superhero, tall and muscular, dressed in a flowing blue robe. A small boy gazed up at him adoringly, as though he'd just been rescued. Someone had drawn a red vertical line through the angel's throat, tracking the poison's journey from his mouth to his gullet. The information printed on the back told me it was Perugino's painting of *The Archangel Raphael with Tobias*, painted around 1500.

'That's the clearest message yet, isn't it? He's not claiming to be an angel, he's showing us how he punishes sinners.'

Burns's expression was even bleaker when I handed it back to him.

'Something else is bothering you, isn't it?' I asked.

His gaze stayed fixed on the ground. 'Taylor's told Brotherton I'm losing my grip.'

'Like he could do better. What does she say?'

'Nothing, so far. She's biding her time.'

I parted company with Burns by the hospital gates, and

watched him slope off. It was hard to guess how he'd spend his evening. Maybe he'd watch Scotland play the All Blacks, cheering for his home team, but I knew he was more likely to carry on working, forgetting to eat a proper meal.

I left work early to go to the meeting Yvette had arranged. At least it helped me forget about Lawrence Fairfield, lying in his freezer compartment in the mortuary. He must have been telling the truth about carrying a secret the Angel Killer wouldn't let him reveal. I hurried north, against the flow of commuters, escaping from brokers' offices. The heat was even more intense than before. It had been gathering strength all day, soaking into every brick and paving slab.

Crossing London Bridge was like entering another world – the architecture grew more grandiose, and the brass door surrounds looked like they'd been hammered out of gold. I checked the address Yvette had given me. The bank was like a smaller version of the Lloyd's building. Ventilation ducts ran across the walls, and a glass lift compartment dangled from the roof at a crazy angle. Huge screens in the foyer were reporting trade on the Nikkei, Dow Jones and FTSE; a row of clocks announced the time in Tokyo and New York. When I asked for Vanessa Harris, the receptionist gave me directions to her office. I called the lift, but it plummeted to the ground at such supersonic speed that I opted for the stairs instead.

Vanessa Harris's office was empty, apart from a desk, two computers and a phone. Her expression was uncompromising, and I got the sense that she didn't suffer fools gladly. She must have been around forty, wearing a smart blue dress, her brown hair so neat it looked like an advert for straightening irons. Her make-up was the kind that Lola describes as war paint: thick foundation a shade darker than her skin, and a slick of red lipstick.

'You know I can't say much, don't you? I signed a gagging order after the tribunal.' Harris's tense body language suggested she was regretting her decision to meet me.

'This is between us, I promise.'

Harris stared at me for an uncomfortably long time, but her need to talk about the Angel Bank must have outweighed her fear of getting sued. 'I was too green to know better,' she said. 'God knows how I stuck it for ten years. The culture was all about public humiliation – they get through staff quicker than anywhere else.'

'Why do people stay?'

She looked at me like I was born yesterday. 'The bonuses are incredible. But the hours are crazy, and anyone who misses a key target gets fired the same day.'

'What was it like for women?'

When she bit her lip, a smear of crimson appeared on her teeth. 'That's why I blew the whistle. The bosses were disgusting. They interviewed girls who applied for internships over dinner. They had to use every trick in the book to get on the ladder.'

It was clear from Harris's expression that she wasn't prepared to describe the tricks they'd turned, and I felt a pang of sympathy. Her tough times at the Angel Bank explained her severe clothes, and the layers of make-up she hid behind.

'Did you hear anything about insider dealing or money laundering?'

Harris's glossy lips sealed themselves. She must have been worrying about writs being thrown at her, because she brought the meeting to an abrupt end. She offered to walk me to the exit, but she came to a halt beside a wall of glass. I could see down to a packed room, with only a handful of women sprinkled through the crowd.

'That's our trading floor,' she said. 'They've got twenty minutes till the FTSE closes, and some of them are up shit creek.'

It was like watching an opera with the sound turned down. The expressions on the traders' faces were either tragic or comical, with no gradations in between. Most had phones clamped to their ears and were gesticulating wildly. People were racing across the room, checking the red-and-green figures that flashed across an electronic board. I caught a whiff of sweat and testosterone, but it must have been imaginary. The glass was two inches thick.

'What's happening?' I asked.

'If they haven't sold enough stocks by close of play, they'll lose part of their bonus. And if it carries on, they're fired.' Harris looked riveted, as though she was watching gladiators in combat. She prised her eyes away to glance at me. 'The Angel's twice as bad. Fights break out on the trading floor.'

Harris turned away abruptly, as though she'd witnessed enough human desperation for one day. I thanked her, then said goodbye.

By the time I set off, my mind was playing tricks on me. The river path was emptier than usual: people must have been staying indoors until the cool of the evening. For some reason I felt sure I was being followed. Footsteps were pacing behind me, but there was no one there, except a woman taking snaps of the river. It was a relief to reach my flat. But when I was getting ready for bed, I heard footsteps again, moving across the landing. The spy-hole was no use, because the outside light had been turned off. For all I knew, some angel-loving maniac was standing in the dark, waiting for me to open the door. I made an effort to steady myself. It crossed my mind to call Andrew, but I didn't want to come over as a neurotic idiot, fretting about noises in the dark. It reminded me of the weeks after my stay in hospital, when every sound made me jump out of my skin – and there was no way I was going back there. I collected a glass of water and forced myself to go to bed.

23

Hari came looking for me in the canteen on Friday afternoon. I'd escaped from my office for an iced tea, but even from a distance I could see it was bad news. My boss's range of facial expressions is quite limited. Most of the time he wears his beatific smile, but when calamity strikes, it's replaced by a mask of absolute calm. He lowered himself cautiously onto the chair next to me.

'I just saw Darren Campbell,' he said. 'I wanted to bring him in straight away, but he ran off before I got the chance. He's got indicators for psychosis.'

'Such as?

'Schizoid symptoms mainly – delusions and auditory hallu-cinations. Some signs of florid paranoia too.'

'Great,' I muttered. 'And it's me he's following around.'

He studied me thoughtfully. 'We need to get him in over-night for a full assessment, and sort out his meds. I'll call his probation officer.'

Hari left me staring into my empty glass. It was several minutes before I could persuade myself to go back upstairs and prepare for my next appointment. It was at this point that I decided not to be afraid. It was a trick I'd learned in my hospital bed. Every time a wave of anxiety hit me, I trained myself to override it. My fellow shrinks would have lectured me about the dangers of repression, but at least it put me back in control. A point-blank refusal to give in to my fears helped my recovery.

I found myself thinking about Poppy Beckwith when a sex addict came to see me that afternoon. She looked nothing like Poppy – middle-aged and overweight, with unkempt hair and an anxious, nicotine-stained smile. Sex was just one of her addictions, alongside whisky and cannabis, but it was the one that scared her most. It sent her into bars, alone late at night, and it forced her to sleep with her best friend's husband. Every man she met was a potential conquest, but sex never satisfied her. It just deepened her self-disgust. It made me wonder how women like Poppy coped with the strain of using their bodies to service other people's addictions. No wonder so many sex workers numbed themselves with drugs and booze. I'd be guzzling gin like it was going out of fashion if I had to sleep with dozens of punters every week. Fallen angels flittered around my head for the rest of the afternoon. It seemed an odd coincidence that Poppy's flat was on Raphael Street, the name of the archangel that had been sent to Lawrence Fairfield on the day he died.

At five o'clock I got ready to leave. My pigeonhole was heaving with mail, so I grabbed the wad of letters and stuffed them into my briefcase. I tried to call Burns, but his phone was engaged, so I set off for Knightsbridge without his permission. No doubt he would give me a piece of his mind for making an unauthorised visit to Poppy, his accent veering north as the rage set in, but calling Taylor was out of the question. Another dose of his verbal machismo was more than I could stand. I was still convinced that the attacks on the Angel Bank were personal. Maybe Gresham had used Poppy as his confidante, and with the right kind of persuasion, she'd open up to me. The killer might even be one of her clients.

I decided against taking the Tube. It would have been like diving into a frying pan, London Underground's ancient ventilation system failing to keep the temperature below boiling point. The bus trundled past the Houses of Parliament. There were no movers and shakers to be seen, only a horde of kids, shrieking at each other in Italian. Gangs of elderly ladies were marching through Belgravia, for a rummage through the sales at Fortnum and Mason.

A man emerged from the door of Poppy Beckwith's building just as I arrived. For a second I thought I knew him. He held the door open and gave me a polite smile, but it wasn't until I was halfway up the stairs that I realised why he looked familiar. He was a presenter from Will's favourite adventure sports programme, forever hanging upside down in biplanes and driving sports cars across Nairobi. Beckwith's client list obviously ran to B-list TV celebrities. I stood on the landing for ten minutes to give her some breathing space before knocking on her door. It opened by a fraction and a perfect eye observed me through the gap.

'What do you want?' Her voice sounded rougher than before, as though she'd spent the whole day smoking extra-strength Gauloises.

'Five minutes of your time, if possible.'

The door closed and I thought she'd decided to ignore me, but I could hear the rattle of chains being undone, and she stepped backwards to let me in. Beckwith's flat was as stylish as ever, but she looked the worse for wear. She had stepped straight out of the shower into a pair of denim shorts and a T-shirt with a hole in the shoulder, her hair gathered in an untidy braid. Without her layers of expertly applied make-up she was pale as a ghost. There was no sign of her heavyweight minder – she must have let him off his leash for the afternoon. The rage on Poppy's face was obvious, but I needed to find out whether she was angry enough to plan a campaign of violence against her clients.

'Why are you here?' she snapped.

I perched on her settee, but she stayed on her feet, the expression on her face still hostile. Maybe she resented squandering even a moment of her free time.

'I've been concerned about you.'

'Really? Been keeping you awake, have I?'

I shook my head. 'Someone's targeting the Angel Bank. They're killing people who work there, and you're too close for comfort, aren't you?' At least I'd caught her interest. She lit a cigarette and waited for me to finish. 'Leo Gresham was a client of yours, and I'm guessing Lawrence Fairfield was too, wasn't he?'

Beckwith's mouth clamped shut, but not before I'd seen a flicker of recognition cross her face. She knew exactly who Fairfield was. And I could guess how they'd been introduced. Leo Gresham would have gone for a drink with him after work. After a few brandies he'd have started bragging about his best call girl. Or maybe Poppy's skills were famous at the Albion Club. Fairfield would have been intrigued enough to book a string of appointments, before prison put an end to his luxuries.

'I never discuss my clients,' Poppy snapped.

'No one's asking you to. I'm just warning you to take care, that's all. You might want to put a camera over your door.'

'You're warning me, are you?' Another flash of anger crossed her face then vanished again. A phone rang in another room and she rose to her feet. 'I'll get that, then you'd better leave.'

She disappeared into the hall and I spotted an appointment book lying on her coffee table. I flicked through the pages; each day's entry was filled with elegant black scrawl. Beckwith's voice drifted from the hall. Her tone was giggly and charming as a schoolgirl; she sounded ecstatic to hear from the man at the end of the line.

'Me too, absolutely. I'd love that. Seven o'clock, the same room as before?'

Her whole life must consist of lies, taxi rides and old men forcing themselves on her. Lavish amounts of money must have helped, but I still wondered how she coped. The fact that she could charge thousands was a reminder of the City's corruption. Compared to her clients' bonuses, her fees were a drop in the ocean. I heard her say goodbye, but as soon as she put the phone down, it rang again. She cursed loudly before greeting her next client in the same saccharine tone. It gave me the chance to open one of the doors leading from the living room. When I glanced inside, it didn't look like a typical call girl's boudoir. There was nothing tawdry about it. The walls glowed in warm terracotta, dozens of cushions scattered across the bed. The only details that gave the game away were a huge mirror on the ceiling, and the collection of Japanese erotic drawings on the wall. Beckwith was still schmoozing on the phone so I opened the door into the next room, then blinked with surprise. All it contained was a single bed covered in a patchwork quilt, a pale carpet, and a crucifix hanging from one of the plain white walls. I managed to pull the door shut just in time to deposit myself on the settee. Beckwith's expression had softened slightly when she returned.

'Look, I'm sorry I snapped,' she said. 'I never let strangers in normally.'

'I can understand that. But you'd be a lot safer if you told the police everything you know.'

Her expression indicated that she knew plenty, but she'd crossed swords with too many policemen in her time. I understood how she felt. Coppers have a list of unrepeatable words for sex workers who indulge in drugs, and she must have been called every one of them. Her tough exterior was cracking when she spoke again, her voice little more than a whisper.

'Leo was different the last time I saw him. He hardly ever mentioned work, but he said there was a problem at the bank. Something that could blow it sky high.'

'Did he give any details?'

She shook her head. 'He was scared, but he wouldn't tell me.'

Tiny lines were appearing beside her eyes, and I couldn't help feeling sorry for her. In my job it didn't matter how quickly I aged, but she would have to invest in Botox before her next birthday, to keep her clients happy. When we reached the landing I turned to say goodbye, and she looked too delicate to hurt anyone. I was beginning to think that my trip across town had been pointless.

'Take care of yourself,' I said.

Her hand grazed my arm for a split-second. 'People are doing that for me. It's your own back you should be worrying about.'

The chain on her door clicked abruptly into place, and my discomfort grew. Poppy had slept with two of the victims, but she didn't seem afraid. Either she didn't realise that proximity could be dangerous, or she knew what was going on. I kept running through the facts, but they refused to slot into place. I gazed out of the bus window and thought about the contrast between Beckwith's two bedrooms. The small, sparsely decorated room probably reminded her of the rehab centres she'd visited – empty and tranquil enough to calm the mind. Or it could have been a throwback to a Catholic childhood. Either way, it would have suited a nun perfectly. I punched the redial button on my phone to get Burns's number but the call was patched through to Taylor instead.

'Burns said he'd get me Poppy Beckwith's file,' I said.

His voice was an irritable whine. 'No problem. We've only got a triple murder investigation to worry about.'

'I need to see it on Monday.'

He grumbled something inaudible then hung up, and my sympathy for Burns doubled. While he drove himself into the ground, Taylor was busy advancing his career.

I took a portion of chicken jalfrezi from the freezer when I got home and slammed it in the microwave. The meal took precisely six minutes to prepare, and tasted of nothing except salt, sugar and E numbers. Fortunately I was too hungry to care. I was about to settle down on the sofa when I remembered my briefcase. I forced myself back onto my feet and emptied it onto the floor. Most of the letters could be thrown away immediately: invitations to conferences, fliers from medical journals and a thick wad of circulars from drug companies. The last letter had a typed address label and, when I opened it, a postcard dropped into my lap. I stared at it for a few seconds. There was something wrong with the image. The angel's perfect oval face observed me calmly, unwilling to take sides. But when I looked more closely there was a reason for her vacant stare. Someone had attacked her face with a needle. There were white spaces where her eyes should have been.

'You bastard,' I muttered.

The killer had discovered where I worked, and he'd sent me the same Leonardo image of *An Angel in Green* that he'd put in Gresham's pocket. The message was obvious – he knew exactly where to find me. Panic was twisting my stomach into knots and it took all my concentration to bring it under control. When Andrew called I was still slumped on the floor, surrounded by junk mail.

'How was your day?' he asked.

I didn't reply. For a second I considered telling him that I'd been fretting about psychopaths and ruined angels, but he'd have questioned my sanity. I heard him swallow a breath at the end of the line.

'I overstepped the mark, didn't I?' he said.

'Not at all. I was about to call you.'

'Thank God.' He gave a sharp burst of laughter. 'I thought I'd blown my chances.'

We agreed to meet on Sunday, and after I'd flirted with him for quarter of an hour, the tension was easing from my shoulders. I went into the kitchen and poured myself a huge glass of wine, my gaze snagging on Will's van when I glanced out of the window. It looked as dilapidated as ever, circles of rust blossoming across the bonnet. Then I rubbed my eyes and looked again. The curtains were drawn, but someone was moving around inside, using a torch to see what he was doing. I tried to tell myself there was no reason to be afraid. Kids had broken in, or some vagrant, searching for a night's shelter, but calling the police would have been pointless. Every spare uniform was patrolling the Square Mile, in case the Angel Killer struck again. I dead-locked the front door then sat in the lounge with the lights turned out, refusing to panic. The headlamps of passing cars dragged yellow stains across the walls, until the patterns lulled me, and I fell asleep on the sofa, fully clothed.

24

Brotherton was speaking to me when I woke up. She was explaining in her sternest voice that the killer was only targeting people with a connection to the Angel Bank. I rubbed my eyes and glanced round the room, but she was nowhere to be seen. The clock radio had switched itself on and the Invisible Woman's tone was even more urgent.

'But it's important not to take risks. If you have to visit the Square Mile at night, we're advising you not to travel alone.'

I felt like telling her to save her breath – hysteria had infected the city days ago. The tabloid stories were getting more lurid every day. The Angel Killer was being compared to Jack the Ripper, stealthy and impossible to track down. They'd even provided maps, because the Ripper's Whitechapel territory was less than a mile from the Angel Killer's favourite streets. The papers were milking the anti-bank feeling that had grown even stronger since the last scandal, when yet another rogue trader had wiped billions off the FTSE. Many journalists seemed unconcerned that bankers were being killed – their stories implied that they were getting the retribution they deserved. I switched off the radio as the forecaster announced that the weather system was changing. High pressure was bringing cyclones and freak storms.

I paused beside Will's van when I left the flat, peering through a gap between the curtains. There was no one inside, and when I slid back the door, nothing had been taken. My brother must have forgotten to lock it, because the door hadn't been tampered with and his sleeping bag was still rolled up on the bunk. Maybe I'd been imagining things – it could have been exhaustion, or a trick of the light.

The tarmac scorched through the soles of my sandals as I began my walk. Outside the Tower of London a Beefeater was welcoming a group of Saturday visitors. Inside that thick scarlet coat his temperature must have been stratospheric. By St Paul's the heat was punishing and I sat down on a bench in the square. Pigeons were strutting across the pavements like they owned the place, and the cathedral was basking in sunlight; an expanse of irreproachable white stone. I shaded my eyes to study its outline. It looked eternal, capable of withstanding whatever life threw at it: earthquakes, bombs, millions of visitors desecrating it every year. A new thought occurred to me as I admired it. Churches were the best place to go if you wanted to enjoy the company of angels. I felt increasingly suspicious that two attackers were at work. I visualised a pair of men sitting together on a hard pew, discussing the paintings on the walls. The second man had even downloaded an image from a stained-glass window to leave by Nicole Morgan's body. I watched some tourists perched on the cathedral steps, writing postcards home, knowing I should tell Burns about the angel I'd received, with its lacerated eyes, but the threat would become real the moment I told him. I forced myself back onto my feet, and a slight breeze skimmed across the river, doing its best to keep me cool.

It was after eleven by the time I reached the Millennium Bridge. I checked my reflection in a restaurant window. There'd been no time to blow-dry my hair, but at least my dark red dress and sandals matched, and my make up was still intact. The riverside was packed with families, enjoying cakes and artisan bread from the Italian cafés. My mother was sitting at a table outside a coffee shop, opaque sunglasses shielding her eyes. She didn't smile when I leant down to kiss her cheek.

'Why didn't you tell me you were running late, Alice?'

I felt like pointing out that she could have used the spare minutes for people-watching, or browsing through her copy of *The Times*. But there was no point. Punctuality is my mother's main obsession. She always reported for work at the library at three minutes to nine, even when my father was beating her black and blue. By the time our carrot cake arrived, she'd defrosted enough to make small talk. She told me about her trip to Crete, producing a brochure from her handbag.

'This is the villa we've booked.'

I studied the photos of a restored olive mill, clinging to the side of a mountain. It seemed ridiculously large for two retirees to rattle around in, and when I glanced at the bottom of the page, a set of numbers made me blink rapidly: my mother's two-week holiday was costing over four thousand pounds.

'And what have you been up to?' she asked.

I considered admitting that I was helping the police investigate the killing spree that was filling the front pages. 'Training,' I said. 'The marathon's in April, I've been getting fit.'

My mother put down her fork. Behind her sunglasses it was impossible to tell whether she was shocked or impressed. 'Is that wise? No wonder you look so drained.'

'I feel great, Mum. You're imagining things.'

She took a sip of tea then closed her mouth firmly, like a final judgement. The expression on her face was sour enough to curdle milk, but I took a deep breath and went for it.

'Will's moved out, Mum.'

My mother finally removed her sunglasses, revealing her pale grey stare. 'Who's looking after him?'

'No one. He wants to take care of himself.'

'Don't use that tone with me, Alice.'

'I'm not using a tone.' I managed to keep my voice steady. 'Will left a week ago. He's back on the road. I've called him every day, but he doesn't pick up.'

She tutted loudly. 'Professionals should be looking after him. I told you that months ago.'

'There's no way Will's going into a home.'

'Some of those places are ideal. They're in the countryside – he could take exercise. You should have taken him to see one.'

'You're not in a good position to lecture me, Mum. You never had Will to stay, not even for a week.'

She replaced her sunglasses, and the sun glinted from the lenses, almost blinding me. After a long silence I steered the conversation back onto safer territory. In between tiny mouthfuls of cake, she told me how disappointing *Top Girls* had been, and that Pilates was reducing her back pain. At one o'clock she kissed the air beside my cheek and set off for the station at a smart pace. No doubt we were equally relieved to say goodbye.

The air was even hotter by the time I got back to Tower Bridge. I kept trying to follow the advice I gave patients with traumatic memories. Limit the amount of conscious time you spend remembering the event, then divert your mind onto something else. I'd given my mother twenty minutes of undivided attention, but I was still struggling to get her out of my head.

I got an unpleasant surprise when I reached Providence Square. Darren was sitting on the grass opposite my building, with his hood back, enjoying the afternoon sun. For a few seconds it felt like my feet had been welded to the concrete. I couldn't believe he had the audacity to wait outside my building in broad daylight and, in retrospect, I did exactly the wrong thing. Every psychology textbook tells you to avoid direct contact. Stalkers are so desperate for attention that even the most negative conversation will be read as an invitation, but my common sense had evaporated. Knowing that he'd been following me made me so angry that I marched straight up to him, without considering Hari's warning. He rose to his feet when he saw me and I tried to bring my voice under control.

'You shouldn't be here, Darren. You know that, don't you?'

He frowned and shook his head vigorously. 'I can't leave you on your own. Anything could happen.'

His stare was the most unnerving thing. I'd seen that fixed, obsessive look on patients' faces before, but it had rarely been directed at me until now. He'd have completed any task I gave him. If I'd asked him to skydive from the tip of The Shard, he'd have followed through, without stopping to find a parachute. But his emotions were so out of control they could flip into violence at any minute.

'Listen to me, Darren. You need to come to the clinic at nine on Monday to see Dr Chadha. But you have to leave now, or I'll call the police.'

I stood there with my hands on my hips, like an irate fishwife. Darren's face reflected a mixture of outrage and disbelief, as though I was yelling at him in a language he didn't understand.

25

The shock hit me when I got inside. Darren was still standing there when I looked out of my bedroom window. The rejection must have hit home, because his expression was even more furious, and it dawned on me that picking a fight with a man who'd spent a year inside for GBH wasn't a great idea, but for some reason I felt more pity than fear. He reminded me of my brother, except Darren had nowhere to hide when his symptoms overwhelmed him. I poured myself a glass of juice, and the next time I peered outside, Darren had disappeared.

My decision to go to church that afternoon had nothing to do with religion; it was to satisfy my obsession with angels. Normally I avoided churches at all costs, because they reminded me of being buttoned into a starched dress and made to sit still while the organ howled. Sundays were always the worst day of the week. My father sat through the prayers with his head in his hands, determined to look penitent. But by the afternoon he'd be pissed again, picking fights with my mother.

I had twenty minutes to kill before I met Lola in Trafalgar Square, so I stepped inside St Martin-in-the-Fields. The church smelled like the one my parents dragged me to as a child – dusty hymn books, piety and candle wax. But at least St Martin's was flooded with sunlight. It streamed from either end of the nave, breaking down into segments of colour. One of the windows was crammed with angels in vivid robes. They looked like a celestial jazz band, blowing bugles and banging drums. I was staring up at them when a man's voice disturbed me.

'They're quite something, aren't they?' The man was grey-haired with a pleasant smile. He was wearing a tatty dog collar, and I wondered if it was his job to identify lost souls. 'Are you a stained-glass enthusiast?'

'Not really. It's the angels I'm interested in.'

'In what way?'

'I need to understand what they mean.'

'I think they're just messengers, sent down to do God's bidding.' The priest smiled at me.

'What about the angels of death?'

He blinked rapidly. 'If you want to learn about them, you should read the Book of Exodus. They punished the Egyptians for their sins. First they turned the Nile into a river of blood, they started plagues, and they threw the whole country into darkness.'

'They sound terrifying.'

His smile slowly reappeared. 'I think the real angels of death are Macmillan nurses. But I like the idea of a guardian angel. Someone to look after you, through thick and thin.'

He walked with me to the wooden doors. On my way out he pressed a flier into my hand, with a schedule of matins and evensongs. He looked deep into my eyes as he said goodbye, as if he was checking the condition of my soul.

Lola was visible from a hundred metres when I reached the square, her crimson dress clashing spectacularly with her hair. She looked amazed to see me leaving a church.

'Have you seen the light?'

I shook my head. 'I'm still mired in sin. Why are you beaming?'

'I've got a job, Al. It's unbelievable. They've asked me to run the kids' drama programme at the Riverside. It's three days a week.'

My first reaction was to wonder if Andrew had been using his influence at the theatre, but I silenced the idea immediately. Lola was more than capable of getting a job on her own merits. I congratulated her, and she enthused about the joys of a regular salary, hands gesticulating wildly. After a while I grabbed her arm and led her up the steps to the National Gallery. It crossed my mind to hunt for Dr Gillick in his underground lair.

'Let's start with the Middle Ages,' I said.

'What are we looking for?'

'Angels. If you see anything with wings or a halo, give me a shout.'

I tried to imagine the killer making regular visits, to stock up on postcards for his enemies. The paintings changed as we walked through the centuries. The earliest angels were like children's drawings – simple daubs on sheets of wood, with stiff blue robes and gold smears for halos. By the time we reached the fifteenth century they were more believable, androgynous, with luminous skin, hovering above the earth. It was the blankness of their faces that bothered me. Maybe the artists wanted to show that they were just emissaries, sent down to earth with tasks to complete, but it was hard to imagine more beautiful go-betweens. After six hundred years their blond hair still shone; their feathered wings glossy with health.

Lola insisted on going to the café after half an hour. She chatted non-stop while we stood in the queue, but my thoughts kept slipping back to the pictures.

'Who would kill people, then leave pictures of angels by the bodies?' I stared into the depths of my iced coffee.

'God, you live in a dark world.'

'Do you think he loves the angels, or hates them? Maybe he defaces them because they scare him.'

'You worry me, Al. You really do.'

Lola seized the opportunity to fill me in on her romance. Life with the Greek god was still blissful – her existence seemed almost as mythical as the pictures we'd been admiring. For the time being she was the poster girl for passionate love affairs.

'The poor boy must be exhausted,' I commented.

As usual she was hurling herself into the relationship, like diving from a cliff blindfolded. Suddenly she focused on me, green eyes sharp as lasers. Lola's always been uncomfortably good at interpreting my body language.

'How are things going with Andrew?'

'Okay, thanks.'

She rolled her eyes. 'God, you're uptight. I should have brought my tin opener.'

'There's nothing to tell. We've got a date tomorrow, if you must know.'

'And?'

'And I'm bricking it. The poor bloke doesn't know what he's getting into.'

She grabbed my hand. 'It'll be fine, Al, honestly. The guy's crazy about you. How much do you actually know about him?'

'Not a lot.' I gave a shaky laugh. 'He loves Chinese food, he lives in the City, and he works for a charity.'

'Andrew set up the Ryland Foundation – he's amazing. I can't believe he hasn't told you about it.'

Fortunately she soon flicked on to the next subject, which was one of her greatest skills. In a single breath she told me her view of the *X Factor* finalists, and the result of her audition for a cameo role in *EastEnders*.

'The sodding BBC,' she groaned. 'I still haven't heard. I'm sure they've got my name on a file somewhere saying "do not employ".'

We parted after an hour. I was determined to sunbathe and Lola was going flat hunting with Neal. We came to a halt in the middle of Trafalgar Square and she gave me a hug. Her feline grin stretched even wider as she watched the pigeons milling at our feet.

'You've got to love them, haven't you? Everything they see is a potential meal.'

Lola rushed away, her dress blazing a trail through the crowd. The next few hours were idyllic. I lay on the grass, drowsing in Southwark Park, then strolled home, determined not to notice any unwelcome admirers. My body felt so heavy and relaxed that I fell asleep on the sofa with the radio on. But something woke me just after midnight. I thought the weather had broken at last, claps of thunder detonating outside my window. But someone was kicking the front door so hard that the hinges threatened to break at any minute. My heart thumped painfully against my ribs. By the time I reached the door, the landing was empty. When I peered through the spy-hole, my neighbour was standing there, looking furious. I didn't blame her; the racket must have woken the whole block.

I leant against the wall to steady myself. Clearly Darren hadn't enjoyed being told to sling his hook. I picked up my phone and started to dial 999, then changed my mind. Someone kicking my door wasn't a good enough reason to call emergency services. Darren would be riding a night bus through the suburbs by the time they arrived. I was too wired to go to bed, so I switched on the TV. An action film was playing, but it didn't help my state of mind – the hero had eight minutes to save the world, even though time kept rewinding. I knew I should turn it off, but it was oddly mesmerising. The man couldn't help himself. He kept boarding the same train, again and again, waiting for it to explode.

26

Sunday was anything but a day of rest. I phoned my brother twice, but there was no reply, and thinking about my date with Andrew made my heart jitter in my chest, like I'd knocked back three double espressos. I ran to Limehouse and back at top speed, but even that didn't help. By the afternoon I was losing patience with myself. Andrew's gift was still sitting where I'd left it, on the hall table. I hung it on a hook in my brother's bedroom. The butterfly made an eye-catching splash of colour against the pale wall, and it made the room feel less empty. All that Will had left behind was the smell of tobacco, and a low-level buzz of worry that grew louder when I was tired.

I arrived at Leicester Square a few minutes early, but at least it gave me time to watch the crowds queuing outside the cinemas. An evening in the dark would be a welcome break from perpetual sunshine, watching other people's stories flicker across the screen. But Andrew didn't look like someone who planned to hide indoors when I spotted him on the other side of the road. He gave an exuberant wave as he rushed towards me. When he leant down to kiss my cheek, I caught a tang of the sandalwood aftershave I remembered from the Albion Club.

'Where are we going?' I asked.

Andrew grinned at me. 'You're in charge, remember.'

'I'm starving, but I never remember restaurants' names.'

'I know somewhere good – it's ten minutes by taxi.'

I've always loved black cabs. They seemed impossibly glamorous when I moved in from the suburbs; I felt like Audrey Hepburn every time I climbed into one. The Covent Garden streets were packed with couples. Young girls in tiny floral dresses were clinging to their boyfriends, arms woven around their waists. Andrew was studying me intently as the cab headed towards the City. It came to a halt on Queen Victoria Street, and I realised we were a stone's throw from the spot where Jamie Wilcox's body had been found on Gutter Lane. The taxi had delivered us right to the heart of the Angel Killer's territory.

'This is an odd place for a restaurant,' I commented.

Andrew smiled. 'I come here all the time, my place is just round the corner.'

We walked towards an imposing building with a polished silver door. The lift was the kind I always avoid, with clear glass doors, forcing you to watch the floors tick by. Andrew must have noticed my expression, because he put his arm round my shoulders as we rocketed towards the sky. At least the destination justified the anxiety. We emerged into a rooftop garden, complete with fountains and grass lawns. From the edge of the terrace, the city looked like a model village, the Thames a thin brown stream, twisting between landmarks. I could see Monument and Mansion House, trapped inside a necklace of roads.

'I'm not sure about this,' I said. 'It's too expensive, I always go Dutch.'

'Treat me next time.' He shrugged nonchalantly.

Almost every table was full, diners sheltering from the evening sun under white parasols. Handbags were slung across the backs of chairs like pennants, to demonstrate that their owners had taste as well as money: Prada and Gucci, in every colour of the rainbow. People were taking forever to consume their hors d'oeuvres, arranged like gem stones on their plates. Andrew sat beside me on a sofa while we waited for our drinks. His clothes were more relaxed than normal; he was wearing a grey shirt over a white T-shirt, and black linen trousers. His five-o'clock shadow had softened the outline of his face.

'You're inspecting me, Alice.'

'I'm just checking you're presentable. Otherwise I'd have to go home.'

'And am I?'

'You'll do, I suppose.'

He spent the next half-hour teasing me, while we waited for a table. He admitted pumping Lola for information when she gave him my number.

'She said you were the smartest girl in school, and I should call you, because it was donkey's years since you'd been on a date.'

'You're lying. There's no way she'd say that.'

He laughed at me. 'I made the last bit up.'

The maitre d' led us to our table, at the edge of the terrace. Lights were coming on across the city, silver chains marking the outline of the river. Andrew asked what I'd been doing at work, listening intently when I told him about receiving the angel card.

'It sounds terrifying,' he said. 'I had no idea you worked so closely with the Met.'

'It's been too close for comfort lately. Tell me what you've been up to, I need distraction.'

He'd organised a lunch meeting with the chief executive of Marks & Spencer. If things went well, the company planned to donate millions to Save the Children. And he'd found time to drive over to Richmond to visit his sister in her new flat.

'The staff are amazing,' he said. 'Someone helped her paint her room, and they're even teaching her how to cook.'

I shook my head. 'My brother knows how to make a meal, it's every other social skill he's forgotten.'

Andrew seemed too interested in watching me to concentrate on eating. Maybe he was as nervous as I was, because he ordered a second bottle of wine before our entrées arrived.

'Can I ask a personal question?' I said.

'Go on then, if you must.'

'What made you switch from banking to working for charities?'

The smile dropped from his face. 'It was the waste. Money leaked through the floorboards – no one cared how much got spilled. It started to keep me awake.'

'You sound like my friend Yvette. She's not mad about bankers either.'

'Who is? Now it's my turn to ask you something personal.'

'I'm not great at all that.'

'Tell me about your last relationship.'

I choked on my mouthful of wine. 'You're joking.'

He grinned at me. 'I'll give you my full romantic history, if you give me yours.'

'Go on then, you first.'

'It's not very impressive, I'm afraid: some hopeless infatuations at school, one amazing girl in my twenties. My thirties were hopeless, because I worked too hard. And here I am, forty-one, regretting my misspent youth.'

'What happened to the amazing girl?'

'Don't try and wriggle, Alice. It's your turn.'

I took a slug of wine. 'One physiotherapist, a tango instructor, and a surgeon I should have hung onto. I'd rather not talk about the last one. He doesn't deserve the air time.'

He laughed at me. 'That's all you're prepared to say?'

I concentrated on my salad. 'I'm not drunk enough.'

'But did you master the art of tango?'

Andrew had a habit of making me laugh, then throwing in a serious question when I least expected it. By the time we'd finished dessert he'd discovered far more than I'd intended to reveal. He picked up our bottle of wine and I followed him across the terrace. We chose two deckchairs with a view to the east. By now the sky was dark blue and I could see past the glitter of Canary Wharf to the shipyards at Tilbury.

'Where do you live?' I asked.

'A stone's throw from here. I'll show you tonight, if you like.'

'You won't.' I shook my head.

He grinned. 'Just as well, probably. I've only been there a few months – it's crying out for some TLC.'

'Go on then. Where is it?'

'Why should I say, if you won't come with me?' His eyes studied the outline of my mouth.

'To impress me with your posh address.'

When I turned to him, his face was so close that I noticed his eyes were a mix of amber, gold and brown. I leant across and kissed him. There was a mixture of pleasure and discomfort on his face when I drew back.

'You're killing me, Alice.'

'Sorry.'

'There are worse ways to go.'

We sat together talking until the restaurant closed, then he walked me back downstairs. The street was deserted as he pulled me into a doorway and kissed me again.

'You're not making this easy.' His hands closed round my waist. 'You'd better go home, or I'll end up ravishing you in an alley.'

I was tempted to go with him, but I knew it was too soon. He was already walking away from me, into the Angel Killer's territory, and I felt like winding the window down to warn him to take care. But the taxi had set off, and my head was spinning so badly, I couldn't guess what direction we were following.

27

Dean Simons must have spent the weekend camping outside the police station. His grey hair was more dishevelled than ever, eyes red from booze or lack of sleep. It crossed my mind to harangue him for invading my privacy, but he would only misquote me, so I ignored him and marched up the steps. One of the photographers lunged in my direction, his flash-bulb blinding me as I passed. The media frenzy must have been fuelling the Angel Killer's sense of power. While stories about him dominated the front pages, he'd believe the whole city was in his grip.

Lorraine Brotherton was already sitting at the head of the table in her office when I arrived for the senior team briefing. She parted her grey curls and gave me a brief nod of welcome, tension emanating from her in waves. My gaze caught on a picture by her desk of a stone house with bright blue shutters.

'It's in the Ardenne,' she commented. 'Nothing to do there except swim in the river, and eat the best food on earth.'

My image of Brotherton fell apart. Maybe her persona changed when she crossed the Channel, her suitcase crammed with gaudy sundresses. Her guard slipped back into place as soon as the investigation team arrived. She became chilly and remote again in the blink of an eye, and the atmosphere in the room was even worse than our last meeting, the air loaded with frustration and pent-up adrenaline. Taylor was the only person smiling as Pete Hancock described his progress on

Fairfield's crime scene. Every staff member and prisoner on B Wing at the Scrubs had been DNA-screened and finger-printed, and a guard suspended for supplying drugs. He was refusing to say where he'd bought the poison that killed Fair-field. The batch of tablets had looked perfectly innocent. Fairfield probably thought he was taking Xanax to help him sleep when he swallowed his lethal dose of rat poison.

Burns was fighting hard to disprove Taylor's claim that he was a liability. He handed out an overview report of events since Gresham died, with a summary of evidence for Wilcox's murder, the attack on Nicole Morgan, and Fairfield's poison-ing. His reporting style was still terse and monosyllabic, as if the idea of lapsing into bullshit terrified him, but Brotherton nodded her approval. She drew the line at congratulating him, but at least she looked impressed. Steve Taylor seemed desper-ate to get in on the act. His bald head gleamed under the overhead light as he described his immaculate command of the incident room.

The team seemed to be listening carefully when I ran through my profile, or maybe they were just too tired to argue. No one interrupted when I explained that the hall-marks from the three killings were still consistent with a category A psychopath, acting out a vendetta against the Angel Bank for personal or religious reasons. Burns had spent days following my advice, getting his officers to trawl through medical records for patients with a history of mental illness and violence, but progress had been slow. So far none of the interviewees was a credible suspect. I was still convinced that the assault on Nicole Morgan had been carried out by someone who knew her, a former colleague or an obsessive fan, because the MO and signature were signif-icantly different from the three fatal attacks. When I mentioned the idea of a copycat again, Taylor muttered something inaudible. Clearly he was still convinced that a single culprit had carried out all the attacks.

I produced the angel card from my bag and passed it to the exhibits officer. 'This came to my work address on Friday.'

'Snap.' Burns blinked at me in surprise.

He put another card down on the table, and on an ordinary day I'd have commented on the beauty of the painting. It was a Pre-Raphaelite archangel, with a lily in his hand. I remembered it from my talk with Dr Gillick.

'You're at the top of his pile,' I said. 'He's given you the most powerful archangel ever. It's Gabriel, telling Mary about the immaculate conception.'

'And that's an honour, is it?'

Brotherton looked concerned. 'We've had dozens of crank calls. It's probably some freak with time on his hands, but we need to be vigilant.'

She kept Burns and Taylor back after everyone else had left the room.

'A quick reminder, gentlemen. I'm monitoring your work very closely. I'll be reviewing your roles after this investigation, so keep your policy and action books up to date. I don't want to hear about any more cock-ups.'

I felt like telling her to change her management style. Threats might be helping her let off steam, but they increased the rivalry between Burns and his deputy, when they should have been working like a well-oiled machine. Taylor still managed to give her an adoring smile before strutting away.

Burns looked unimpressed when I confessed to visiting Poppy Beckwith. He reminded me in no uncertain terms to get his permission before acting alone.

'I think she needs protection, Don. She's inside the danger zone, isn't she?'

He shook his head firmly. 'Poppy's never worked for the bank. He doesn't care about anyone else, and she's got her bodyguard, hasn't she?'

Burns handed over Poppy's file reluctantly. It felt substantial as I stuffed it into my briefcase on the way out – she must have been in trouble since the day she was born.

My clinical supervisor, Sandra, came over from the Maudsley at ten o'clock. Our supervision sessions had fallen into a pattern over the past five years. She was one of the few people I relied on for unbiased professional advice, and I'd grown used to her sympathetic smile. Her white hair had been cut so short that she looked like Judi Dench's doppelgänger.

'You look tired, Alice. How are you juggling your caseload with all that forensic work?'

I didn't want to admit that my date with Andrew had kept me awake, fear and elation flooding my system. 'I'm spinning a few too many plates, that's all.'

'What would happen if you let one drop?' she asked.

I pictured myself in the middle of a room, the floor thick with broken crockery. I took a deep breath but didn't reply.

'Listen, Alice. I've seen people burn out, and it's not pretty. Keep doing everything for everyone, and they'll just keep piling more onto you.' Sandra touched my wrist. Her touch was gentle but firm, as though she was taking my pulse. 'How are things at home?'

'Better, thanks.' It crossed my mind to confess that I was still adjusting to the space Will had left, getting used to the echoes.

'Did you hear I'm taking early retirement? They finally agreed to let me go.'

It felt like a body blow, but I managed to congratulate her, and she told me about the Indonesian cruise she was planning. It was difficult to imagine someone else taking her place.

The rest of the day was a blur of heat and conversations. Patients arrived, unburdened themselves, and left, until I felt like a collection service, waiting for them to hand over their parcels full of woes. I made a conscious effort to leave their stories behind when I set off for my run. I decided to aim for pace instead of distance. If people could run marathons in the tropics, I could manage a few miles at top speed, even in forty-degree heat. Every muscle was screaming for a reprieve by the time I reached Cherry Garden Pier, the sun scorching my face. I stretched my arms over my head and gasped in some oxygen. Thank God I was doing the marathon, not a hundred-metre sprint. The training would have killed me. I stood by the railing and watched a man fishing from the end of the pier, line bobbing with the tide. I couldn't believe anything edible survived in such murky water. If he had any sense he'd buy his fish from Sainsbury's like the rest of us.

I was so desperate to dive into the shower when I got back to my building that I didn't notice anything unusual as I scrabbled for my keys. It was only when I heard footsteps that I turned around. Someone was standing there, almost hidden by shadows. I flicked on the landing light and Andrew stepped towards me. There were dark hollows under his cheekbones, and I wondered if he'd been sleepless too. It was clear that something was bothering him. I smiled at him and unlocked the door.

'Come in while I grab a shower.'

I left him in the living room, inspecting my bookshelves. I was towelling myself dry before I realised that I hadn't told him my address. I pulled on a blue dress and found him lounging on the sofa, flicking through a walkers' guide to Nepal.

'You've got fifty-one travel books, Alice.'

'It's wish fulfilment – I never go anywhere.' I passed him a glass of orange juice. 'How did you get my address?'

'Take a guess. Which one of your friends can't keep secrets?'

I rolled my eyes. If Attila the Hun had asked for my number, Lola would have passed it straight over.

Andrew carried on watching me expectantly. 'The thing is, it's my sister's birthday tomorrow.'

'And you're going to Paris.'

'Just for a few days. I was hoping you'd come with us.'

I had to explain that my work couldn't be cancelled. If Brotherton knew I'd absconded to Paris, she'd have me struck off instantly. Andrew looked crestfallen, and when I met his eye, I realised I'd stopped seeing him clearly. All I could see was his irrepressible smile. It took an act of will to stop myself touching him.

'Tell me about your last relationship, Alice,' he said quietly.

A band of panic tightened round my chest. 'Why are you asking?'

'You should get it out of your system. Go on, give me the whole story.' His hand was resting on my shoulder.

I told him as much as I could and, to his credit, he didn't flinch, even when I told him about the women who'd died. The violence didn't seem to affect him. He listened without interrupting, as if everything I said was easy to believe. And when I finished he didn't break eye contact. He just reached out and pushed a strand of hair back from my forehead. The gesture almost undid me. It was so gentle that I hardly felt his fingers glance across my skin, and when I leant over to kiss him, I meant business – I'd forgotten we were supposed to be taking it slow. Andrew gave an agonised laugh when the phone rang in the hall.

Burns was talking so fast it sounded like he'd swallowed a mouthful of helium.

'I can't hear you. Slow down, Don.'

'We've caught him, Alice. He's here at the station.'

'You've got immaculate timing.'

'Unbelievable, isn't it?' Voices were rising to a shout, as if he was standing in a jubilant football crowd. 'I can't talk now. Just get down here, quick as you can.'

A look of disbelief passed across Andrew's face after I told him the killer had been arrested. He stumbled to his feet blindly when I asked for a lift to the station.

28

'This is my life story,' Andrew said, as we left the flat. 'The girl who's seducing me always runs for the hills.'

'Not by choice. I'd rather switch off the phone and keep you here.'

It was after midnight by the time we got into his car. I was too distracted to notice what make it was, but it felt luxurious. It smelled of brand-new leather and air freshener, as though he'd just collected it from the showroom. Andrew told me about his trip to Paris as he drove. He and Eleanor were leaving first thing next morning on the Eurostar and she was overflowing with excitement. If the trip went well, he'd take her on a longer break later in the year.

'When are you coming back?' I asked as he pulled up outside the station.

'Wednesday night. I'll see you then, won't I?'

'If you're lucky.' I gave him a hasty kiss then ran up the steps.

For once there were no journalists in sight. The incident room was pulsing with energy, and a young policewoman barged past, holding her coffee aloft, like she was carrying the Olympic flame. Clusters of detectives were hanging around in groups, a mixture of relief and exhaustion on their faces. Burns must have been high on adrenaline, because he looked fresh as a daisy, even though he'd been at the station for sixteen hours. He led me towards the interview rooms. When he told me the name of the man they were holding, I came to a halt in the middle of the corridor.

'Liam Morgan's been arrested for the angel killings?'

'Not yet, but he's got himself a lawyer.'

I stared back at him. All I could remember was the way Morgan had served tea to his wife, gently setting the cup in front of her, keeping his overdeveloped muscles firmly under control.

'You've got enough evidence to prove he attacked Nicole, then pitched up at the hospital to nurse her half an hour later?'

'Not yet. That's why you're here.' Burns gave a tense smile. 'He hasn't opened his mouth – I need you to do an assessment.'

At least I was back on familiar territory. I'd carried out dozens of psychological assessments at police stations and prisons. Sometimes the reports were used in court, or they helped prison governors decide whether an offender should be transferred. Often the suspects hardly spoke during the interviews I witnessed, falling back on repetitions of 'no comment'. But physiology can be revealing. Someone's state of mind is easy to measure through body language, eye contact and avoidance methods. I pulled out a copy of the assessment pro forma and made myself comfortable in the observation room. It interested me that Taylor was conducting the interview – Burns must believe he would learn more from watching Morgan than asking the questions himself.

Taylor had chosen the worst interview room the station had to offer. It looked like a Honduran interrogation cell – windowless, with a neon strip-light bringing the temperature to boiling point. I half expected to hear the screams of torture victims being water-boarded when Liam Morgan was finally led in. He was wearing a tight shirt and I noticed again how exaggerated his physique was – the weightlifter's classic inverted triangle, with bulky shoulders tapering to a narrow waist. He looked as if he'd spent years honing every muscle. His eyes looked glazed, and when he lowered himself onto one of the plastic chairs, I could see the outlines of his military tattoos. For the first time it struck me that he was a trained killer – he must have witnessed hundreds of deaths during his tours overseas. His solicitor sat down beside him, an elderly man with his briefcase balanced on his knee.

Taylor flicked a switch on the digital recorder and stated the date and time of the interview. He looked as tense as his suspect. No doubt he was desperate to run into Brotherton's office to brag that he'd got a result.

'Here we go again, Liam.' He gave an exaggerated sigh.

Morgan was too busy studying the surface of the table to reply. It showed a legacy of neglect: rings from a hundred coffee mugs, and scorch marks from the days when suspects were allowed to smoke.

'Your housekeeper says you went out to the annexe in your garden to use the gym, the night Nicole got hurt. But you could have gone anywhere, couldn't you? No one would have heard the car.' Taylor's voice sounded cold and insistent. 'We've got reason to believe you attacked your wife, Liam. You must want to deny that, don't you?'

Morgan's face looked like it had been chipped from granite. He was still staring at the table intently, burning a hole in the Formica with the power of his gaze. After a few minutes his solicitor turned to Taylor.

'My client's dealing with the shock of his arrest. As far as I can see, you've got no evidence for detaining him.' The man's expression was a mixture of outrage and disbelief.

Taylor ignored him and carried on, his voice rising to a nasal whine. 'Your housekeeper's concerned, Liam. She says you've been acting strangely, talking to yourself and breaking down in front of your kids. And your mountain bike's gone missing. That's a coincidence, isn't it? The man who attacked Nicole was riding a bike.'

Morgan's shoulders twitched violently.

'And if you're the kind of bloke who could cut your wife's face to ribbons, chances are you killed them all.'

'You can't talk to my client like that,' the solicitor snapped. 'It's harassment.'

'Ten of our boys are combing your house right now, turning over every knife and fork.' Taylor was grinning, his skull glistening with sweat. 'It's best you tell us now, isn't it? Juries love a sob story; you can say it was post-traumatic stress.'

Liam's calm was fraying at the edges. His legs bounced under the table while he struggled to keep his mouth shut.

'It's your kids I feel sorry for.' Taylor leant closer. 'This'll take a lot of explaining, won't it?'

Morgan's face was turning purple. He must have been fantasising about putting his combat skills into practice, and his solicitor looked thunderous. The old man was murmuring threats about reporting Taylor to the authorities when Burns and I escaped to his office. I talked him through my assessment form. Morgan's score was almost off the scale. He was registering high numbers for agitation, stress and avoidance, but it still didn't amount to a confession.

'Going on his body language, he attacked her, but it hasn't registered yet,' I said. 'I don't think he had anything to do with the others. Some crisis with his wife triggered the attack.'

Burns shook his head. 'We have to look at him for all the attacks. It's Nicole who's suffering. She's got another operation tomorrow – the press are round the Cromwell like flies.'

By the time we got back to the incident room, Taylor was holding court, flirting with one of the telephonists. No doubt he was explaining that he alone was capable of bringing the

Angel Killer down. He was too busy staring into the depths of the young woman's cleavage to give Burns his usual look of contempt. It occurred to me that he must genuinely believe he was a ladies' man – that explained his slipknot tie, the aftershave and snug trousers. They were the tools he used to increase his masculine charm.

'What do you know about Morgan's military record?' I asked Burns.

'Ten years in the Royal Yorkshires. The bloke's a decorated war hero. He got a gong for carrying an injured mate across a minefield in Afghanistan. He's been out six years.'

'And he's still brutalised.'

He massaged the back of his neck. 'Liam's been with Nicole ever since the attack. He hasn't left her side.'

'That's not unusual. Last year an ex-squaddy in Birmingham shot his wife in the back, then drove her to the nearest hospital. He was inconsolable.'

'But it doesn't explain why he killed the other three, does it?'

'That's because he didn't. I'm sure this is domestic.'

His expression was neutral. Taylor might be convinced that the hunt was over, but Burns seemed to be struggling to make up his mind.

As the squad car drove me home, my mind kept drifting back to Liam Morgan. Part of me wanted to believe that the investigation had ended successfully. But Liam was a million miles from the killer I'd profiled. I'd been certain he was a graduate, with a love of culture and religious interests. And why would Morgan kill so many people? Maybe his wife's banking friends had snubbed him at too many dinners, or being her slave had finally unmanned him – his rage spreading to every corner of her exclusive world. I gazed out of the window at rows of unlit houses. Something about the theory struck me as wrong. Husbands attacked wives for all sorts of reasons: lying, infidelity, disappointed dreams. But it was hard to see why he'd kill three of her colleagues. Whatever he'd done, I didn't envy him. Taylor would dream up new ways to fracture his ego overnight, then he'd be dragged back into the interview room. Voices would keep hammering at him, until the cracks began to show.

29

I ate the world's unhealthiest breakfast the next morning: a huge fry-up, followed by a banana to salve my conscience. The cashier at Brown's beamed as she passed me a complimentary copy of the *Sun*, but the headline spoiled my appetite. ANGEL KILLER'S REIGN OF TERROR! I dropped the paper back onto the table, and wondered how Liam Morgan had spent the night. Taylor was probably still shining a searchlight into his eyes. The police hadn't released details of his arrest yet, in case it added to the feeding frenzy around Nicole. I watched the businessmen racing along the riverside, dressed for another day of sub-Saharan heat. By now Andrew and his sister would be halfway to Paris. I felt like chucking my briefcase in the river and jumping on the next train.

The manila folder in front of me was covered in greasy fingerprints – dozens of coppers must have thumbed through it over the years. Poppy Beckwith's file made me blink rapidly. Her father was a viscount, living in a stately pile in the Cotswolds. When her parents divorced she was exiled to boarding school. An incident involving a Bunsen burner, petrol and minor damage to the science block got her expelled at sixteen. Her early twenties were a nightmare – pills, booze, soliciting in public toilets and a ten-month stretch in Holloway. It was miraculous that Beckwith had fought her way back to the top of the pile, with a flat in Knightsbridge and a list of millionaire clients.

Her perfect face floated in front of me. The idea that the killer was connected to her was still refusing to go away, even though Burns didn't agree. The killer could be one of her clients, just like Gresham and Fairfield, unable to cope with sharing her. Once he found out where her most regular clients worked, the Angel Bank had become his target. I closed my eyes and tried to conjure him. He seemed to be revelling in details. It must have given him so much satisfaction to taunt the police by sending a postcard to a man he'd already poisoned. I wondered if Max Kingsmith knew that another of his associates had died. Even the sheer walls of Wormwood Scrubs had failed to protect Lawrence Fairfield. But Sophie was the one I felt sorry for – she'd be on the receiving end of her husband's rage.

Darren was perched on the railings, peering into the sun, when I reached the hospital. I watched him from the side of the building, trying to decide what to do. His expression reminded me of the boys who always waited by the school gates, lovesick but trying to disguise it, longing for a glimpse of their favourite sixth former. My stomach twisted as I phoned the emergency mental health team. They did their best to be discreet, but the operation still looked like a scene from *One Flew Over the Cuckoo's Nest.* The doctor from the acute psychiatric ward was wearing his white coat, a nurse and three ward orderlies trailing behind him. Darren obviously had no intention of going quietly. I felt like covering my eyes as they grabbed his wrists and marched him away, because I knew what was in store. He'd be left in a secure room, with nothing to distract him. If he was more co-operative by morning, the drug regime would begin. They'd keep him high as a kite until his mood stabilised. When I glanced down, my fists were so tightly clenched that my nails were cutting my palms. Being sectioned was Darren's best chance of a proper diagnosis, but I still felt guilty. It took me back to the morning when Will had been sectioned. I'd travelled with him in the ambulance, but the paramedics had had to sedate him because he kept screaming at the top of his voice. The breath I'd been holding slowly released itself as I stepped back into the sun.

I meant to go and check on him at lunchtime, but a GP called and told me about a young female patient. The girl's self-harming involved razors and matches, and it sounded so extreme that I spent the next hour arranging an emergency bed for her. The rest of the day was packed with phone calls, appointments and emails. I didn't even have time to check the texts that kept arriving from Andrew, while the air conditioning groaned in the background, as though it was mortally wounded.

A young policewoman pulled up in a squad car at six o'clock and I climbed into the passenger seat. She spent the next half-hour describing her boyfriend's efforts to qualify as a chartered surveyor. By the time we reached Notting Hill, we were on first-name terms, and a dull headache was thumping at the base of my skull. Burns was leaning against the railings outside Kingsmith's house when we pulled up. I wasn't sure why he needed my help. Maybe he just wanted company, because his deputy was fighting him at every step.

'How's Mr Morgan?' I asked.

'Keeping his trap shut. It looks like you were right. He's got alibis for all the other attacks, apart from Nicole's.' He gazed up at the Kingsmiths' house. 'I thought you'd want to see the great man's palace.'

Burns looked stunned when I told him that I'd already visited. 'He must have a hide like a rhino to throw a party with all this going on.'

Two men in dark suits were standing outside Kingsmith's

front door; they looked more like hired assassins than private security guards. Burns tutted impatiently while one of them grunted into his walkie-talkie. When the door finally opened, Louise was standing there, her grey hair caught in an untidy ponytail. The gold crucifix she'd worn at the party was almost hidden by the collar of her blouse. Her face lit up when she saw me.

'Alice, how lovely to see you again. Thank you both for coming.'

'Is everything okay, Mrs Emerson?' Burns asked. 'Your message was passed through to me.'

She led us to a room I hadn't seen before. It looked like a Fifties time capsule. A comfortable armchair sat in the corner, beside a basket full of yarn and knitting needles. There was no sign of a TV or a computer. Louise motioned for us to sit down on a narrow, old-fashioned settee.

'Nice and restful in here,' Burns commented.

'You need it when there's a baby around. These bits and bobs are from my house in Cornwall.' She shifted awkwardly in her seat. 'The thing is, Inspector, I had to talk to you. I've been so worried . . .' Her voice petered out.

'About your son-in-law?'

'Good Lord, no. Max can look after himself.' Her expression hardened, and I caught another glimpse of her dislike for Kingsmith. 'Nothing affects him.'

'You don't always see eye to eye?' Burns asked quietly.

Her cheeks reddened. 'He treats my daughter like a slave. Since Molly was born, it's as though Sophie doesn't exist. She's the one I'm concerned about. She's so busy looking after everyone else, but she's terrified. I hear her wandering around in the middle of the night.'

'Where is your daughter today?' Burns asked.

'I made her take Molly to the park – a walk always relaxes

her. I've been trying to persuade her to go out more with her friends, because Max leaves her alone so much, but she hardly ever does. She goes to the gym, and that's about it.'

Burns seemed to be struggling to get comfortable on the hard settee. 'Is something in particular worrying you?'

'A letter came for her today.' Louise's gaze dropped to the floor. 'I always open the bills for Sophie, I've helped with that side of things since Molly came along. This morning I opened a private letter by mistake. It was so awful, I didn't let her see it.'

She reached inside one of her magazines and pulled out a plain brown envelope, handing it to Burns quickly, as if it was contaminated. The typed address label was identical to the one I'd received. He produced a pair of plastic gloves from his pocket, and I inhaled sharply. The angel in green had become so familiar, I could see her with my eyes closed, brown curls framing her delicate features as she played her violin. This time a smear of red had been daubed across her face. It was hard to tell whether it was ink or blood. When I glanced at Louise, her face was tense with strain. It was easy to understand her anxiety. There was no way she could have imagined a crisis like this when she sacrificed her peaceful retirement.

'Could I keep this, please?' Burns asked. 'It's important your daughter doesn't go anywhere alone, for the time being.'

'I understand.' Louise gave an emphatic nod, as if she was planning to lock her up for the foreseeable future.

Burns did his best to reassure her, but she still looked worried when we left. I scribbled my mobile number on the back of a business card and handed it to her.

'Sophie's got this already, but could you remind her she can call me any time?' I asked.

Louise gave me a grateful smile. She stood on the doorstep as we drove away, flanked by her taciturn security guards, hand half raised, uncertain whether to wave goodbye. She must have been longing to pack a suitcase and escape to Cornwall.

Burns filled me in on the work that had been done since the last time we spoke. Every Angel Bank employee had been interviewed, and hundreds of clients, and he'd been liaising with SOCA and the Serious Fraud Office. They'd cast a wide net, investigating rivalries with other banks and talking to business investors. It reminded me how much he'd changed. The old Burns wouldn't have been capable of such a systematic approach. He didn't mention our visit to Kingsmith's house again until we got back to King's Cross.

'Those are ex-SAS boys guarding the place – no wonder the old girl's scared. She must be expecting a siege at any minute.' He seemed reluctant to get out of the car. 'We're getting nowhere with Morgan. He still hasn't opened his mouth.'

'That's because he can't accept what he's done. He's the loneliest man in the world right now. You could spend time building a rapport, chatting about where he grew up, his time in the army, his kids. The indirect approach should do it.'

He gave a reluctant nod. I sensed that Burns had reached the point where the old-fashioned methods were starting to look appealing. He'd be prepared to use blackmail, truth drugs or a cattle prod to gain a confession from him. When we got back to the incident room I was hit by a fug of coffee, hopelessness, and smoke lingering on people's clothes. Liam Morgan had been their only strong suspect. Judging by the team's faces, they were running out of steam. Taylor was busy circulating, making sure Brotherton clocked his efforts to rally the troops.

Burns found me a spare computer, then left me to my own devices. I logged onto the HOLMES system while people raced past my desk. The room was in frantic motion. At least a dozen telephonists were answering calls from members of the public, each caller certain that they knew the identity of the Angel Killer. Their expressions were jaded – they must have spent hours listening to unlikely fantasies. On the other side of the room huge photos of the victims gazed down at the flurry of activity.

My phone buzzed loudly as I started my work. It was another text from Andrew. He'd sent a string of photos since the morning: one of his sister outside Notre Dame, the pair of them boating down the Seine, and the last of himself, standing in bright sunlight outside a café. I was still smiling when my phone vibrated in my hand, and my brother's name appeared in the window. I stepped into the corridor to speak to him.

'Hello, sunshine.'

His reply never came. I couldn't even hear him breathing, and I was afraid he was in trouble, unable to tell me what was wrong. I forced myself not to panic. The most likely reason was that he'd tripped the redial button by mistake.

'Will, are you there?'

All I could hear was a fizz of static, so faint that it sounded like it was being beamed from another planet. I slipped my phone back into my pocket and returned to my seat. Will was so far out of reach, there was no point in worrying. I took a deep breath and started picking through the evidence files, lit up in red, flashing across the screen.

30

I'd been concerned about Darren since I'd seen him being frogmarched into the psychiatric unit. But he must have calmed down overnight, because he'd been moved to a standard room, beside Robinson Ward. The nurse I spoke to looked under the weather. The skin on his face had broken out in a sore-looking rash.

'We had to give him a mega-dose of risperidone last night,' he admitted.

'And he's coping with that, is he?'

'We had no choice, the lad was bouncing off the walls. The head psych wants to see him later.'

I didn't envy him his job. Acute mental illness has always been the sharp end of nursing; it's a wonder they don't end up in straitjackets themselves. I looked through the observation hatch into Darren's room. He was lying in bed, staring groggily at the TV, barely able to keep his eyes open. I've always hated risperidone. It slams a lid on the symptoms of paranoia, but they come back immediately when the patient stops taking it. The side effects are no fun either – slurred speech, migraines and renal failure. I glanced at my watch and decided to come back when the head psych had done his rounds.

I'd planned to use the afternoon to work on my paper for the BPS conference, but by two o'clock I was starting to wilt. The air conditioner had developed such a racking, consumptive cough, it sounded in need of a course of penicillin. I picked up the phone and called Burns.

'Making progress?' I asked.

'Morgan's about to let rip. Can you get over here?'

'I'm on my way.'

Taylor was the first person I saw at the station. His smug grin was absent for once. Maybe he was aggrieved because his new boss's sideways approach had worked miracles. Morgan had begun to talk the instant his aggressive questioning stopped, but the strain had taken its toll on Burns. He was talking in the controlled monotone of someone using all his energy to keep calm.

'I don't want anyone standing up in court saying he was coerced. I need a full assessment, Alice.'

He didn't even register my nod of agreement, but I already knew my report had to be one hundred per cent accurate. I would have to testify to every sentence if the case went to court and Morgan pleaded diminished responsibility. The tabloids would go into meltdown if he was found guilty.

It was clear that Morgan was at cracking point when he reached the interview room. His skin was paler than before, tan bleached to a dull indoor pallor. His solicitor was so gaunt he looked as if he'd been on a sympathetic hunger strike.

The moment Burns's finger hit the recorder, Morgan started talking. His voice was a dry whisper at first, as though silence had weakened it.

'She's been seeing someone, right under my nose,' he muttered. 'She laughed in my face when I found out.'

'Who's the bloke?' Burns looked sympathetic.

'Fuck knows — she didn't deny it though. She said I was cramping her style.' Morgan's mouth gagged in disgust.

'That's unbelievable. How did you take it?'

'I lost it with her, I suppose.' His shoulders jerked upwards in an involuntary spasm.

Burns's voice dropped a level, as if they were friends, trading secrets in a pub. 'It'll go in your favour that you're opening up. And it sounds like you had your reasons. Just take us through it, step by step.'

'I read about the pictures he leaves. I couldn't get them out of my head.' Morgan's voice was faltering. All the words he'd swallowed over the past few days seemed to be sticking in his throat.

'So you made it look like the Angel Killer did it?'

Morgan was too busy studying the backs of his hands to reply.

'It's okay to take your time,' Burns said quietly. 'Can you tell me where you left your bike, Liam?'

He cleared his throat. 'Clerkenwell.'

'Are you ready to explain what happened?'

He gave a miserable nod. 'She kept struggling. I only wanted to give her a scare.'

'Did you carry out the attack, Liam? I need a yes or a no, for the recorder.'

There was a long pause. 'It was to teach her a lesson, that's all.'

'A lesson?' Burns's tone hardened suddenly. 'It was a bit more than that, wasn't it? You left her in shreds. She almost lost an eye.'

I caught a glimpse of Morgan's relief. It passed from his face in an instant, like a cloud lifting. Destroying his wife's beauty was a price worth paying. It had given him so much pleasure, a ten-year stretch would feel worthwhile. When I glanced at him again, he was doing his best to look contrite.

'You went after her in the car, didn't you?' Burns had regained his calm.

Morgan described downloading the angel picture from a website. He'd loaded his bike into the boot of his car, parking in Clerkenwell, then cycling to the Square Mile. Afterwards he hid the bike in someone's back garden. He drove home to Mayfair in a state of shock. When the phone rang, he got back in the car and raced straight to the hospital.

'I couldn't believe what I'd done.'

'Right.' Burns's eyebrows shot up. 'It was a great big accident.'

'I didn't lay a finger on anyone else.'

'But you know who's behind the other attacks, don't you?'

Morgan spent the next half-hour denying responsibility. He claimed that his wife's behaviour had provoked him, and he had no idea who the Angel Killer was. After that, every new question met with silence. We were about to leave when he finally spoke again.

'When can I see my kids?'

Burns's glare indicated that his parental rights had been cancelled for the foreseeable future. He still looked pale with tension when I followed him out into the corridor, even though he'd got a result.

'One down, three to go,' he said, frowning. 'Brotherton says Scotland Yard'll replace me if we don't catch him soon.'

I wanted to say something comforting, but he marched away before I could open my mouth, as though his life depended on reaching his next destination on time.

The heat was still breathtaking when I got outside, and the bus dropped me by Butler's Wharf. I found a chair in the shade, and ordered a lime soda. A tour boat was drifting on the tide, and the Angel Killer was still out there, on the loose. I couldn't stop thinking about Liam Morgan, and all the other men who maim their wives. I'd carried out an assessment once on a man who'd thrown acid in his girlfriend's eyes. He was pleading temporary insanity, but I'd never met anyone more rational in my life. He'd worn exactly the same look of mock-regret that I'd seen on Morgan's face.

All I wanted when I got home was a long bath and a night in front of the TV. With any luck some ancient black-and-white movie would be playing, like *High Society* or *Roman Holiday*. But I'd only been in the bath five minutes when the doorbell rang. I heaved myself out of the water, cursing loudly. Lola was on the landing, wearing an expectant smile and clutching two bottles of pinot grigio.

'Surprise!' she yelled, barging past me into the kitchen.

Within half an hour she'd updated me on the Greek god's efforts to secure a recording deal, and Craig's failure to find love on match.com. And she'd pumped me for every detail about my date with Andrew at Le Coq d'Argent. I lay flat out on the living-room floor, letting the day's tension drain away while she chattered. When my mobile rang at nine o'clock, I didn't move a muscle.

'I'll get it.' Lola reappeared immediately, struggling to contain her excitement. 'It's Andrew,' she whispered.

'How was it?' I asked him.

'Extortionate. Guess how much a coffee on the Champs-Elysées costs these days?'

'Go on, shock me.'

'Ten euros. But at least Eleanor had a great birthday; I'd love you to meet her some time.' There was a thunderous noise in the background, like he was standing beside a motorway.

'Where are you?' I asked.

'Out for a drink. Listen, Alice, can I come round later?'

'Lola's here. Can we make it tomorrow, about seven?'

He groaned. 'That's a long wait.'

'You never know, I might push the boat out and get us a takeaway.'

'The luxury never ceases.' Another car roared by, then I heard a girl's voice, calling his name. 'I can't wait to see you.'

He rang off before I could say goodbye, and a pang of jealousy hit me. I wanted to be the one sitting opposite him in the pub, listening to his stories, not some mystery woman with a braying laugh. Lola gave me her widest Cheshire Cat grin before going back to her monologue. She was so busy explaining her plans for future happiness that I was free to dream about the following night. Her chatter washed over me and, for the first time in days, my ribs expanded properly when I breathed.

31

Lola had forgotten to go home. She was elegantly draped across the bed in Will's room. I switched on the coffee machine, went back into my room and flicked through my wardrobe. There was nothing remotely seductive for my date with Andrew. He'd have to put up with a sundress and my usual black cotton underwear, but with any luck he wouldn't complain after waiting so long. Lola picked up on my state of mind straight away. Her smile was glued in place as she ploughed through an enormous bowl of muesli. At least my nerves provided her with some early-morning entertainment.

The sky was the usual relentless blue when I set off, but the weather seemed to be turning. The air hung in front of me like a smokescreen, muggy and hard to breathe. Andrew kept appearing in my thoughts. It was easy to imagine waking up with his arm round my shoulders; the idea felt surprisingly comfortable. I was still fantasising when Hari stopped me by the hospital gates. He was beautifully turned out as usual, wearing a well-cut suit and his permanent smile.

'You look happy, Alice. Is it the sunshine?'

'That must be it.'

'Got time to visit our Mr Campbell? I want to see how he's doing.'

'Isn't it too early?'

Hari's calm gaze assessed me. 'I need to check how he responds to you. Don't worry, I'll be there too. Nothing can happen.'

I followed him across the quadrangle reluctantly. An elderly man was banging his head against the wall at three-second intervals when we arrived at Robinson Ward. There was a look of grim satisfaction on his face, as though the impact was knocking his thoughts into shape much more effectively than his medicine. Two ward orderlies were struggling to coax him into a wheelchair.

A blissed-out smile crossed Darren's face when he saw me. He was sitting up in bed with his hands gripped tightly together, as if he was clasping something precious. He didn't even register Hari's presence.

'I knew you'd come,' he whispered.

'How are you feeling, young man?' Hari asked.

'It's all making sense now.' Darren's gaze was still glued to my face. 'Can I leave here soon?'

'Not for a while. You need an assessment first. How much do you remember about the last few weeks?'

'Everything.' He stared straight back at me.

'You were following me, Darren. Do you remember that?'

'It's for you, not me.' His words were slurred by the risperidone, but his tone was resolute.

'That's what you think, is it?'

'One day you'll understand.' His dark eyes blinked in slow motion, then he tapped his temple with his index finger. 'I've got second sight; my mum had it too. Someone needs to take care of you.'

Hari's smile had faded by the time we left Darren's room.

'It's not looking good,' I said.

'I wouldn't say that.' He rubbed his beard thoughtfully. 'He's calmer than before.'

'It's acute phase schizophrenia, isn't it?'

'Too early to say. I'll do the verbal fluency and stress tests with him later.' Hari glanced at me. 'Relax, Alice. We've got him on a Section Two order – he's not going anywhere for twenty-eight days.'

We went straight into the case conference. Hari and the head psych discussed Darren's treatment, and I tried to remind myself of the statistics: fewer than three per cent of paranoid schizophrenics commit acts of violence. I'd treated dozens of patients with the condition over the years, and most of them held down jobs and relationships, just like the rest of us. But I couldn't help remembering a patient from the Maudsley when I was doing my training. He refused to take his medication and his delusions grew worse, until he believed that government spies were plotting to assassinate him. He stabbed a girl on the underground, convinced she was sending telepathic signals, ordering him to kill himself. I made myself tune back into the discussion. The head psych was planning to keep Darren hospitalised until his delusions were under control. I had a month, at least, before he was back on the streets.

There was no time to think about Andrew, or to check the texts that kept arriving. My phone was on silent, but it buzzed steadily in my pocket throughout the day. I saw three new referrals and scrambled to complete my paperwork between appointments, determined not to take anything home. The phone on my desk rang at six o'clock, just as I was switching off my computer. It was a surprise to hear Lorraine Brotherton's voice, sounding calm and businesslike.

'Do you know where Lombard Street is, Dr Quentin? I'd appreciate an hour of your time.'

I put the phone down in a state of irritation. It was bound to be something routine, and I was beginning to regret letting Burns press-gang me into getting involved. The investigation had stalled since they'd arrested Liam Morgan, and the visit would make me late for Andrew. I left a message on his phone as I trotted down the fire escape. He had back-to-back meetings that afternoon, but hopefully he'd check his voicemail before he set off.

Lombard Street was a ten-minute taxi ride across London Bridge. I peered up at the elegant Georgian building. It would have belonged to a wealthy merchant or trader when it was first built, but it had been divided into separate offices, a row of company logos printed beside the door. Their rates would be astronomical because the block was right at the heart of the City, a stone's throw from the Angel Bank. I couldn't guess why Brotherton had summoned me to a broker's office, but at least the view from the stairs made the climb worthwhile. From this vantage point I could see the entire Square Mile. The Bank of England was basking in late-afternoon sunshine, secure in the knowledge that it was impregnable.

When I reached the top floor, crime scene officers in white suits were crawling over the landing. I had to get through a cordon, and a SOCO bustled past clutching a plastic box. She glanced at my ID card then waved me into a wide hallway. It was painted charcoal grey with huge monochrome photos of London's skyline filling the walls. I guessed that it was someone's apartment rather than an office. The place felt like a bachelor pad, because there was no sign of softness anywhere – not so much as a cushion or a houseplant. I could hear people talking in the distance, but there was no one in sight.

'Hello?' The word bounced back at me from the dark walls.

Burns's voice was jabbering behind a closed door, and Pete Hancock scribbled my name on his register before letting me through the containment cordon. He was as monosyllabic as ever when he handed me a Tyvek suit and plastic shoes. I could tell he thought that shrinks should stay in their offices instead of tampering with evidence. His black monobrow lowered to half an inch above his eyes.

'Your hair's not covered,' he snapped.

I tucked the loose strands inside my hood, then pushed the door open. I was standing inside a state-of-the-art bathroom, big enough to accommodate a rugby team. A cluster of men was huddled in front of me. Glossy black tiles ran from floor to ceiling, shelves loaded with towels. But everything else about the picture was wrong. A SOCO was dusting the mirror, and the floor was awash with several inches of water. Burns must have been overheating inside his plastic suit, because his grin looked feverish, a sheen of sweat glistening on his forehead.

'You won't believe this,' he said. 'Are you ready to take a look?'

'Do I get a choice?' I picked my way across the wet tiles to join him.

The water in the bath was overflowing, tinted the colour of pink gin. I rubbed my eyes hard, but the picture stayed the same. I recognised the man who was staring up at me blankly, through a foot of liquid, but the information didn't make sense. Trails of blood were seeping from slash marks on his wrists, his hair floating like threads of seaweed.

32

I could see that it was Andrew, but my brain kept cancelling the idea. The fact hovered somewhere nearby, waiting to hit me if I closed my eyes.

'Are you all right?' Burns's voice was travelling from miles away.

I don't remember him leading me outside, but he must have done, because I was in a vast living room, and SOCOs were buzzing past, photographing every object in sight. Time had switched to slow motion. Brotherton's mobile was clamped to her ear, her grey hair hanging in rats' tails. When she turned to speak to Steve Taylor, her body twisted too slowly, as though she was wading through a swimming pool.

I rubbed my forehead, trying to push my thoughts back into place. Yesterday, Andrew had been alive and well, begging to come round. I felt sure I'd wake up soon, and the day would start again, in the normal way.

'It's the bloke who chatted you up at the bankers' do, isn't it?' Burns said.

I shook my head. 'I was seeing him.'

'Since when?'

'A few weeks.'

The colour slowly drained from Burns's face. 'I'd have kept you away, if I'd known. I'm afraid it looks like he was involved, Alice.'

'What do you mean?' The room was still swimming, furniture hovering a foot off the ground.

Taylor was monitoring the conversation. He looked drunk on a cocktail of ego and triumph, grinning from ear to ear.

'We found this lot in his office,' he bragged, pointing at a row of evidence bags on the coffee table.

One was stuffed with white feathers, and another held a stack of postcards. The angel on top of the pile was gazing at the ceiling, like butter wouldn't melt in his mouth. The tightness in my chest was squeezing the air from my lungs.

'They're not his,' I said. 'He'd never hurt anyone.'

Taylor ignored me. 'You won't believe the kit in here. Pity the camera by his front door was on the blink – we'd have mug shots of all his mates by now.'

He hurried away and I forced myself to stand up. Burns was watching me closely, as if I might fall at any minute. I wanted to go back to the bathroom to make sure they were taking care of him. Andrew must still be lying there, gazing through a lens of water, in a T-shirt and boxer shorts. More than anything I wanted to scream at them all to get out, so I could say goodbye, but I made myself walk from room to room. The flat seemed as unreal as a film set, so obsessively tidy that it already felt like a mausoleum. I remembered him telling me that he'd just moved in. He'd spent little time there because he was so busy. There were no newspapers or books lying around, hardly any personal items on display.

When I reached Andrew's bedroom, the sheets had been thrown back, as though he'd just leapt up to make coffee. I rested my hand on my collarbone, holding back a wave of nausea. If I'd let him come round last night, he might still be alive. Taylor's comments were starting to sink in. Maybe I'd been wrong about him all along. I would have been the perfect target – lonely and gullible enough to miss all the clues. But there'd been no sign at all. His odd flashes of temper had disappeared as quickly as they came. I rubbed my hand across my eyes and reminded myself of his gentleness, and the time he sacrificed to helping other people. It was wrong to start doubting him. I couldn't live with myself if I let him down.

I made myself carry on walking. The flat's previous owner must have been a James Bond fan, with a limited supply of taste. A monochrome version of Marilyn Monroe covered a whole wall in one of the spare bedrooms, and behind another door there was a fully equipped gym and sauna. It was like a hi-tech hotel that had lost its personality. The study was the only place where Andrew had left traces of himself. Biographies and history books lined the shelves: *Stalingrad* and *Shackleton's Last Voyage*. Maybe he'd been yearning for adventures, longing to travel just like me. The scene-of-crime team had already emptied his desk. Credit card statements and letters were arranged in piles, and his Filofax sat on top of his in-tray, wrapped in an evidence bag. I glanced around, but the team had moved on to another room. I thumbed quickly through the pages, my stomach lurching when I saw my birthday circled on his calendar, with my name scribbled by the date. I don't know what I was hoping for, but I fumbled to the back and found his parents' address, staring at it until it lodged in my memory.

Taylor ambushed me in the kitchen, gazing at me like a lost cause. 'How well did you know him?'

'We went out a few times, that's all.'

'Did he tell you he worked at the Angel Bank?'

'Of course, but it was years ago. Who waits that long to get even?'

The contempt on Taylor's face was turning to disgust. 'You don't get it, do you? He was working with Morgan. He couldn't have killed Wilcox, because you and Burns saw him at the Albion Club, but he knew Gresham and Fairfield. Maybe they got him fired.' His words spilled out in a gush of excitement. 'Piernan heard Morgan had been caught. He knew it wouldn't be long before we knocked on his door, so he topped himself instead of facing the music.'

I glared at him. 'There's no way Andrew killed himself or anyone else.'

'He left it all here for us to find. And guess what? There's a pint of Rohypnol in his bathroom cabinet.' His blasé, sing-song tone made me want to slap him.

'Someone planted it there.'

'Who? The neighbours say he was never home. No one came by, except some bloke, once or twice a week. Maybe he was protecting his cash. After all, Mummy and Daddy own half of Berkshire.'

I tried to argue, but I was running out of strength. He turned away before I could yell at him that he was wrong. Burns appeared as I slumped on a stool by the window.

'Come on,' he said quietly. 'I'll take you home.'

'Not yet. I need to see him first.' My legs felt unsteady as I marched towards the bathroom, but Taylor was guarding the door.

'You're not in a fit state, are you?' he sneered.

I could see Andrew through the doorway. They'd lifted him out of the bath and he was lying on the floor, facing me, in the recovery position. It looked like he might come round at any minute. I tried to reach him, but the floor lurched up to greet me, and when I came round I was in Burns's car, heading along the Embankment, still wearing my blue sterile suit. I tore at the zip, desperate to free myself, and my mind kept flitting over everything I'd seen. The blurred film of Gresham falling under the train, and Jamie Wilcox's body dumped beside the rubbish bins. But it was different now, because I was involved. I'd laughed at Andrew's jokes. I remembered running with him in Regent's Park, and the first time he kissed me, in the middle of a crowded restaurant.

'He's loving it,' I said, under my breath.

'What?' Burns glanced across at me.

I stared at the buildings going by on Upper Thames Street. 'The killer's conned you lot into thinking you've found your man, so he's free to carry on.'

Burns didn't reply. Maybe he believed Taylor's ridiculous theory that Morgan and Andrew were a double act. When we got back to Providence Square he turned to face me. It was hard to read what he was thinking, but it looked suspiciously like pity. He rested his large hand on my shoulder, but it didn't feel comforting. In fact it made me want to punch him, so I jumped out of the car before I lost control. The shock hit me when I got inside. My whole body was shaking, and I didn't have a clue what to do with myself. Crying wasn't an option. When I looked out of the window, the sky was a bleached, unnatural white, and my eyes were so dry that my corneas itched when I blinked. I tried to call Lola, but there was no answer. A new text had arrived on my phone. When I opened it, the message was from my mother. Her villa was even more luxurious than the pictures in the brochure – she was having the time of her life.

33

It was impossible to sleep. Every time my eyes closed I was swimming in shallow water, trying not to look down because the seabed was thick with corpses, hair waving like the tendrils of anemones. When the alarm went off I considered calling in sick, because a numb feeling of shock was still lodged under my breastbone. But there was no way I could face staying by myself at home.

I bumped into a delivery man on the landing. The bouquet he was carrying was so large that he staggered slightly as he heaved it onto the kitchen table. Even at the best of times, I've never been a fan of florists' bouquets. There's something disturbing about watching dozens of perfect blooms slowly dying in front of your eyes. There was no card in the box, but my heart raced as I looked at the docket. Andrew's name was printed at the bottom in thick black type. He must have placed the order as soon as he got back from Paris. My first impulse was to lug the flowers out onto the landing, so I wouldn't have to look at them, but I sealed the door behind me and set off for work. It was difficult to think straight as I walked down Tanner Street. Taylor might be convinced that Andrew had masterminded the attacks, then committed suicide, but his diary was full of events and meetings. I could still hear his voice, saying that he couldn't wait to see me. Misshapen windows stared down from the apartment blocks, and everything my gaze fell on looked wrong. The street looked like a picture game of spot the mistakes.

I realised as soon as I got to work that I was a liability, because I'd stopped listening. Normally it's easy to tune out distractions and give my whole attention to each patient as they tell me their stories, noticing the symptoms that hide in the pauses between words. But today I was missing whole sentences. I carried on nodding and asking questions, but nothing registered.

I sat in Hari's office and told him what had happened. He made small, sympathetic grimaces as I spoke, then invited me to stay with him and Tejo. I thanked him, but explained that I needed some time alone.

'I'll tell HR you're on compassionate leave,' he said. 'Call me tonight, and let me know you're okay.'

Hari stood in my office and watched me pack my briefcase. I got a strong feeling that he wanted to escort me from the building, and I didn't blame him. He had a duty of care, and I was in no fit state to make a diagnosis.

Journalists had already gathered when I reached Pancras Way. They must have got wind of Andrew's death, and now they were desperate for a scoop. Maybe Taylor had been leaking vile rumours, saying that the Angel Killer had been found dead in his bath. They were jostling each other, prepared to trample over their colleagues to get the shot. I put on my dark glasses and turned up my collar. In an ideal world I'd have hurled a smoke bomb and watched them scatter. Dean Simons came scuttling over the instant he saw me.

'How's it going, Alice?' His forehead was dripping with sweat. 'Made any progress?'

'Leave me alone,' I snarled.

He leered at me. 'Is the stress getting to you again? You should jack the job in, shouldn't you? Let someone more qualified have a go.'

I elbowed past him and ran up the steps. But when I reached

the incident room I knew I'd stepped out of the frying pan into the fire. Taylor's toxic grin was even more unpleasant than the journalist's.

'I've brought Stephen Rayner in. We're about to interview him,' he said. 'He got caught on CCTV outside Piernan's building the night he died. Looks like he was Piernan's buddy, not Morgan. He's not playing ball, though – I think he prefers the feminine touch.'

Taylor swaggered along the corridor beside me, the contempt in his voice increasing with each stride. He glanced around to check there were no witnesses.

'You're a laughing stock. Do you realise that?' he hissed. 'You give us all that pathetic psychobabble, then it turns out you're shagging the main man.'

By now I was aching to wrap a crowbar round his head, but Burns emerged before I could follow through. His level gaze seemed to be measuring my state of mind.

I stared back at him. 'You realise there's no way Andrew killed himself, don't you? People don't forward-plan when they're about to commit suicide. His diary was full for the rest of the year.'

Burns gave a slow shake of his head. 'Stay in the observation room, Alice. Fill out a report form, if you feel up to it. We'll talk after the interview.' He closed the door before I could argue.

I watched Taylor and Burns preparing themselves through the observation window. Two metres of clear space between their chairs showed that no truce was in sight. The next person to enter the room was Rayner's lawyer. She was a pretty Asian woman, and she was wearing a shocked expression. The state of Rayner's face explained why. His jaw was so swollen he could hardly speak, a string of bruises littered across his neck. I felt like leaving immediately – Taylor's arrest methods must include attacking people in their own homes. But I knew my only hope of helping Andrew was to remain professional and keep my wits about me. I fumbled in my bag for a pen.

'We've lodged a complaint,' the lawyer snapped.

Taylor folded his arms. 'You resisted arrest, Stephen. It took two officers to pin you down.'

'That's not my understanding.' The lawyer frowned her disapproval.

When he began to speak, Rayner's sentences were so full of gaps, he seemed to be struggling to breathe. 'You lot haven't given me any peace since Leo died. It was getting to me – that's why I went to Andrew's. I wanted to talk to a friend. I told you, he was out when I got there. He didn't pick up his phone.'

'Trying to decide who to shove under the next train, were you?' Taylor scowled. 'We know you don't mind a bit of violence.'

Rayner stared back at him, his arms resting at his sides, body language unusually controlled. 'I just wanted to do something normal, that's all.'

'Did Piernan let you in, Stephen?' Burns's deep voice was a relief after Taylor's aggressive whine.

'I rang the bell but no one answered.'

'Rubbish,' Taylor sneered. 'The CCTV on the street caught you at 10.05 p.m., then again at 10.31 p.m. You had plenty of time to chuck him in the bath, then dump the feathers and postcards on his desk. Your fingerprints are everywhere – they're even on his kettle. Make yourself a cuppa afterwards, did you?'

'Slow down, Steve.' Burns leant over and looked him in the eye. His expression reminded me of someone walking an attack dog in the park, using all his discipline skills to keep it under control.

Rayner's hands lay motionless in his lap as he began to speak. 'I waited for him on the landing. I've known Andrew since he worked at the bank; we met up for a few beers most weeks.'

My pen hovered above the page. It made perfect sense; Andrew would have taken pity on Rayner's isolation. Maybe he was grateful for someone to wind down with, on his few evenings at home.

'Does it give you a thrill, Stephen?' Taylor leant across the table. 'You get a kick from killing these rich, powerful blokes. Is that where the photos come in? D'you take a few snaps after, to excite yourself?'

Burns gave him a warning look, then hissed a caution that was too quiet to hear.

When Rayner spoke again, his voice was trembling, odd pauses separating his words.

'I've told you, I've got nothing to hide. I went to see my friend, that's all. I don't know why he was killed. It's so terrible. First Leo, then Andrew.'

It was hard to tell whether Rayner was crying, because his shoulders were heaving, but he wasn't making a sound. By the time Burns found me, I felt calm for the first time since Andrew's death.

'It's not him, Don. But it's obvious he's lying about something. All the signs are there.'

Burns sat opposite me, huge shoulders braced for an outlandish theory.

'I could see it in his body language,' I said.

'What do you mean?'

'When someone lies, they stop making gestures. They're so busy concentrating on building the lie, their hands stop moving. Often they don't gesticulate at all, even when they're accused. Didn't you see how frozen he was? And the stress patterns in his speech were out of sync – long pauses, then periods of babbling. His eye contact was too strong, trying to convince you he's telling the truth.'

'You're not making sense.' Burns rested his hands on the back of his neck, as though his head was too heavy to support.

'It can't be him. Andrew went out for a drink with someone – he wasn't there when Rayner called round. But he knows something. He's trying to hide it, and he's cracking under the strain.'

'Rayner's prints are everywhere. He's the only face we can identify on the CCTV.'

'Look at it again. I bet he visited every week, just like he said.'

'It's got to be him. We've interviewed all the bank's employees, going back five years, and drawn a blank.'

'Look closer to home then. What about relatives and acquaintances?'

'I'm telling you, there's nothing there.'

'I'm sorry, Don. I think you're barking up the wrong tree.'

Burns looked exasperated. 'Look, Alice, I'll take on board what you've said, but I think you should go home now and get some rest.'

I gritted my teeth, because he'd stopped listening, and I expected better from him. Being treated like a child goes with the territory of being a puny, five-foot blonde, but it always rankles, especially when I'm right. I stuffed the form back into my bag and marched out of the room, before I said something I'd regret.

34

On Saturday I disposed of Andrew's flowers. I'd been avoiding going into the kitchen, but the smell of gardenias was strong enough to make me gag. I felt a pang of guilt as I abandoned them in the rubbish bin, but it was part of my coping mechanism. The only way to keep going was to avoid thinking too hard. Hopefully the numbness would last until the killer was found. But it was a struggle to keep myself occupied. I'd been through the latest HOLMES printout twice, combing for clues and coming up with nothing. It felt like trying to build a house from thousands of mismatched bricks, but I couldn't stop thinking about it. Watching TV was out of the question, because as soon as I sat still, my mind defaulted to Lombard Street.

There was only one way to keep calm. Normally I hate getting my hair cut, but for once the tedium was comforting. The stylist at the salon on Elizabeth Street was too polite to comment when she inspected my split ends. Under the harsh lights I looked gaunt and dry-skinned. Other women's voices buzzed in the background, discussing their love lives and the finalists of *Big Brother*. I emerged with shiny, expensive-looking hair, and a vacuum where my thoughts should have been.

A headline caught my eye when I passed the newsagent. ANGEL BANK STOPS TRADING. I rushed inside to buy a copy of the *Independent*, and wondered how the Angel Killer was felt destroying the bank's empire. The story didn't give much away, but it explained that the FSA had withdrawn their licence while 'serious irregularities' were investigated. The bank's golden reputation would be badly tarnished, if it ever reopened. For some reason Henrik Freiberg came to mind. He'd coped with his boss's egotism for years – at least now he'd be liberated. I considered stopping at a coffee shop on the way home, but I couldn't face a crowd of people enjoying themselves.

I caught sight of myself in the hall mirror that afternoon. My hair skimmed my shoulders, and for once I looked present-able. Andrew was standing behind me, wearing a smile of approval, but he'd vanished by the time I turned round. I don't know how long I stood there, with my hand pressed over my mouth.

By the evening I'd run out of displacement activities. I'd scrubbed the bathroom floor, dusted the bookshelves, and annihilated every germ in the flat. When the phone rang I was sitting on the floor in my bedroom, unable to move. The woman at the end of the line sounded delirious. My brain was working so slowly that it took a while to realise it was Lola, babbling with excitement.

'I got the part. The theatre's letting me do three episodes of *EastEnders*. They've given me my own storyline!'

I managed to congratulate her, but my tone must have lacked conviction.

'What's wrong, sweetheart?'

'Can I come round, Lo?'

'Of course you can. I'll be waiting for you.'

I can never fool Lola about my state of mind; she notices if my voice is even a fraction off-key. Normally she flings her arms round me, but when she opened the door to her bedsit on Borough Road, she just stood there with her hands motion-less at her sides. I followed her into the tiny flat and collapsed on the sofa. When I told her what had happened, her eyes widened in disbelief. She held onto my hand while I told her the details, studying my face for danger signs.

'I can't believe it,' she whispered. 'Who's sick enough to do something like that?'

She made me a cup of tea and I glanced around her studio. I could see why she was flat-hunting. It was twelve feet square, with an all-night off-licence doing a roaring trade downstairs. She fell asleep every night to a lullaby of winos arguing about overpriced beer. But at least the rent was cheap – an actor friend had lent it to her while he worked in New York. He'd plastered the mildewed walls with posters for West End shows. The cast of *Matilda* beamed down from the chimneybreast, wearing showbiz smiles, as if life was one long miracle. Lola passed her hand in front of my face, as though she was checking my vision.

'You're not really here, are you?'

'How do you mean?'

'You're in a bubble. I bet you haven't even cried.'

I shook my head. Maybe it was my inability to let go that set Lola off, but once she started, there was no stopping her. She can weep for Britain at the best of times. My only option was to put my arm round her shoulders and wait for her to stop. After a while she began to rally, but her eyes were two shades darker than before, and her light-bulb smile had fizzled out.

'It's you who should be blubbing, not me,' she gulped.

'I have to keep going. I've got to find out who it is.'

'I'll help you, Al. Just tell me what to do.'

She did everything in her power to persuade me to stay. But I couldn't face any more talk about Andrew, or dealing with her distress as well as mine.

It was dark by the time I set off, but I ignored the cabs revving on Borough Road. A taxi ride would have reminded me too much of my last journey with Andrew. People were knocking back last orders from the pubs below Tower Bridge. I paused by the railings to watch a disco boat full of pensioners heading for Greenwich, the Bee Gees screeching their hearts out. The hectic falsetto of 'Night Fever' was trailing a few beats by the time it reached the shore.

My determination was finally making a comeback as I drew level with the Design Museum. Maybe the fresh air helped, but I realised that grieving had to wait until I'd tracked down Andrew's killer. In the morning I would go through the evidence files again, to make sure I hadn't missed anything. A crowd of people was hanging around by China Wharf, but their noise dropped away as I followed the boardwalk, then the path emptied. The only thing on my mind was going to bed and hiding under the covers. Maybe I was too numb to recognise the signs when I took a short-cut through the car park. I didn't hear a thing, not so much as a footstep, but suddenly my vision failed. My hands were scratching at thin air, and there was nothing in front of me except a mile of blackness.

35

Someone had pulled a hood over my face. Every time I tried to breathe, plastic filled my mouth, making me gag. Shock paralysed me for a few seconds, but I knew I had to fight, or I'd end up with a face like Jamie Wilcox's – another corpse for Burns to find. My heels were dragging along the pavement as he pulled me backwards. I lashed out, elbows thudding against his ribcage. It must have caught him by surprise, because he released one of his hands, and the plastic flapped loose around my throat. I still couldn't see anything, but at least I could breathe. I flicked my leg back with all my strength. The heel of my sandal must have hit his shinbone, because he gave a high-pitched yelp of pain. Then my mouth was stifled again, before I had time to scream.

A door creaked a few metres away, and I was thrown forwards onto the ground, footsteps drumming past me towards the river. My eyes took a while to adjust to the orange streetlight when I ripped the bag from my face. An old man was peering down at me through thick bifocal lenses, his irises milky with untreated cataracts. Air poured from my lungs in ragged gasps, and for a few seconds I felt completely calm. Nothing cancels self-pity quicker than fighting for your life.

'You okay, love? I bet you tripped on that bloody step, didn't you? I keep telling them to put a light out here.'

'Did you see someone running away?'

'I only came out for a fag, dear.' The old man looked confused. 'I didn't see a thing.'

I wanted to tell him that his nicotine craving had probably saved my life, but he was already tottering away to enjoy his cigarette. I raised myself to a sitting position. Luckily I'd landed on the grass rather than the pavement. There would be no evidence of my encounter – not so much as a bruise. The bag he'd put over my head was made of thick black plastic, and it looked perfectly innocent, but it could have smothered me in minutes. It was identical to the one the Angel Killer had used to cover Jamie Wilcox's face in Gutter Lane. But why had he attacked me? He only targeted people who'd worked at the Angel Bank. Nothing was making sense, and the adrenaline hit me before I could stand up. My hands trembled as I dialled Burns's number. There was a buzz of music and conversation when he answered, and I guessed he was in the middle of a crowded pub.

'Stay put, Alice. I'm on my way.' He sounded aggrieved, as though he was the one who'd been attacked.

I inspected myself in my bedroom mirror, checking for damage. There was a tear in my skirt and grass stains across my top, but it was my face that gave the game away – my eyes stared back at me, hollow with shock. Burns looked unusually smart when he arrived. His dark hair had been combed for once, and he'd even ironed his shirt. Even though he'd lost so much weight, he still looked like a rugby full back, solid and dependable, with the kind of shoulders you could cry on for hours.

'You look like hell on earth,' he exclaimed.

I collapsed on a kitchen stool. 'Cheers, Don.'

Burns was keeping busy, rooting through my cupboards. Eventually he found a bottle of brandy and poured a huge measure into a tumbler.

'Knock that back. It's medicinal.' He followed me into the lounge, watching me intently while I described what had happened. When I handed him the ripped piece of plastic, he held it at arm's length, as if he hoped it would disappear.

'I'll give it to the lab tomorrow. Taylor won't be thrilled – this blows his theory that Stephen Rayner's our man. He's still in a holding cell.'

The shock seemed to be affecting Burns too. His hands were clenched so tightly it looked like he was trying to crack Brazil nuts with his bare knuckles. Until a few minutes ago he'd been celebrating, keeping his fingers crossed that he'd arrested the right man and the second Angel Killer was safe under lock and key.

'You should be in protective custody, Alice.'

'I'll pass on that one, thanks.' I'd spent enough nights in airless hotels during the Crossbones case to last me a lifetime.

'Why didn't he just sling you over his shoulder?' Burns murmured.

'He was strong enough. If the old man hadn't come along, I wouldn't have stood a prayer.' When I glanced at him again I noticed that his five-o'clock shadow had disappeared. 'Where were you tonight, anyway?'

'Out with a colleague. Someone from work invited me for a meal.'

A look of embarrassment crossed Burns's face and I felt a flicker of guilt. He'd probably been out on his first date since his divorce. It took him a moment to snap back into professional mode.

'Right, you can't stay here by yourself. I'll sleep on the settee.'

'Don't be ridiculous. I've got good locks on my door. I don't need a bodyguard.'

'I'm staying, Alice.' His colossal shoulders were squared for a fight, and I realised there was no point in arguing. It would take a bulldozer to shift him, so I scurried away to make up the spare bed.

I didn't get much sleep that night, and neither did Burns. I could hear the bed creaking in Will's room as he tossed and turned, but I still couldn't work out why I'd been targeted. So far he'd only chosen men who worked at the Angel Bank. Maybe my relationship with Andrew had angered him, or he'd begun to focus on the investigation team.

It was dawn before I managed to drift off, and when I opened my eyes, Burns was standing in the doorway, clutching a mug of tea. He dumped it on my bedside table and made a swift exit. It felt as though I'd woken up in the wrong body. The muscles across my shoulders were tight enough to burst. I must have strained them, fighting to get away. Taking a shower helped, the jets of water scouring me awake. I stepped into some shorts and a T-shirt.

'You're never going for a run.' Burns gaped at me. 'Someone attacked you, for God's sake.'

I wheeled round to face him. 'Hiding in here like a frightened rabbit won't help, will it?'

'Christ. It's like negotiating with Darth Vader.' He held up his hands like I was throwing things at him.

He ignored me and carried on brewing the coffee. He made toast and scrambled eggs, and my image of him started to crumble. A few years ago he'd existed on junk food, munching king-sized McBreakfasts in his car.

'What are you doing today?' he asked. 'I'm taking my boys to Hyde Park. Come with us, if you like.'

'Thanks, but I think I'll just take it easy.' For some reason I couldn't tell him about the visit I was planning.

'Fair enough.' He glanced down at his empty plate. 'Don't stay on your own tonight, though. I'll get surveillance here tomorrow morning.'

Burns was gone before I could thank him. I checked my mobile before setting off for my run. A message from Hari had arrived the previous night, just after 10 p.m. Normally his voice was soporific, but this time he sounded strained.

'Call me when you get this, Alice. I'm afraid there's some bad news.' He took a long breath. 'Darren's gone missing from the ward.'

36

The sky was a blank sheet of light as I crossed the bridge. By Shadwell Pier the Sunday strollers had disappeared, and the towers of Canary Wharf were filling the horizon. Heat haze made the buildings shiver, no longer attached securely to the ground, and the endorphins flooding my system were as effective as anaesthetic. Maybe the Angel Killer had nothing to do with my attack. Darren had made his way to my building, fresh from Robinson Ward, outraged by my lack of interest. But why would he use a plastic hood, just like the Angel Killer? I felt sure he was more likely to rant about his fantasies than hurt me again. I'd seen his horrified expression after he punched me, as though he'd witnessed a stranger knocking a woman to the ground. I slowed to a jog by Wapping station, choking on mouthfuls of overheated air.

After my shower I tapped the postcode I'd memorised from Piernan's Filofax into my sat nav, and let the GPS take control. When I arrived in Richmond, the mansion was so huge that I checked the postcode again, but it was definitely the right address. I parked my car and looked down at the cattle grazing on Petersham Meadows, the river winding east towards Westminster. I remembered Andrew saying that his parents had sold the ancestral home. If this was their idea of downsizing, their estate must have been the size of a small town. The house had too many windows to count, and an imposing flight of steps leading to the door. I was beginning to get cold feet when an old man strode towards me. The skin on the back of my neck contracted, because the likeness was so unsettling – Andrew had come to life again, but the clock had spun forwards by thirty years, the red tones in his hair replaced by grey.

'Are you looking for someone?' he asked.

'I was a friend of your son's.'

The man blinked rapidly as he held out his hand. 'Come inside, it would do my wife good to see someone.'

I glanced at the portraits in the hallway. The faces sprang from the same gene pool, framed by white eighteenth-century collars and, judging by their expressions, they objected to strangers invading their territory. Piernan's father paused by a set of wooden doors and whispered to me: 'Miriam can see you, but I'm afraid she's not herself.'

The woman sitting in an armchair by the window seemed too young to be Piernan's mother. Her head was bowed over a photo album, but when she raised her face to me, it was child-like, almost free of lines. The thing I noticed first was her expression. I'd seen that combination of rage and disbelief before. The stories the police had told her must have been terrifying. She closed the album and looked at me expectantly, and I told her how sorry I was about Andrew's death.

'People have been staying away,' she murmured. Her eyes were like her son's, pale brown and inquisitive.

'I wanted to ask you a question. I thought you might know who Andrew was with on the night he died.'

'It's too late for questions,' she snapped. The anger on her face was quickly replaced by distress. 'I'm sorry. It's just that talking about it seems so pointless. Neither of us can face telling his sister.' Her mouth twitched uncontrollably. 'Andrew worked so hard, he didn't notice everything he was missing.'

'He didn't like putting himself first, did he?'

Her eyes suddenly blinked back into focus. 'Were you his girlfriend?'

'We'd just started seeing each other.'

'The psychologist. Of course, he told us about you.' Miriam's face brightened. 'Would you like to see some photos?'

I leafed through the pages of her album. They showed Andrew at football matches, acting in a school play, sitting in a tree house with his sister. He looked the same in every shot, lanky and full of mischief, thin fingers hiding his uneven smile. When I glanced at Miriam her head had fallen again, tears dropping into her hands. Her husband appeared in the doorway, but he didn't seem to notice his wife's distress. I thanked him for letting me intrude and he paused to speak to me on the way out.

'I don't know what to tell her. None of it makes sense.'

It was difficult to think of a reply, so I rested my hand on his arm for a moment.

'The thing I need to understand is Andrew's link to the Angel Bank.'

He seemed agitated when he spoke again. 'They were his biggest benefactor. A few months ago, Andrew came to see me. He told me that he hated doing business with them. He wanted to cut his losses and walk away.'

'How did you respond?'

'I told him not to be a fool. The charity needed as much help as it could get.' His voice quavered. 'I wish I'd told him to follow his heart. Maybe he'd still be alive.'

'I'm sure it's not your fault.'

The old man's eyes were brimming. 'You'll come and see us again, won't you?'

'Of course I will.'

He was still standing at the top of the steps as I drove off. All I could hope was that Burns and Taylor didn't release any

259

information. The couple would break into a thousand pieces if they knew their son was a suspect for the angel killings.

I parked on a side road when I reached the centre of Richmond. The village looked like a parallel world, where nothing ever went wrong. Cricketers were playing on the green in immaculate whites, and throngs of locals were sunning themselves outside the pubs. But the idyllic setting couldn't remove my worries. I was wondering why Andrew had never found a partner – dozens of eligible girls must have pursued him. It would have taken a strong will to keep turning them down. A woman drifted past, a brood of perfect, blonde-haired children trailing behind her. The family looked like an illustration from *Country Life*. If the locals knew I was sitting there, contemplating murder and destruction, they'd have chased me out of the neighbourhood.

37

Yvette had gone up in the world since she worked at Guy's. Her new flat was on the fifth floor of a swish apartment block by Butler's Wharf, and from her doorstep I could see yachts packed tight as sardines in St Katharine Docks, and the warehouses of Wapping and Shadwell. When she threw open her door she looked fabulous, as usual. She was wearing a bright red dress, and she seemed to be modelling herself on the old school divas, like Shirley Bassey and Diana Ross. She hugged me so tightly that my bruised ribs twinged, then she led me into her living room and we collapsed on armchairs overlooking the river. I was hoping she wouldn't ask about Andrew, but it's not Yvette's style to beat about the bush.

'Tell me about him,' she said.

'I don't think I can. Not yet, anyway.'

'You poor soul.' The look on her face was a combination of sympathy and fear. 'Do you still think it's to do with the Angel Bank?'

I nodded. 'Someone's obsessed by the place. Your friend Vanessa said the Angel was hell on earth when she worked there. It's even worse now.'

'Vanessa told me how they select their juniors.' Yvette pulled a face. 'One year the interns were a hundred per cent female. Like Hollywood in the good old days – if you did okay on the casting couch, the job was yours.'

'It sounds like the Dark Ages.' I remembered Vanessa Harris

hinting that women had been exploited. Clearly the Angel Bank was a lousy place to work, for female employees as well as gay men. The only person having fun was the straight white male who called the shots.

Yvette did her best to distract me. She made me dinner, and told jokes about her attitude to bankers. According to her, every yard of the Square Mile was morally bankrupt.

'You're not their biggest fan, are you?'

'Put it this way, not many of them go to church. Our paradigms are unlikely to collide.'

I did my best to smile. 'Lucky you've got strong convictions, or some hedge fund manager would have seduced you by now.'

By ten o'clock I was exhausted and Yvette led me to her spare room. She seemed embarrassed when she opened the door – evidence of her love-hate relationship with money was scattered everywhere. Dresses in garish colours were draped across chairs, the carpet knee-deep in Jimmy Choo and Manolo Blahnik shoes. It took a long time to clear enough space to crawl under the sheets. But in the morning I woke up convinced that Andrew was still alive, until I saw the shoe boxes stacked beside the bed, and the facts flooded back into my mind. I got up immediately and wrote a note to Yvette.

I called in at Guy's to see if there was any news about Darren. The junior doctor on Robinson Ward looked embarrassed as she led me to his empty room.

'We checked on him every fifteen minutes, but he broke the window lock,' she said.

When I peered outside it was clear how easy his escape route had been. All he'd had to do was drop ten feet onto the grass below, then run through the gates onto Newcomen Street.

'Let's hope they pick him up soon.' The doctor glanced at me. 'He was saying some pretty disturbed stuff about being on a special mission. He kept ranting about guns and knives.'

The discussion failed to reassure me. I had to remind myself that Darren was just a distressed young man with mental health problems. He was unlikely to return with an AK-47 strapped to his back.

The temperature was still tropical when Steve Taylor called me on my mobile.

'You're needed at the station, pronto.' He rang off before I could ask why.

In the taxi I kept hoping that the case was closed; the Angel Killer was banged up in a holding cell somewhere. But Taylor looked even shiftier than normal when he met me in reception. He led me to Brotherton's office with an unpleasant smile stretched across his face, like a mask that could be peeled off at any minute.

'The boss is in a meeting, and Burns is out running errands.' He threw himself into Brotherton's chair like it was his rightful throne.

'Why did you call me?'

Taylor observed me through half-closed eyes. 'To give you the chance to explain yourself.'

'Sorry?'

'If people knew what you've been up to, you'd be struck off. You were picking blokes up at a dinner we paid you to attend.'

'You've got your facts wrong. A mutual friend gave Andrew my phone number.'

'Piernan spent a fortune on you, didn't he? I bet you got everything you wanted.'

'What do you mean?'

263

He waved a piece of paper at me. 'This is his bank statement. He gave a hundred grand to Guy's for starters, then he spent twelve grand at the Bruton Gallery. And those flowers he sent you cost two hundred quid.'

I didn't argue, too busy trying to make sense of it. Andrew must have paid for my therapy groups to continue, insisting that his donation stay anonymous. And he'd lied about the butterfly print being a free gift, to save embarrassment. The experience was beginning to feel unreal. Taylor must have spent days plotting how to get rid of me, to leave Burns without an ally.

'You've been running rings round poor old Don, haven't you?' Taylor's tone was loaded with fake pity. 'He's put a hole in our budget, while you went after a rich boyfriend. You'd better tell me exactly what happened.'

In the end I gave him the dates when I'd met Andrew, just to get him off my back, and he made an elaborate show of recording them on an evidence form: Lola's workshop, running in Regent's Park, the private view, and dinners we'd shared. I didn't tell him about Andrew's late-night visit to my flat, because I had no desire to make his day. He studied the list ponderously.

'All these dates, but you never suspected a thing. Aren't you meant to be the big expert on human behaviour?'

'I've already told you, Andrew wasn't involved.'

'So it's a coincidence that the attacks have stopped, even though there's a shed-load of evidence at his place? Burns told us about your little adventure, by the way. You've only got yourself to blame. Muggers are bound to have a go if you wander around by yourself at night.'

I ignored him. 'It'll happen again. The bank's fallen apart, but that won't satisfy him. He hates the people, not the business itself.'

Taylor lay back in his chair, hands relaxed on the armrests. 'One more thing, for the record.' His gaze travelled from my legs to my chest. 'Was your relationship with Piernan sexual?'

I stood up so fast that my chair bounced off the wall. 'There are therapy groups for men like you.'

'Brotherton won't be thrilled when she hears all this.' The look on his face was triumphant. 'You should jump before you're pushed.'

I gave the door a cathartic slam as I left. The discussion had made me so angry, I felt like smashing something. It was easy to see why kids threw bricks at shop windows – for the shattering noise, and the river of glass flooding across the pavement. I decided to walk home to try to calm down. The temperature was still warm enough to raise a sweat as I reached Victoria Embankment. A sign was inviting tourists to visit HMS *President*, but she didn't look welcoming. Her hull was the lacklustre grey of a whale's skin, exposed too long to the air. When I reached Broken Wharf it was clear that the area had repaired itself years ago. The river path was lined with wine bars, and the men sunning themselves were wearing such smart suits that business must have been booming. I was about to call Burns while I queued for a drink, but my phone rang before I could find his name in my contacts list. My brother's name appeared in the window.

'You again, sunshine. What are you up to?'

When he finally replied, his words were strung out like beads on a necklace. 'It's amazing down here. You don't need to worry about me.'

'That's good to hear.' A tight knot of distress was forming in my stomach. Will sounded as lost as I felt. I seemed to have lost my ability to protect people, even myself.

'Take a look at the clouds, Al. You should be careful, there's something weird happening in the sky.'

I wanted to ask more questions, but his voice was breaking up, and then the line went dead. I collected my iced tea, and for some reason I felt obliged to follow his instruction. I scanned the horizon carefully, pivoting on the spot, but there wasn't a cloud in sight. All I could see was a plane flying overhead, its white vapour trail slicing the sky neatly in two.

38

The air had stopped circulating. It hung motionless above the river, and even the barges looked lethargic, drifting slowly with the tide. The police were in the same position, changing direction with every new current, never making any headway. I sat down on a bench and tried to imagine what would happen if the Angel Killer wasn't found – more people would die, Taylor would crow about his boss's failures, and Burns would lose his job. I scanned the pages of my profile report. It was covered in scribbled notes and splashes of highlighter, but it still wasn't helping. The killer had planned his attacks so coolly, working obsessively to cover his tracks, with no overt sexual motive. His obsession was with all the staff, past and present, who'd worked at the Angel Bank. It seemed like anyone who signed their employment contract was on his hit list.

My mind raced as I stared at my notes. I felt certain of just two things: Stephen Rayner had been concealing something during his interview, and Poppy Beckwith was implicated in some way. Gresham and Fairfield's pillow talk must hold clues about why they were killed.

When I looked at my watch it was almost seven. Any rational person would have gone home, but the echoes in my flat were still too loud. I made a snap decision and caught a bus heading west. When I finally reached Raphael Street, I knew there was no point in ringing the doorbell – Poppy's human

Rottweiler would savage me if I bothered her again, so I sat on a low wall opposite her building, hoping the branches of a lime tree would hide me if she looked out of her window.

The parade of men going in and out of Poppy's flat was enough to make a diehard romantic cynical. A careworn businessman marched up the steps at eight o'clock. He looked like he'd worked all day at the Treasury, balancing important sums. When he emerged half an hour later, his demeanour was brighter. He'd abandoned his tie, and a dumb grin covered his face. Poppy's next client was a musician I vaguely recognised. He glanced around furtively before going inside, and when he reappeared he gazed up at Poppy's window longingly. Then he lit a cigarette and sauntered away.

By half past nine I was beginning to regret my fool's errand. I was about to leave when a dark blue BMW pulled up. It parked in a narrow space outside Poppy's building, and I pretended to check my phone messages. When I looked up again, my jaw dropped. Henrik Freiberg was getting out of the car, still dressed in the ill-fitting suit he'd worn at the Angel Bank, even though the auditors had closed the place. He disappeared into the apartment block before I could react. A red curtain was fluttering from one of the windows of Poppy's apartment, like a flag of victory.

I dialled Burns's number but it was constantly engaged. Just as I was about to give up, Freiberg reappeared. For once he had a spring in his stride, as though someone had given him an injection of courage. I crossed the road and stood beside his car. A series of emotions crossed his face: anger and embarrassment, swiftly followed by shame. He tried to dive into his car, but as soon as I heard the click of his central locking, I jumped into the passenger seat. Shock had rendered him speechless, and he shrank behind the steering wheel as though he expected me to attack him.

'Let's go somewhere quiet, please, Mr Freiberg,' I said.

He followed my instructions to the letter, and I realised how he'd hung on to his job as Kingsmith's deputy. He was a typical beta male, happy to submit to anyone with a stronger personality. Poppy probably walked all over him in six-inch heels. The car smelled of expensive soap. He must have chosen the deluxe service, then taken a shower, so he'd be squeaky-clean when he went home. Freiberg drew up in a cul-de-sac off Albany Street, staring through the front window as though the car was still moving.

'Why are you following me?' he mumbled.

'How long have you been visiting Poppy?'

His gaze bounced from my face, like a tennis ball glancing from a hard surface. 'I was visiting a business associate, not that it's any of your business.' He was beginning to stammer, beads of sweat gathering on his top lip.

'Look, I'm not doing this to embarrass you. You could be in danger. Some of the victims were Poppy's clients. You know that, don't you?'

Freiberg was coming apart at the seams. His mouth opened then snapped shut again, like a mechanical toy, grey hair flopping across his forehead. I was afraid he might be ill, so I leant over and tried to make eye contact.

'I try to stop seeing her, but it never works. Don't tell my wife, please. I'll do anything.' His words came out in a high-pitched whimper. The idea of disclosure seemed to terrify him more than the danger he was in.

'It's none of my business. Of course I won't tell her.'

My reassurance failed to convince him. Freiberg carried on gazing ahead, gripping the wheel like it was his one chance of retaining his sanity. After a few minutes I got out of the car and left him to finish his panic attack. Confronting him had served no purpose. All it told me was that yet another member of the Angel Bank's staff was enjoying Poppy's services. I might as well have carried on sitting on the wall, watching the stars come out.

It was after eleven when I finally started the trek home. A half-moon was hovering over the roofs of Knightsbridge, pale and sickly against the light-polluted sky. I had plenty of time to study it, because the bus ride took forever. I was starting to regret confronting Freiberg. The combination of concealing his visits to Poppy and the auditors crawling over the bank seemed to be pushing him to the limits.

The bus ground to a halt at Victoria beside a group of travellers. Their faces had that lost, expectant look that people always wear when they start a long journey. My mind drifted to Andrew's last trip to Paris, but I managed to silence the thought as soon as it arrived.

When I got back to Providence Square, a fire engine was blocking the road. A summer party must have gone spectacularly wrong, the bonfire raging out of control, because firelight was reflecting from the white faces of the buildings. Locals were hanging around, hoping for a better view. And when I turned the corner, I could see why. Will's van was alight. It looked like a giant firework, with flames shooting through the windows into the night sky. I tried to push past the crowd, but three officers were holding everyone back. The intensity of the fire was growing, and they must have been afraid it would spread to the cars nearby. My eyes closed as I remembered the years when Will lived on the road, and nothing could persuade him to come inside. When I opened them again, I saw Darren on the other side of the square, sitting on a white scooter. He rode away before I could move a muscle.

It took a long time to find a policeman and explain that the van belonged to my brother. He gave me a disapproving look then made a note of my details.

'It'll be kids,' he grumbled. 'They do this sort of thing for a dare.'

'I know who started it.'

I gave him Darren's name, explaining that he'd escaped from Guy's. The policeman looked amazed as he scribbled everything down. He seemed to find the story more intriguing than *EastEnders* on a good night. I stared past him at my brother's van. Water was pouring through the front window, and there was a muffled explosion as the bonnet blew open, the gutters flooding with oily water. I walked back to my flat. I was too tired to worry about potential attackers as I climbed the stairs – Darren would be miles away by now, and it was hard to see why he'd targeted the van. Maybe it was because my name was printed on the sign by the parking bay. It seemed odd that the sight of Will's van burning like an effigy hadn't upset me. A young man with a head full of guns and knives was targeting me, but it didn't seem to matter. The only thing I cared about was finding Andrew's killer. My emotions were so blunted, my safety mechanism had shut down, and that was a problem. I should have been scared, but warning signs didn't affect me any more.

39

I called Burns before breakfast the next morning, and left a garbled message, telling him about Freiberg's visit to Poppy. The morning sky was grey instead of blue when I went down to inspect Will's van, but it felt more sweltering than ever. The van looked even worse by daylight. All that remained was a blackened shell, the seat cushions reduced to a tangle of charred leather, every window shattered. The heat had been so intense that the tarmac had melted under the front wheels, fusing the axles to the road.

Hari rang as soon as I got back inside, and for once his calm had deserted him. He sounded horrified when I told him it looked as though Darren had started the fire.

'Why didn't you call me, Alice? You could have stayed with us.'

'Maybe I'm overreacting. I don't think he means any real harm.'

'How real do you want it? He's attacked you once already, we can't take any chances.'

I did my best to keep busy all day. I logged into my work email and found an invitation from a teaching hospital in Seattle to fly over and train their interns. In an ideal world I'd have jumped on a plane immediately. I could stroll by Puget Sound, and spend the evenings listening to music on Jackson Street, pretending nothing had happened. My mobile rang again while I was planning my escape. There was a pause, then a woman's quiet voice greeted me.

'It's Sophie here.'

I took a second to recognise Max Kingsmith's wife. 'It's good to hear from you.'

Her voice sounded strained as she asked me to meet her for coffee.

'I could come to your house,' I offered.

'Actually, I'm climbing the walls. I'd rather get out.'

I suggested meeting in Covent Garden, and there was a quake in her voice as she said goodbye. It sounded like her anxiety levels were hitting the roof. So many of her husband's colleagues had died, everyone must have started to look like a potential culprit.

The rain clouds were darker when I left home that evening, scudding in rows across the sky. People were clutching umbrellas as I caught the bus at Tower Bridge, and a spatter of raindrops hurled themselves against the glass then disappeared. A gang of women in leotards were queuing outside a dance studio on Floral Street when I reached Covent Garden, and I felt like joining them. An hour of high-impact aerobics would be the ideal way to burn off some stress.

Sophie gave me the awkward smile I remembered from our first meeting, and it struck me again that she didn't tick the boxes for a millionaire's partner. She was attractive, but she wasn't calling attention to herself. As far as I could tell she was wearing no make-up, apart from a dab of transparent lip gloss. Only her diamond earrings gave her away: she could have exchanged them for an Alfa Romeo. We'd been walking several minutes before I noticed a man in a dark shirt trailing us along Betterton Street.

'Is he yours?' I asked.

'He's worse than a Labrador.' She gave an embarrassed nod. 'He even follows me to the loo.'

The man loitered outside the Poetry Café as we ordered

our drinks. Every time I looked over my shoulder he was peering through the door, but it was hard to believe the place was dangerous. Most of the tables were occupied by young men with foppish haircuts, scribbling verse in their note-books, while photos of Rupert Brooke gazed down approvingly.

'The police told us about Andy Piernan,' Sophie's voice faltered. 'I didn't know him that well, but I admired him. He was someone with a conscience.'

It crossed my mind to admit that I'd been seeing him, but it would have hijacked the conversation. She seemed frailer than last time we met, her skin waxy with sleeplessness.

'How've you been coping?' I asked.

'Not great.' She attempted a smile. 'I snap at everyone, and if a door slams I have a heart attack.'

'The police are making progress, you know.'

'Are they?' Her face brightened. 'Have they arrested some-one?'

'Not yet. They've got some strong leads though.'

'Not strong enough to help Nicole. I heard about what Liam did. It's incredible, he seemed so crazy about her.' A deep frown settled on her face, making her look years older.

'And how's your husband doing?' I asked.

'Same as ever. If he's scared, I'd be the last to know. When he said the bank was closing, I thought he'd spend more time at home, but he's with his lawyers all day long. They're plan-ning an appeal.'

'Doesn't Max ever talk about how he feels?'

'Not if he can help it. To be honest, all I've ever wanted is more time with him. But he's in his own world – Molly doesn't get a look in. Sometimes it makes me want to beat him to a pulp.' She let out a short laugh, then clapped her hand over her mouth. 'Sorry. I think I'm losing it.'

'I'd be more worried if you were calm. But at least you can talk to your mum if it gets too much.'

'She's been amazing.'

'How does she get on with Max?'

'Mum says I should leave him.' She gulped down a breath. 'She thinks I deserve better. She's wrong, of course. He's not always like this. He's just under so much pressure.' Sophie's anxious gaze settled on my face. 'And what about you? You live with someone, don't you?'

I shook my head. 'Work keeps me pretty busy.'

'No time to relax.' She gave me a sympathetic look. 'It's the same for me. I haven't even been swimming. The friends I go with are from the bank – the police have told us all to stay indoors.'

Sophie and I talked for another hour. Her statements kept circling back to her husband. She told me more about how their relationship began. At first she'd turned him down, worried by the age gap, but he wouldn't take no for an answer, bombarding her with letters and phone calls until she finally crumbled. She hinted at the conflicts between them, then fell into an awkward silence. I felt like telling her about his method for recruiting female executives, but I managed to keep my mouth shut. We were about to leave when she glanced across at me.

'Sometimes I wish I didn't care about him so much, if that makes sense.'

'Of course it does. It makes everyone feel vulnerable.'

'It's Molly I'm scared for, not me.'

When I looked at her again, her eyes were round with fear.

'You'll be okay. Your Labrador's keeping an eye on you.' I nodded at her security guard, still stationed by the window. 'Call me any time, won't you?'

Sophie hugged me impulsively when we got outside. Her

bodyguard was stifling a yawn. The poor man must have been longing for something dangerous to happen to brighten up his day. I watched them walk back to the Tube, ignoring each other, like a couple after an almighty row.

I took my time walking through Soho. It's always been one of my favourite neighbourhoods; hemmed in by smart shopping streets, but determined to stay disreputable. Old men were hanging around outside lap-dancing clubs, adult book-shops and massage parlours concealed by smoked-glass windows. Tiny Chinese restaurants were doing a roaring trade. It was hard to remember the last time I'd eaten a proper meal, but even the smell of Peking Duck didn't tempt me. Watching couples enjoying a romantic dinner would be too much to bear.

At nine o'clock I caught a taxi home, with my phone buzzing in my pocket. But at that moment I didn't care how perfect my mother's holiday was, or how urgently Burns needed to talk. My devil-may-care attitude lasted until I got back to Providence Square. I forced myself to march up the stairs. I was beginning to feel relieved, until a sound came from the living room. My feet had fused themselves to the floorboards, even though I knew I should be running. Someone had got there before me, and he was standing a few metres away, on the other side of the door.

40

'What are you doing, Al?' Lola stumbled into the hall, rubbing her eyes.

I was brandishing a wine bottle to cosh over the intruder's head. 'I thought you were a burglar. Why didn't you turn the lights on in there?'

'I fell asleep on the sofa. You didn't answer your phone, I've been worrying about you.'

I didn't have the heart to explain that sympathy wouldn't help. If anyone tried to look after me, I'd come apart at the seams. I went into the kitchen to make us some tea, but my hands were shaking, and milk slopped across the counter.

'Your friend came round earlier,' Lola said. 'He couldn't stay long. He said he'd come back later.'

'Who do you mean?'

'Darren.' She was busy stirring sugar into her tea. 'He seemed pretty urgent about it. Maybe you should give him a bell.'

I reached over and grabbed her arm. 'Listen to me, Lo. He's the one who's been following me. He's dangerous. Don't talk to him again.'

'He's a stalker?' Lola looked astonished. She's always had strange ideas about human nature. The inmates on Death Row could convince her in seconds that they were pure as the driven snow. She was still studying me intently. 'Look, Al, I'm going to stay here for a bit. You shouldn't be on your own.'

'What about Neal?'

'He'll cope.' Her feline grin flashed on for a moment. 'It'll keep him on his toes.'

I gave her a hug then went to search for clean sheets for Will's bed. The light was flashing frantically on the answer-machine, so I forced myself to listen. The first message was from Taylor, letting me know that he'd told Brotherton about my supposed professional misconduct. He paused dramatically between sentences, as if he was puffing on a Cuban cigar. Any day now my contract would be cancelled. The next message was silent. Someone breathed quietly for thirty seconds, then hung up. And the last was from Burns, his accent thick as Scotch mist. I deleted them all and dived into bed.

Burns was waiting for me in Browns the next morning. His skin had a greyish cast as he stared at his uneaten toast. I wondered whether he knew about his deputy's latest efforts to get me fired, but I could see it was the wrong time to share bad news.

'Stephen Rayner told us his little secret,' he said. 'When I got your message about Freiberg's visit, I asked him what he knew about Poppy, and out it came. Once he started, he wouldn't shut up.'

'What did he say?'

'Rayner overheard someone at work saying Poppy was the top guys' favourite girl, and it wasn't hard to get her address. He went to Raphael Street two or three nights a week, taking photos. He was planning to use them for blackmail if the bank tried to fire him. Then he made a mistake. He told a friend about it at a party, and a few days later his camera got nicked. Pictures of half a dozen Angel staff were in there, including all the victims.'

'And you think the killer's using the pictures as a blueprint. Anyone from the bank who visited Poppy recently is on his list.'

Burns's phone rang before he could reply, and his eyes widened as he listened to the voice at the end of the line. He stuffed the phone back in his pocket as soon as the call ended.

'Henrik Freiberg's gone missing,' he said.

There was a grim expression on his face as we got into his car, and I knew what he was thinking. Freiberg was one of Poppy's loyal customers. Rayner would have had no trouble snapping him as he went into her building.

I thought about Stephen Rayner as we drove. He'd been convinced that his boss was his only ally. Maybe he believed that if Gresham retired, his job would be on the line. He'd seemed so frail when I interviewed him. If his photos were being used by the Angel Killer, the guilt would drive him to the edge. I glanced out of the window as we reached the West End. Mayfair was home to more millionaires than any other neighbourhood in the city, but the pedestrians were determined not to appear rich. Most of them looked scruffy and bohemian, like artists, or resting actors.

Burns pulled up on a narrow road. A view of Hyde Park unfolded at the bottom of the street, but the Freibergs' house looked too dilapidated to belong to a banker. It was a mess of shambling eaves, with a climbing frame in the centre of the front garden. The family seemed to be advertising their home as a kids' paradise before you'd even stepped inside. The woman who welcomed us must have been a beauty once, with dark, deep-set eyes. She was in her fifties, thickening around the waist, her hair a bright, artificial auburn. When she ushered us into her living room, a young woman was standing by the window, her face tense with concern.

'This is my daughter, Rina,' said Mrs Freiberg.

I sat down on a worn-out sofa and it was easy to see what had caused the wear and tear. A horde of grandchildren gazed out from the mantelpiece – more pictures of babies and toddlers than I could count. There was a portrait of Freiberg at the centre, wearing a patriarchal smile. I couldn't help wondering how his wife would react to the news that her husband had been paying a fortune for sex, every week, on his way home from work.

'Can you tell us what's happened, Mrs Freiberg?' Burns asked.

'Sonia, please.' Her smile was slowly unravelling. 'Henrik answered the phone around 3 a.m., then he got up and left. I thought it must be one of the kids, but they're all fine.'

Rina was holding her mother's hand tightly, as though she was in danger of floating away. I tried to picture Freiberg relaxing in one of the tatty armchairs. His body language at the Angel Bank had been so self-effacing. The pressure of being Kingsmith's right-hand man seemed to weigh heavily on him, yet he'd kept his pleasant, history teacher's manner. It was easy to see why he was terrified of exposure. It would jeopardise his whole family.

'Henrik wouldn't just leave. We've been married thirty years.' Sonia's voice rose in protest, as though she was giving her husband a piece of her mind. 'He's been in a terrible state for months – some days he hardly says a word. I keep telling him to see the doctor.'

The tears arrived suddenly, as though someone in another room had opened a valve.

'Calm down, Mum. Nothing's happened, he'll be fine.' Rina's arm closed around her shoulders and her mother's sobs paused for a second.

Burns rose to his feet. 'We'll do everything to find your husband, I promise.'

I followed him back along the overgrown path, and he pulled the passenger door open without glancing in my direction. He listened intently to the message his police radio was broadcasting, but there was so much static I couldn't hear properly. After a few minutes Burns jabbed the off button and swore quietly under his breath.

'What is it?' I asked.

'Freiberg's car's at Pacific Wharf.'

'That's good news, isn't it?'

'Christ knows.' His shoulders heaved upwards. 'The message says it's been torched.'

41

It took an hour to cross the city, cutting a line southeast from Mayfair, through heavy traffic. By the time we reached Bermondsey we'd swapped extravagant villas for grey social housing. I knew Pacific Wharf well, because I ran past it on the way to Rotherhithe. The neighbourhoods grew less salubrious the further east you travelled, and Pacific Wharf hadn't profited from the housing boom. Property developers had lined the river with apartment blocks, knowing the views would fetch high prices, then they'd run out of cash. Concrete skeletons towered above the pavement, ribs of metal exposed to the elements.

Burns parked on Rotherhithe Street and we headed towards the river. The water was gunmetal grey, reflecting the clouds massing overhead.

'The heavy brigade got here before us,' he commented.

Two squad cars, a scene-of-crime van and a fire engine had arrived already, clustered in front of a half-built apartment block. Only the foundations and ground floor had been completed. A mess of steel girders and concrete sections lay abandoned, as though the builders had suddenly downed tools. Burns spoke to one of the firemen, then we crossed the outer cordon to an underground car park. The developers must have had big plans – it could have accommodated hundreds of cars, but the space was empty now, apart from the stink of burnt rubber. Our footsteps echoed as we crossed the concrete.

'Wait here, Alice.'

Pete Hancock was checking people in and out of the crime scene. I watched him frowning at Burns as he pulled on his blue suit, then they disappeared behind a row of screens. When Burns finally re-emerged, I could tell that it wouldn't be pretty. It was his pallor that worried me most. Only his pride was stopping him from dispatching his breakfast behind the nearest pillar.

'He's here all right,' Burns mumbled, his eyes blank with shock. 'In your shoes, I wouldn't look. Save yourself a few nightmares.'

I drew in a deep breath and walked past him. I was beginning to hate putting on crime scene overalls, the dry fabric scratching against my skin. Behind the screen, a layer of black smoke hovered below the ceiling, the smell intensifying with each step. It had a sickly edge, like someone had turned the oven on, then forgotten the Sunday roast. It left a salty, chemical taste at the back of my mouth. A few metres away, a burnt-out car was still smouldering. It was impossible to tell whether it was Freiberg's BMW, because the fire had scorched away every trace of pigment, the chassis stripped to raw metal, windows and tyres melted away. God knows how many gallons it had taken to bring the flames under control. Pools of water were standing on the tarmac, a handful of white feathers drifting on the wet concrete.

'Where's Freiberg's body?' I asked.

'Right there.' Burns gritted his teeth. 'He hasn't been moved.'

I bent down to peer inside the car, then straightened up immediately and closed my eyes. Burns was keeping busy, studying the splinters of glass that littered the ground. It was a long time before I could force myself to look again. The body inside the car didn't seem human. It could have been a sculpture, made from charcoal or black metal. The fire had stolen everything from him: clothes, skin, even his lean tissue. And it must have been fast, because he hadn't even tried to escape, his bird-like hands melted to the steering wheel. I circled the car slowly, with a handkerchief pressed over my mouth. Freiberg's empty eye sockets stared at me accusingly. He'd sat in exactly the same position in Knightsbridge, but it was his wife I pitied. Sooner or later she would find out that her husband's body was unrecognisable, only his dental records could identify him.

'That's enough,' I said, under my breath. I don't know why I was so angry. Maybe it was grief for Andrew bubbling to the surface, or the fact that another life had been lost. Either way, when we emerged into the fresh air, my legs were trembling, but I didn't feel weak, just determined to stop it happening again.

'He left us another message.' Burns handed me a postcard, wrapped in transparent plastic.

The angel was the sweetest yet. A cherub's blue eyes shone back at me, skin made of porcelain, his mouth breaking into a smile. He looked as innocent as Freiberg's legion of grand-children. I glanced at the back of the card; the picture was a close-up from Filippino Lippi's *An Angel Adoring*, hanging in the National Gallery. I felt like ripping it to shreds. It crossed my mind that the cards might have no meaning at all. They were just a taunt, reminding us that we were useless guardian angels.

'I'm going back to the station,' Burns said when we reached the car. 'I'll drop you at home. Taylor'll go bleating to the boss if he sees you.'

I shook my head. 'I'm still officially employed – Brotherton hasn't fired me yet.'

Burns was polishing his glasses. 'I don't get it, Alice. Why do it again? He tried to set Piernan up. I thought he'd walk away and get on with his life.'

'It's an addiction. He wants to stop, but he can't. The compulsion's too strong.'

A row of ghosts was waiting for us at the station. Someone had enlarged the angels' faces from each crime scene, and the effect was uncanny. They gazed down through clear, inhuman eyes, judging us all unworthy. There was no sign of Brotherton. Maybe it was her policy to turn invisible when the incident room was busy, only materialising again when things calmed down.

My phone rang as Burns was racing from desk to desk, handing out instructions and answering questions. The voice at the end of the line had a broad West African accent. It was Sam Adebayo from the City YMCA, and I remembered asking him to call if he saw Darren.

'He stayed here last night,' he said. 'But he left early this morning.'

'Did you talk to him?'

'For a while. He didn't make much sense though. He seemed angry – I couldn't get him to sit still.'

I gave Adebayo the number for the emergency mental health team, and I don't know what prompted me to ask where Darren had been working when he lost his job. Adebayo didn't reply immediately. I heard the sound of pages being turned, and realised he was flicking through Darren's file.

'The employment agency sent him to the Angel Bank. They fired him for being late, six weeks ago.'

I thanked him and hung up, but the information took a while to sink in. Darren had been one of the cleaners who rose at the crack of dawn to scour the bank's marble floors. When I glanced around, the room was in motion, people whirling from table to table. It seemed odd that it had taken another death to revive the team. Burns's face was lit with manic energy when he arrived back at my desk.

'Did you interview all the temporary workers at the Angel Bank?' I asked.

'Almost, but a couple are no fixed abode. Why?'

'One of my patients got sacked from a cleaning job there, six weeks ago.'

His expression grew more serious when he heard that Darren had served a year for GBH, and that he was a diagnosed schizophrenic, with anger management issues.

'Let's get this straight.' Burns stared at me. 'The bloke got fired from the Angel, he has a breakdown and starts talking about guns and knives. Then he sets fire to your brother's van, and you didn't even tell me about him?'

'Don't get carried away, Don. It's not him. He's too ill to plan something like this.'

'We still need to check him out.'

I tried to argue, but he was already typing commands into the computer at a furious speed.

'Unbelievable,' he said, staring at the screen. 'The bank didn't even log his name.'

'I'm not surprised. Agencies must send thousands of temps into the City every day.'

'But they haven't all been inside for nearly killing someone, have they?'

He started handing out orders to a woman at the table opposite. He asked her to contact Darren's probation officer, and send a squad car to collect him if he returned to the YMCA. When I looked up again, Steve Taylor was standing on the other side of the room, looking as shitty as ever. Luckily Burns was on the move again, grabbing his car keys. I was glad to escape without facing another showdown, but my relief was short-lived.

Darren had parked his scooter on the yellow lines outside

the station and he was staring straight at me. Something in my expression must have triggered alarm bells, because he set off immediately. I caught sight of the number-plate, and Burns repeated the numbers into his phone as we jogged down the steps, but I knew it was pointless. Who could track down one lost soul in a community of eight million? There was no clear suspect, and Burns was clutching at straws. It was beginning to feel like almost anyone in the city could be the Angel Killer.

42

Burns was concentrating on the endless flow of traffic on Baker Street, and I'd already guessed where he was taking me. Our visit would follow the usual pattern. Poppy would be wearing another gorgeous outfit, preparing for her next client, but Raphael Street was deserted. Not a single punter arrived during the fifteen minutes we sat outside, while Burns barked instructions into his phone.

The door to Poppy's building had been left ajar, and I wondered why she carried on with her work. She could easily have persuaded one of her boyfriends to pay for another bout of rehab. Maybe she couldn't face being a viscount's daughter again, condemned to a life in the country and marriage to a chinless wonder. There was no answer when Burns rapped on her front door. He leant down to peer through the letterbox.

'Something's wrong,' he said. 'The place has been trashed.'

Burns made me stand back before launching himself at the door. There was a sound of wood splintering as the lock broke – not many obstacles could have survived a full-frontal attack from a man of his scale. He massaged his shoulder gingerly as he stepped over the threshold. The hall was a mess. A cabinet had been pushed over; letters, keys and photographs were strewn across the floor.

The place was oddly silent. If Poppy had been at home, she'd have confronted us by now, furious about our intrusion. There was hardly any damage in the lounge, just a few pictures askew, and pieces of broken glass on the floor. Nothing seemed to be missing. The kitchen was undisturbed. Someone had made coffee recently; the red light on the percolator was still glowing.

When I got back to the lounge, Burns was opening the door to Poppy's bedroom. I saw him recoil, then fumble for his phone, cursing under his breath.

'Don't go in there,' he barked at me.

I heard him asking for back-up: a scene-of-crime team, eight uniforms, a pathologist. It didn't take a clairvoyant to realise she was dead, but I still wasn't prepared. Poppy was sprawled across the bed in her favourite pink dress, except it wasn't pink any more. It looked like it had been tie-dyed in different shades of red. She'd been stabbed dozens of times – the wounds visible through the torn fabric. But he'd saved his energy for her face. It was unrecognisable. There was a hole where her nose should have been, her features a blur of livid flesh. The brown mess on the pillow must have been the remains of her eyes. The scene didn't seem to bother Filippino Lippi's angel. He was propped against the headboard, surrounded by white feathers, gazing at me innocently.

My first reaction was rage, and most of it was self-directed. I'd failed to convince Poppy to take more care. It made me wish I'd worked harder to convince Burns to give her protection. I couldn't forget our last conversation, and the dry graze of her fingertips on my wrist when she said goodbye. It sickened me that her death had been more violent than all the others.

I spotted her appointments book lying on a coffee table. 'His name'll be in there, won't it?'

Burns put on plastic gloves and riffled through the pages. 'There's nothing under today's date. She must have taken the day off.'

The SOCOs had already arrived, head to toe in white, tying security tape across the door. I caught a glimpse into the second bedroom, and spotted something new. From a distance the room still looked innocent, with its plain furniture and the crucifix on the wall, but two pairs of handcuffs were locked to the bed frame. I felt a pang of sympathy for Poppy. She must have pretended to be a schoolgirl countless times, for yet another old man to deflower.

'You shouldn't be in here.' One of the SOCOs shooed me along the hallway, as if I was a dangerous contaminant.

Clouds were circling overhead like towels churning in a tumble-drier. I leant against the car and imagined calling the hospital in Seattle to tell them I'd changed my mind. Maybe I could forget everything I'd seen, and go swimming every day after work. Burns's return neutralised my daydream. His movements were so jerky and unpredictable, it looked as though his nerve endings were hooked to the national grid. Poppy's appointment book was still clutched to his chest. He slipped into the driving seat and started leafing through the pages, working backwards from today's date.

'I knew it,' he muttered.

'What?'

He stared back at me. 'Kingsmith went to see her last month.'

'You should warn him, Don.'

'I can't.' Burns's jaw was working overtime, muscles ticking in his cheek. 'He's blaming us for the FSA ruling. He'll sue us if we contact him.'

He dropped the appointment book in an evidence bag then placed it on the back seat, out of my reach.

'Can I see?' I asked.

He grunted something inaudible, and his scowl was the equivalent of a point-blank refusal, so I kept my peace and looked out of the window.

'The tabloids would pay a fortune for that,' he said.

My curiosity grew even stronger. The pages would be stuffed with famous names – actors, footballers, business magnates. Maybe a few cabinet members had found their way to Poppy's door. No wonder Burns looked tense. For the first time in his life, he was the guardian of state secrets.

'We've got a predicament, haven't we?' he said. 'Kingsmith's on the Angel Killer's list, but he won't let us anywhere near him.'

I held his gaze. 'It's not just him we need to worry about. If he gets attacked, his family are in danger too.'

Burns didn't bother to reply, but his tyres gave a thin scream as the car pulled away.

43

'I'll drop you at a taxi rank,' Burns said, 'then I'll get over there.' His driving had taken a nosedive. He was taking corners too fast, shoulders hunched over the wheel.

'I'll come with you.'

It was the thought of Sophie that made me volunteer. She'd have heard about Freiberg by now – at least the sight of us waiting outside might reassure her. It was after seven when Burns pulled over by a parade of shops. He shoved two jumbo cups of coffee into my hands, then drove the last half-mile to the Kingsmiths' house.

'There's enough caffeine in here to kill a horse,' I said.

'It'll keep us awake.' From the set of Burns's jaw, it looked like he was prepared to wait until the next millennium.

Two sentries were still standing either side of the Kingsmiths' door. They looked like actors auditioning for the next Bond movie. Apart from their presence, the house was the same as its neighbours – prosperous and too large, like an overfed businessman. It dawned on me that Lola was still waiting at my flat, determined to keep an eye on me. I stepped out of the car to call her. The clouds were even darker than before, marking the sky like smudges of charcoal.

'Have you seen Darren?' I asked.

'Not yet.' Lola sounded disappointed.

'That's good news. Call the police if you do. Promise you won't talk to him.'

I gave her the incident room's number, but I'm not convinced she wrote it down. Knowing Lola she was more likely to dash outside and minister to him herself.

Burns was knocking back huge swigs of coffee as though it was a universal cure. He was so preoccupied that I had the chance to study his new image. He was an inch away from being handsome. Two more stone and his transformation would be complete: a thin man stepping free of the fat suit he'd dragged around for years, Oliver Hardy morphing into Stan Laurel. I kept expecting his former self to reappear, desperate to vanquish him. Suddenly he strained forwards in his seat.

'There she is,' he said.

Sophie Kingsmith was standing in the doorway, chatting to her sentries, offering them mugs of tea and charming them with her anxious smile. Burns gazed at her approvingly.

'How did that tosser get a girl like her?' he muttered.

'It's a mystery. She must have low self-esteem.'

As soon as the men had finished their drinks, Sophie went back inside and lights appeared in the downstairs windows. I wondered what Max had been doing since the bank closed. He'd been advised to stay safe at home, but being trapped indoors, unable to work or play golf, must have been sending him into meltdown.

I flicked through Burns's CD box to keep myself occupied: Curtis Mayfield, Ry Cooder, Al Green, Matthew P, Amy Winehouse. There were a few dubious choices hidden under the passenger seat – the Proclaimers and Adam Ant – but it was the wrong moment for criticism. When I looked up again, the house was a blaze of light. Maybe it was part of the family's game plan. If the killer was lurking nearby, it gave the impression that the place was a fortress, and everyone inside was wide awake. Burns seemed determined to stay all night.

'You'll have to talk, to keep my eyes open,' I said.

'About what?'

'Anything. What made you leave Edinburgh and come here?'

Burns's shoulders twitched irritably, and I wondered if he disliked talking about his past as much as I did. 'I grew up in Midlothian. There's nothing in my village except miners' cottages, a graveyard and a Spar, with everything past its sell-by. The pub was full to the rafters on Mondays when the dole cheques came, empty the rest of the week.'

'So you escaped?'

'I made a crap job of it.' He kept his gaze fixed on the house. 'Edinburgh Art College gave me a scholarship, but they chucked me out after a year for bad behaviour. I got the train down here with my tail between my legs. My father wouldn't let me back in the house.'

I was too surprised to reply. My image of Burns didn't include a wayward past, or a talent for life drawing. 'Why did you choose the police?'

'There weren't many options. It was the army, the navy or the force. All I had to offer was my immaturity and a couple of highers.'

'But you didn't have to stay in, did you?'

He looked across at me. 'What is this? Late-night psycho-analysis with Dr Alice Quentin?'

'I'm just trying not to sleep.'

'Okay then. Here's my dirty little secret. I thought I'd hate the job, but it fits me to a T. Someone's got to slap these monsters behind bars. And what would I be doing now if I'd gone to art school? I'd be grinding my soul to dust, teaching kids to draw in some shite school in Midlothian.'

'And what's your biggest ambition?'

'Man alive. You don't let up, do you?' He thought for a moment. 'I want my boys to have more choices. They can be deckchair attendants for all I care. I won't pressure them.' Burns looked stunned by his own candour. 'Go on then. What's your big dream?'

'To learn to dive, on the Barrier Reef preferably.'

He rolled his eyes. 'Go and see *Open Water*. That'll cure you.'

Burns's fingers jittered across the steering wheel, and it was clear that the conversation was over. God knows how many shots he'd put in his coffee. I felt like pointing out that the killer was unlikely to approach a building with guards at every entrance. The 007s must be armed to the teeth. If he came anywhere near, he'd be riddled with bullets. When I looked up again, the front door had swung open, light spilling across the pavement. Max Kingsmith stomped over to us, wearing a furious expression. Burns groaned quietly as he got out of the car.

'Go home, Inspector, before I call Scotland Yard,' Kingsmith snarled. 'You've done nothing to protect us, and you're stopping my men from doing their work.'

He didn't wait for a reply before pacing back up the steps.

'Charming,' Burns muttered.

Kingsmith's order made me furious, but it was a blessing in disguise. Nothing had changed in the past two hours, and Burns looked like he was hallucinating, his eyes stretched uncomfortably wide. Maybe he was afraid to shut them in case his body lapsed into sleep. Lights were still blazing in every window, and the bodyguards had been replaced by clones in identical suits. Even the radio had fallen silent.

Burns drove slowly on the way home. When he turned to me, it was too dark to read his expression.

'Were you keen on that Piernan bloke?' he asked.

I nodded, but couldn't reply. When I glanced at him again, he'd never looked more dejected. Going home must feel like admitting defeat; he was probably wishing he'd followed his original destiny to become an artist. He insisted on traipsing up the stairs to my flat, yawning deeply as we reached each landing. I watched him stumble back to his car with an odd, rolling gait. When he got home he'd go out like a light, immune to the loudest alarm clock.

A headache thumped at the base of my skull and I headed for the bathroom in search of Nurofen, tiptoeing past Lola's door. It took me forever to fall asleep. I tried not to imagine the terror Poppy Beckwith had gone through. All I could hope was that the killer had shown her some mercy and sedated her first, but it seemed unlikely. His violence was escalating out of control.

I must have drifted off eventually, because a shrill, rattling noise woke me just after three. My mobile phone was flashing on the bedside table, but I couldn't tell who was speaking. For a second I thought it was my mother, calling from Crete to harangue me for some unknown crime. Then I realised it was Sophie Kingsmith. Her voice was somewhere between a whisper and a scream.

'Help me, please.'

I could hear her uneven breathing, and another voice in the background. She was talking so fast her words tumbled over each other, and by now I was sitting bolt upright.

'Slow down, Sophie. I can't hear you.'

'He's inside the house,' she whispered. 'We can't get out.'

Noises buzzed behind her voice. Someone was whimpering; it was impossible to tell if it was a man or a woman. I was about to reply, but there was a loud, shattering noise, like a plate smashing against a wall, then the line went dead.

I went into panic mode, racing to put on my jeans. We should have ignored Kingsmith's threat and stayed put until morning. I stuffed my phone and car keys into my pocket then ran downstairs to the ground floor. Will's predictions about the weather had finally come true. Huge raindrops were plummeting from the sky. The smell of rain hitting the parched ground should have been a relief, but I hardly noticed it. Water coursed down my face, like I'd just climbed out of a swimming pool.

When I reached my car I made a hurried call to Burns, but there was no reply. Fortunately there was hardly any traffic, except a straggle of taxis, ferrying the last party-goers home. My windscreen wipers were working overtime as I crossed Tower Bridge – even on the highest setting they were struggling to clear the deluge. I drove west, triggering half a dozen speed cameras. Mooring lights flickered across the surface of the river as I tried to steady my breathing. Hopefully the police would be there already, and Burns would get his moment of glory when Sophie's family were rescued. But I'd been too optimistic. There were no squad cars in sight when I reached Mayfair, and the black-suited security guards had disappeared. Rain gushed down the windscreen in torrents, as though someone was flinging buckets of water at the car. The house blurred then came into focus again. Sophie and her mother must be locked inside, cowering in their palatial living room.

Then it dawned on me that the killer always acted fast. My stomach contracted as I realised I'd arrived too late. By now the white feathers would have been scattered, yet another angel gazing up at the ceiling. And the bastard would be miles away, congratulating himself on a job well done. My impulse was to run straight up the steps and peer through the letterbox, but I could imagine the rage on Burns's face. I dialled his number again but there was still no answer, so I left a message, then waited for him to call back. For once the city was keeping its mouth shut. All I could hear was rain pelting the roof of my car, the whine of a solitary motorbike, then silence. I remembered Burns's unsteady walk. He'd be asleep by now, deaf to even the loudest ring tone. I would have to make my decision without help from anyone.

44

Worst-case scenarios kept running through my head: Sophie could be lying wounded inside the mansion, with Molly in her arms. Or maybe he'd slaughtered them all. My eyelids clamped shut to wipe the images away. The killer must have vanished into the back streets as soon as his work was done. Apart from the light pulsing from the windows of the house, there was no sign of life. It was hard to imagine anyone angry enough to kill a whole family. How could someone get inside, unless one of the Kingsmiths' guards let him walk through the door? I picked up my phone and called 999. The woman who answered sounded disbelieving when I explained the situation, as though I might be a fantasist. I rang off immediately and climbed out of the car, the rain drenching me again. Anyone looking out of the windows would have seen a drowned rat, scurrying up the steps.

The door was open and there were no sounds coming from inside the house. He must have done his work and vanished, just like the other attacks. I gulped down a deep breath and reminded myself that it was too late for panic – all I had to do was search for survivors. My mouth felt like I'd swallowed a handful of salt as I stepped over the threshold. The first thing I saw was one of the black-suited security guards, slumped against a radiator, as though he was trying to keep warm. I knelt down and pressed two fingers against the artery in his neck. His skin was still warm, but there was no pulse. Blood was dripping from his shirt, and I knew that checking for wounds would be pointless – I had to concentrate on helping the living. Inside the man's jacket I spotted his empty gun holster, and information started to slot into place. No one could overpower four armed security guards. The killer must have been waiting inside the building, ready to attack.

I knew I should wait outside, in case I contaminated the crime scene, but the sound of a man's voice stopped me in my tracks. The low, guttural noise drifted from the other end of the hall, where another security guard was lying on the wooden floor. He'd been gagged, hands tied behind his back, a broad gash in the centre of his forehead. The wound was an ugly, inflamed red, but at least he was alive. His eyes kept blinking, as he fought to stay conscious.

'It's okay,' I said quietly. 'You're safe now.'

My voice made him panic, his shoulders heaving like he was under attack. His eyes rolled wildly as I tried to undo the ties around his wrists. They were bound together with a length of plastic twine, and I was wrestling with the knots when a sound detonated, loud as a thunderclap. I didn't register that it was a gunshot until the bullet ploughed into the wall in front of me. The next one came a second later and the guard slumped forwards, gouts of blood dropping to the floor. I set off up the stairs, my heart thudding against my ribs. My phone dropped from my back pocket as I ran, the plastic case clattering down the wooden stairs.

The lights went out as soon as I reached the landing – the killer must have found the fuse box and thrown the switch, and there was nothing to cling to except blackness. I flailed my arms like a windmill, desperate to touch something solid. A seam of light appeared in the dark. I slammed the door shut behind me, but when I reached down there was no lock, and the wooden panels felt flimsy. He could shoulder it down in seconds. I groped around until I found a chair, but when I jammed it under the handle, I knew it wouldn't save me. All it could give me was a few extra moments to plan my escape. The footsteps had stopped. Maybe he'd tripped in the dark, or he was standing on the other side of the door, biding his time.

The only sounds I could hear were my breathing, raw with panic, and raindrops crashing against the window. For some reason I was convinced there were no survivors. Maybe he'd forced Kingsmith to watch while he shot Louise, then his wife and baby. I pressed my back against the wall. The most important thing was to stand away from the door. A single bullet would convert the wood to matchsticks.

The darkness lifted for a second as moonlight flooded through the window. The only furniture I could make out was a narrow single bed, a cabinet and a cupboard. It looked like I'd chosen one of the Kingsmiths' spare bedrooms as my hideaway. I did my best to open the sash window but it was locked, and kicking out the panes wasn't an option. The noise would give me away. He'd be waiting for me when I hit the ground, and I'd be trapped in the garden with nowhere to hide. My claustrophobia was getting the better of me. The oxygen supply seemed to be running down, dizziness overwhelming me. And then I heard it again. His footsteps on the landing, slow and deliberate, like he had all the time in the world. A thin beam of light appeared under the door – the bastard must be shining his torch through the gap. I held my breath until it felt like I was drowning, then he set off again, the floorboards creaking under his weight. He was searching for me in another room, peering under beds and tables.

I kept willing the rain clouds to evaporate so I could see again, but all I could rely on was my sense of touch. I wrenched the cupboard door open and inhaled the scent of lavender. It made me pity Sophie. She'd tried to make the place comfort-able, putting lavender bags in every wardrobe, but it hadn't protected her. My thoughts cleared for a second. The killer must know the house like the back of his hand, because he knew where the fuse box was, and he could find his way around with the lights switched off. His footsteps were closer now, gaining momentum, like he owned the place. And then the picture started to sharpen. Maybe the man striding from room to room was Kingsmith himself. That would explain why he'd sent us away. Somewhere along the line, his narcis-sism had tipped over into psychosis. He was destroying his own empire, because his dreams were about to be destroyed. The world he'd created was riddled with corruption. I remem-bered Andrew telling me that Kingsmith tried to destroy his enemies. Sacrificing the people closest to him would make him invincible. The power of life or death lay in his gift, like an Egyptian pharaoh.

My hands fumbled blindly across the cupboard's top shelf. I was hoping for scissors, or a vase to smash over his head – but there was only a pile of towels, neatly folded. Then I heard something that made me hold my breath. The noise was so faint I thought it must be imaginary, but it came again, shrill and unmistakable. Hiding wasn't an option any more, because a baby's cry was drifting from the floor above. There was no way I could leave Molly by herself.

45

Sophie must have hidden Molly somewhere safe when she realised her husband had lost his mind, praying she wouldn't make a sound. But I wasn't the only one who'd heard her crying. The footsteps were moving faster now, thundering across the landing, starting to climb the stairs. The muscles in my throat constricted like a vice tightening – Kingsmith had switched his search from me to the baby. My first impulse was to fling the door open and chase upstairs to find the baby, but I stopped myself. I had nothing to fight with – not so much as a bottle to smash over his head. He was pacing the floor above me, relentless as a sleepwalker. If I set foot outside I'd be on the losing end of his game of cat and mouse. I scrabbled frantically in the cupboard again and my fingers closed around a small metal cylinder. It was too dark to see whether it held hairspray or deodorant, but it didn't matter. At least I had something to spray in his eyes.

I pressed my ear to the thin wood. For a moment there was no sound, then I heard him rushing down the stairs. A thread of torchlight appeared under the door but it was gone in seconds. I wondered why he was hurrying, then a sick feeling of panic churned in my stomach. Maybe Molly was dead already. He was running through the house with her body in his arms. My eyes were growing used to the dark; I could make out the swirling flowers on the wallpaper as I strained to hear the next sound. I didn't have to wait long. Molly was wailing pitifully, as though she understood exactly how much danger she was in. I yanked the door open and floundered through the dark, without questioning what I was doing. I tripped twice on the stairs, but managed to keep going. The baby's yells grew louder with each step, guiding me towards her.

Sophie had chosen a good hiding place. Molly was safe in her Moses basket, under a gabled window, with moonlight flooding into the room. There was a key in the lock, and suddenly I could breathe more easily. It would take a while to kick down such a sturdy door. The baby's cries had softened to a dull whimper – maybe she'd sensed that she wasn't alone. When I reached into the basket, her hand grabbed my finger tightly, unwilling to let go.

Suddenly the lights flashed on again. At first they were so bright I could hardly see, but when my vision cleared, Molly was blinking up at me and I was standing in the middle of a junk room. A whole wall was lined with cardboard boxes and crates, old furniture stacked in piles. I was still desperate to find a weapon, but when I opened the first box, my fingers sank into softness. I pulled back the lid and stared inside. The container was packed with long white feathers, tickling the palms of my hand. For a second I was too shocked to move. When I flipped back the cardboard lid of the next box, an angel stared straight into my eyes, his expression calm and forgiving. Dozens of angels were crammed inside the container, competing for space. My thoughts were slowing down. Kingsmith had been so arrogant – he hadn't even tried to hide his paraphernalia.

I heard him pace across the landing, then I saw the doorknob twist, and my heart pumped even faster. He knew I was in here with Molly. All he had to do was fire his gun at the lock. But he moved away, and a familiar smell hit the back of my throat, strong enough to make me gag: the sharp reek of paraffin. That explained why he was wandering from room to room. Fire would cleanse everything, just like it had when he killed Freiberg. It would consume the bodies of his family, and the items he'd been leaving at the murder scenes. The place would be an inferno by the time the emergency services arrived, and he'd walk away unscathed. He'd be free to build himself a new world. I dragged in a deeper breath. I had to act now or I'd end up like Henrik Freiberg, a lump of human charcoal no one could identify.

Running back downstairs wasn't an option. He'd shoot me on sight. The window rattled in its frame, but refused to open. When I peered through the glass, the drop to the flat roof below looked suicidal. It was at least twenty feet, but it was my only chance. I'd have to jump, with Molly in my arms, while he was busy splashing paraffin into every room. I raised a chair over my head and hurled it at the glass, the panes shattering into jagged pieces. There was an outside chance that I'd land without injuring myself.

The baby must have cried herself into an exhausted sleep because she made no sound when I reached into the Moses basket and picked her up. There was a blanket and a pillow in the basket and I swaddled them round her. She was a soft, warm mass against my chest as I cleared fragments of glass from the windowsill with the flat of my hand. The stink of paraffin was growing stronger, and I knew that jumping was my only choice. Soon the house would go up in flames, and there was no sign of rescue. Even if the police broke down the front door, Kingsmith would shoot them immediately. I tried to remember what a surgeon told me once, about people who survive falls. It was best to relax. If the body's tense, the impact breaks more bones. I swung my legs through the opening with Molly clasped in the crook of my arm and stared down at the drop. Then I heard a voice. It was raw with fear, but I recognised it instantly.

'Help me, please.'

Sophie's voice was coming from nearby. Her words were a breathless sob, almost too weak to hear. She must have been hiding in a room on this floor. Somehow she'd managed to crawl out onto the landing. God knows what the bastard had done to her. I lowered Molly back into her basket.

'Sophie, are you okay?' I called.

There was no reply, but I knew I had to help her. With any luck I'd be able to drag her back into the junk room. At least then we'd be together. The lights flicked off again, and this time the darkness was complete. The moon had gone into hiding. My hands groped along the wall, and there was a low grumble of thunder, then all I could hear was Sophie's incoherent moans. It was the thought of her lying there injured that made me unlock the door.

46

A powerful light dazzled me, and my hands flew up to shield my eyes from the glare. Sophie was on the floor, slumped against the wall, clutching a torch. Her image swam as I moved towards her.

'Stay where you are.' Her words were distinct and hard as ice cubes.

'Has he hurt you?'

I was afraid that Kingsmith was waiting to spring out of the shadows. The light blinded me again as I tried to look at her. She was taking rapid, panicked breaths, and I understood why she was on the edge of hysteria. Watching her husband rampage through the house with a gun would have challenged anyone's sanity.

'Come on, Sophie, you have to stand up.' I took another step towards her. 'We need to get out of here.'

'Don't touch me,' she snapped.

I squinted into the light. Her outline was clearer now. There was a can of paraffin beside her, a gun clutched in her right hand. My panic dropped away instantly – maybe I realised that calmness was the only thing that could keep me alive.

'It's all right,' I said. 'I'm not moving.'

'I brought you here to listen to me.' Sophie's voice was almost too low to hear.

'I am. You can tell me everything.'

'No one heard me, except you. But you were as bad as the others. You flirted with him at the party, just like all the rest.'

Her anxious smile had been replaced by a sneer, and I wondered how I'd made such a fundamental mistake. She wanted someone to confess to before the place went up like bonfire night. My thoughts scrambled to rearrange themselves, but logic's hard to achieve when a gun's pointing at your chest.

'They called themselves angels, but they all fucked her, every one of them. The whole gang. Leo and the new boy—'

'Jamie Wilcox.'

'Who cares about his name? It was a club. Max and Henrik were the founding members.'

'I know, Sophie. I saw what you did to Poppy.'

The beam of her torch dropped from my face, and I realised how broken she was, shoulders slumped like an abandoned rag doll, the gun hanging loosely from her hand.

'They thought they were God's gift.' Her words faded into a sob. 'But they were filthy, all of them, and Max lied through his teeth.'

'I'm sorry,' I murmured.

'Stephen's pictures made up my mind. They walked out of there, grinning like idiots, but she was so stupid. I told her I was delivering a present that was so big, two men were carrying it upstairs. The greedy little bitch believed me.' She gave a cold laugh. 'Andrew saw her for months, you know. He was part of it.'

I stared back at her. I'd been trying not to consider whether Andrew had visited Poppy. I forced myself back into the present, and when I glanced down, I saw that Sophie's clothes were soaked. It wasn't just the carpet she'd doused with paraffin. When she struck the match, her skin would be the first thing to burn. Setting light to Will's van and Freiberg's car had been dress rehearsals for the main event.

'It's over now, Sophie. There are no angels left. Put down the gun and let's go.' I heard a police siren on the street outside, but they were too late to help me.

'You'd say anything to walk out alive, wouldn't you?' Her short hair was standing on end, her eyes staring. 'But you won't. Neither of us will.'

'We can leave right now. Tell the police whatever you like, I won't stop you.'

'Shut up, you bitch,' she snarled. 'Don't patronise me.'

Her anger had revived her strength. She was on her feet again, towering over me, the gun aimed squarely at my face, and I realised there was nothing to lose. I could say exactly what I thought.

'You loved it, didn't you?' I said. 'Killing them was the only thing you could control, while your husband was out there, screwing anything that moved. Do you know how many girls fucked him in his office, just to get a job?'

'Shut up!'

The barrel of the gun was less than a metre away. If she pulled the trigger, she'd leave a two-inch gap between my eyebrows. Everything speeded up after that. With perfect timing, Molly started to cry, and Sophie's expression changed. For a split-second she looked like any other anxious mother, eager to comfort her child. And that's when I reached for the gun, but someone knocked me to the floor. I heard the gun fire, and a man's voice groaning. When the torch rolled past my face I managed to grab it. The man was lying on the ground, and Sophie was coming for me, but this time I knew what to do. I smashed the torch into her face with all my strength. There was a crunching sound. I must have broken her cheekbone or her eye socket, but I was too busy searching

for the gun to care. When I finally grasped it, she looked piti-
ful. Tears were streaming from her eyes, the side of her face
grossly swollen. She was fumbling with the box of matches
but I knocked it from her hand.

'Don't move a fucking muscle,' I snapped.

Darren was lying on the other side of the landing. He'd
pushed me out of the way when the gun fired, and now he was
staring at the ceiling, moaning softly to himself. I couldn't go
to him because I was afraid to take my eyes off Sophie, even
for a moment. The squad cars seemed to take forever to arrive,
sirens blaring on the street outside. Someone called my name,
but I couldn't reply – I hardly noticed the gang of uniforms
streaming past me, leading Sophie away. When I knelt beside
Darren, I could see the exit wound in the middle of his chest,
through the torn cloth of his T-shirt. The bullet must have
shattered his spine. His ribcage was rising and falling much
too fast.

His eyes were losing focus when I knelt beside him. His
hands felt icy, as though he'd been lying for hours on frozen
ground. The expression on his face was hard to read, but he
seemed to be smiling as he looked up at me.

'You needed me after all, didn't you?' His voice was a raw
whisper.

I tried to reply, but no words arrived, so I leant down and
kissed his forehead, keeping my face inches from his. I saw
how young he was. God knows why he'd scared me so much.
The years were dropping away from him already. He could
have been twelve years old; a schoolboy with no concerns,
about to fall asleep.

'Stay here, Darren,' I said. 'Come on, keep talking to me.'

He clutched my hand tightly, then slipped out of reach. I'd
seen people die before, when I was doing my medical training,
but this time it was different. His history erased itself from his

face – all the filthy hostels he'd lived in, the crooks who'd bullied him in jail, the freezing park benches where he'd slept rough. The burdens disappeared one by one, and when his eyes closed, he was innocent again.

I don't remember how long I knelt there, holding his hand, but a paramedic helped me to my feet. When I turned round, Burns was leaning against the wall, watching me. His lips were clamped shut, like he was doing his best not to scream.

'Why didn't you wait, Alice? You're lucky to be alive.'

'Disassociation.'

He frowned. 'Spare me the long words.'

'It's like when you cut yourself. You're numb, until the pain kicks in.'

Burns carried on gazing at me, as though I was speaking in Latin. When I showed him the angel cards, he stared into the box in disbelief, as though he was waiting for them to fly away. I spotted a blonde wig hanging from a hook on the wall. It was beginning to sink in that Sophie had been prepared for her child to die with her when she set the place alight.

'Where's Molly?' I asked.

'Safe,' he replied. 'She's being looked after, you don't need to worry.'

It felt like hours before I could leave, and my body was starting to let me down. I had to lean on Burns's arm when we got outside, too dizzy to care about the rain. Burns gave me an anxious look as he settled into the driving seat, water gushing down the windscreen. He asked me something as we pulled away, but I couldn't reply. All I could see was Darren's scooter, still parked on the corner, his crash helmet dangling from the handlebar, slowly filling with rain.

47

It was hard to tell whether I was shaking because my clothes were soaked, or because shock had finally set in, but it was a struggle to climb the steps to the police station. A crowd of photographers were already heading in my direction, with Dean Simons leading the pack.

'Been up to your usual tricks, Alice?' His voice was too loud, roughened by gallons of cheap booze.

Burns cut a swathe through the crowd and I kept my head down, ignoring the voices yelling at me, and the dazzle of flashbulbs. As soon as we got inside I turned to him.

'Can you arrest that bloke for something, please?'

'Harassment or invasion of privacy?' Burns asked.

'Both.'

'I'll see what I can do.'

When we reached the incident room my hands were fluttering against my sides, and Steve Taylor was refusing to meet my eye. His low spirits must have been due to wounded pride – there was no way on God's earth that he could claim victory this time. If Brotherton made cuts, he'd be the first one to receive his P45. Burns strutted past and led me to his office. He made me coffee, then passed me a packet of digestives.

'Get those down you,' he said. 'I'll be ten minutes.'

I crammed a biscuit into my mouth, then tackled the mug of coffee, my teeth clattering against the china. I was trying to understand why I still couldn't cry. Distress was churning in the pit of my stomach but, at this rate, it would be there until the end of time. Hari would say it was Alexithymia – the inability to express emotions – or clinical depression, the nation's favourite cause of insomnia and eating problems. When Burns finally returned I was staring blankly at the wall, but at least I'd managed to eat half the biscuits.

'She's talking already,' he said. 'The doctor's trying to fix her face, but she won't shut up.'

'Is her mum okay?' I asked.

He nodded. 'She'd locked her in a room on the ground floor. She sedated her, and the security guards. The ambulance blokes thought the old girl was having a heart attack when she came round. She hasn't been told what Sophie's done yet – they're waiting till she's stronger.'

'And Kingsmith?'

'She saved him until the end. Maybe she was hoping he'd change. But he wouldn't apologise for seeing Poppy, so she shot him, point blank.'

I winced. 'Where did she get the Rohypnol?'

'It's not hard, is it? She probably bought a job lot on the internet for less than a hundred quid.'

I rubbed my hand across my eyes. 'So she killed them all for sleeping with Poppy. But why did Jamie Wilcox go to her? It doesn't make sense.'

'Peer pressure. I bet the bigwigs took him for a drink, and the next thing you know, they're having a whip-round to send him to their favourite girl.'

'An initiation ceremony.'

Burns's eyebrows rose. 'Beats biting the head off a chicken, I suppose.'

I stared back at him and his image wavered. I remembered the film clip he'd shown me of the young, broad-shouldered man in a hooded top, coolly pushing Leo Gresham to his death. Sophie must have bought a tracksuit somewhere, and carried out her plan without a flicker of guilt. And when she transformed herself into a long-haired blonde, she became someone else. The kind of woman who could pick up men in a crowded bar, or persuade a prison guard to carry drugs into Wormwood Scrubs.

I was still struggling to understand how she'd got hold of Rayner's camera. But I remembered her complaining about all the events she had to attend. As the boss's wife, she would have known all the executives, and overheard plenty of indiscreet conversations at champagne-fuelled dinners. It would have been easy to borrow her husband's master key to unlock Rayner's office.

'Did you know she was mates with Piernan, too?' Burns asked.

By now my mind was on overload. I closed my eyes but the pictures wouldn't go away. She must have sedated him, then hauled his body into the bath, slitting his wrists for good measure. The details had been so carefully planned. She'd incriminated him by leaving the angel cards and Rohypnol in his flat. And she'd even sent herself a card, to make sure she looked innocent.

'It was her who attacked me, wasn't it?' I asked.

He nodded. 'You're not her favourite girl. But at least you got your own back tonight.'

'Her barrister's bound to say it was postnatal psychosis.'

Burns shook his head briskly. 'I reckon she was planning it before she got pregnant. We just got hold of her medical records. She had a psychotic episode in her teens and tried to top herself. But I don't think that's the reason. It was just a fucked-up version of love — she got wise to her husband's tricks, so she made them all suffer.'

'Why did she bother with the angel cards and the feathers?'

'Her dad was a vicar. Maybe she couldn't stand all that sin.'

I remembered the discreet crucifix her mother wore, how could a religious upbringing result in so many deaths?

'She said something else,' Burns carried on. 'She was planning to go after Nicole, for having a fling with Max.'

The idea took a moment to register. It made sense that Nicole would aim for a multimillionaire as her next husband, even if they were both still married. It seemed ironic that Liam had saved her life. If Sophie had got there first, dissecting her face wouldn't have been enough – she'd have slit her throat too.

Burns looked more upbeat than he had in weeks. I could tell from his expression that his confidence was returning. If Taylor had appeared, he'd have hurled him out of the window.

'Give me a minute then I'll drive you home,' he said.

His idea of a minute could stretch to an hour, depending on how many distractions came his way. As I tried to get comfortable on my plastic chair, I noticed Poppy's appointment book on his desk. I tried to restrain myself, but it was a losing battle. The pages made fascinating reading. Men from all walks of life had used Poppy's services: a game-show host; my favourite stand-up comedian; even a world-class tennis player. On the second page I saw Andrew's name, and I realised that Burns had been trying to protect me, as usual, even though it was blindingly obvious. It still hurt to see his surname written in Poppy's looping scrawl. Andrew had booked a weekly slot in her schedule until a few months ago. I stared out of the window and tried not to judge him. He'd driven himself so hard that there'd been no time for a personal life. In his shoes I might have done the same. I knew how it felt to work yourself into a stupor, then go home to an empty bed.

Outside the window, the sky was lightening, and when I

glanced at my watch it was almost seven. The rest of the city would be eating breakfast by now, or taking a shower, preparing for another day at work. I was ready to leave when Burns finally came back. My hands were still shaking, but I was determined to walk to my car unaided, without anyone propping me up. The ground rocked when I got to my feet, and Burns reached out to steady me. He was standing in front of the window, shoulders broad enough to block out the light. There was a mix of emotions in his eyes – surprise, pity, maybe even a hint of admiration. I wondered if he was about to deliver more bad news, because I'd never seen him look so serious.

'Can I go home now, Don?'

'Not just yet.' He was still refusing to smile.

It was a surprise when he put his arms round me, but I should have remembered that comfort is Burns's speciality. My cheek rested on his shoulder and it felt like trying to embrace a giant. Neither of us pulled away, until someone walked past, heels clicking on the lino outside the door. He was still looking at me as I drew back, with a complicated expression on his face. When I glanced down I noticed a dark stain on the arm of my T-shirt, as big as a fist, beginning to turn brown. My clothes were covered in patches of dried blood. No wonder Burns had taken pity on me. I must have looked like the archetypal pathetic blonde – white-faced and shaking like a leaf, almost too shocked to move.

48

I got some odd looks as I marched through the station, covered in bloodstains, with messy, uncombed hair. Lorraine Brotherton's office door was half open, and I caught a glimpse of her. She was wearing a dark grey dress, which matched the clouds outside. Luckily she didn't spot me. She was too busy examining the contents of her filing cabinet to haul me in for a lecture on safety protocols. No doubt she was longing to slip back into anonymity when the furore died down. She'd probably already booked the car ferry to St Malo.

For once the press ignored me when I got outside. They were too busy taking pictures of Dean Simons resisting arrest. He was shrieking about injustice as two uniforms dragged him up the steps.

I skirted round the side of the crowd and got into my car. It was the middle of the morning rush hour, and everything was still coated with a layer of artificial calm. Andrew would have felt the same in the moments before he died, afloat on a sea of Rohypnol. But something changed when I put my hands on the steering wheel. I felt steadier, and even the traffic was soothing, the mechanical routine of driving as easy as running. All I had to do was shift gear and let my instincts protect me – with luck I could avoid knocking anyone down. At first I drove without any sense of purpose, apart from escaping everything I'd seen. I wasn't ready to go home, even though I was desperate for a shower. It was only when I passed the edge of Regent's Park that I realised where I wanted to be. The paths were almost empty, rain falling in long, unbroken sheets. Even the most obsessive marathon runners had stayed at home.

It took less than half an hour to double back into the City. I parked my car on Lombard Street, then dug around on the back seat for my mac, buttoning it up to cover my filthy clothes. I felt too weak to use the stairs, which presented me with a problem. The concierge smiled reassuringly as I stepped into the glass-bottomed lift. The first moments were the worst; listening to the doors click shut, knowing it was too late to escape. But the aversion therapists are right – avoidance is not an option. The only way to tackle a phobia is to feel the fear and do it anyway. I tried not to hold my breath as the numbers ticked by.

Luckily there was just one policeman guarding Andrew's flat, and he looked fresh out of Hendon.

'DI Burns sent me,' I told him. 'I need to go in, please.'

'Have you got some ID?'

I flashed my NHS card at him and the young man nodded politely. He was so green that yesterday's lottery ticket would probably have done the trick.

The flat was exactly as I remembered, with a row of huge black-and-white photos lining the hall. The skyscrapers were packed so close together that they looked like schoolkids, standing in line, vying to be the tallest. I felt sure Stephen Rayner had taken them. They had the same sharp-edged beauty as the landscapes in his flat, and I couldn't help wondering how he'd cope with the fact that the snaps he'd taken of his Angel Bank colleagues had condemned them to death.

I rummaged through the cupboards in Piernan's kitchen until I found his supply of booze, then filled a shot glass with

Irish malt. I stood beside the panoramic window as the alcohol scorched my throat. Rain was pelting the streets, but London was carrying on regardless, executives sheltering under umbrellas as they raced from one transaction to the next. I could see the Angel Bank building, still standing tall, even though it had been shut down and its directors were lying in the mortuary. The Square Mile didn't seem to give a damn. Soon another bank would take over the lease and start operating again, led by a new financial guru.

I don't know how long I stood there. But I remember going back for a refill, trying to dissolve the tightness inside my ribcage. All my coping strategies had deserted me for the time being. Normally I worked hard to avoid acknowledging pain: burying myself in work, sprinting for miles or hitting the town with Lola. But today it was inescapable. I closed my eyes but Andrew refused to appear. I'd been wrong to imagine that I could come here and say goodbye to his ghost. It had departed a long time ago. The only things he'd left behind were expensive furniture, a shelf full of adventure stories and the sterile smell of loneliness. But at least the whisky was taking hold. Soon I'd be strong enough to go home and face the inevitable tsunami of sympathy from Lola, and the Warhol butterfly, trapped in its wooden frame. I perched on the edge of a stool and made a string of rash promises to myself. In future I'd work less and see more of my friends, stop worrying about my brother. And I'd run the marathon in a decent time, so no one could ever see me as a weakling again. I gazed at the cupola of St Paul's, its stone pallid against the dark sky. Burns's skin had been the same colour today, chalk white with tiredness and relief. I drained the last drops from my glass and forced myself back onto my feet.

The rain was falling more gently when I left the building. My clothes were already so drenched that I didn't bother to hurry back to the car. I stood on the pavement, letting the droplets massage my face, and a man went by on a scooter, slowing down for a better look. It's funny how the simplest thing can undo you. His Lambretta was a newer, cleaner version of Darren's, and suddenly I was kneeling beside him again, watching his eyes lose focus. For once it was easy to cry, and the weather provided the perfect camouflage. The drivers in passing cars would never have guessed. All they'd have seen was a thin blonde in a white coat, with her face to the sky, celebrating the end of a long drought.

ACKNOWLEDGEMENTS

I would like to thank Teresa Chris for being a fierce angel and Ruth Tross for being a ministering one; without your excellent help this book would not have been written. Thanks are also due to Andrew Martin for your kind encouragement and a fine glass of wine at Harrogate. Much gratitude to Hope Dellon, Dave Pescod, Miranda Landgraf, Penny Hancock and the 134 club for their readings and sound advice. The helpful staff of the National Gallery gave me some invaluable guidance on angels and art history. Many thanks to DC Laura Shaw for her good company and for setting me straight on police matters.